"We could…kiss and see."

"See what?"

"If it felt okay. I mean, you did call me your brother earlier."

"Gross." She smacked his chest. "I didn't mean it literally."

"Well, that's a relief."

"It's just that I don't want this to change anything. And I feel like this could do all sorts of changing. Throughout everything, you've been my one constant."

"Here is what I know. You're thinking that I never thought about you like that. You are wrong. I have. More than once. More than twice. More than I might want to say."

"Are you joking?"

"Not about this. You are smart, but also so oblivious sometimes. You have no idea how gorgeous you are. Trust me, every guy who talks to you thinks about it. I'm just being a pal and letting you in on the truth."

She searched his face, but there was no hidden joke to his words.

"Okay then, kiss me," she said, pushing back her shoulders. "Kiss me, and let's see if we even have chemistry."

Praise for Phoebe Mills

A Wedding on Sunshine Corner

"Mills captures the small-town atmosphere beautifully, populating it with down-to-earth characters who are easy to care for. This uplifting tale will leave readers eager to return to Heart's Hope Bay."

—*Publishers Weekly*

"Mills makes good use of the best-friend's-sister and enemies-to-lovers tropes and creates delightful chemistry and fun in this engaging contemporary small-town romance."

—*Booklist*

The House on Sunshine Corner

"A lovely second-chance romance."

—Harlequin Junkie

"[A] small-town, second-chance romance with humor, heart, a likable cast of characters, and just enough steam…"

—The Romance Dish

Starting Over on Sunshine Corner

BOOKS BY PHOEBE MILLS

Starting Over on Sunshine Corner

A Sunshine Corner Novel

Phoebe Mills

FOREVER
New York Boston

Copyright © 2023 by Grand Central Publishing

Cover design by Susan Zucker
Cover copyright © 2023 by Hachette Book Group, Inc.

Forever
Hachette Book Group
1290 Avenue of the Americas, New York, NY 10104
read-forever.com
twitter.com/readforeverpub

First Edition: February 2023

Forever is an imprint of Grand Central Publishing. The Forever name and logo are trademarks of Hachette Book Group, Inc.

The publisher is not responsible for websites (or their content) that are not owned by the publisher.

The Hachette Speakers Bureau provides a wide range of authors for speaking events. To find out more, go to www.hachettespeakersbureau.com or call (866) 376-6591.

ISBNs: 978-1-5387-2528-3 (mass market), 978-1-5387-2529-0 (ebook)

Printed in the United States of America

OPM

10 9 8 7 6 5 4 3 2 1

Starting Over on Sunshine Corner

Chapter One

Jackson Lowe fished his phone from the back pocket of his worn denim jeans and leaned against the company truck. The sea fog had burned off by midday, and the sun-warmed steel soothed the tight muscles in his lower back. After punching in his passcode, he flicked over to the surf app, groaning at the perfect afternoon forecast: light offshore winds and waves five to eight feet high. It seemed unlikely he would be able to fit in a sneaky surf session, but maybe one little ride out wouldn't hurt.

He and the rest of his landscaping crew had busted tail on Mrs. Keller's property for the past three hours. While the guys had pruned, he'd let her give him a private tour around her beloved rhododendrons, showing where a few were developing leaf spot. He'd removed and destroyed all the visibly affected leaves and promised to come back early next week to add extra mulch. She was happy, and now he was happy because he could sneak out for a quick surf session before picking up...

"Jack!" a baritone voice yelled.

Jackson startled, having been so engrossed on the app that he hadn't heard his father's approach. His dad's elbow jutted out of the window of a white pickup identical to his own with the green company logo and LOWE'S LANDSCAPING: PROUDLY SERVING THE CENTRAL OREGON COAST emblazoned on the door.

"Hey, Dad." Jackson shoved the phone back in his jeans, while grinding his molars back and forth.

"Working hard or hardly working there, son?"

Jackson tried to ignore the sinking feeling that he'd just been busted, as if he wasn't a thirty-one-year-old crew leader who'd finished a job well done. His dad always had that effect on him, even now as he regarded him from below his Trail Blazers hat with those serious blue eyes that belied his half smile.

"Just finished up here. Do you need something?" *Or are you checking up on me?* Jackson left the last question unspoken, but it hung in the air between them. Why did he always feel like such a loser whenever his dad shot him one of those long, searching looks? It wasn't like he was a major life screwup. He worked hard, stayed out of debt, didn't smoke or have more than a few beers at the Last Chance Bar on a Saturday night. He didn't sleep around or get in trouble with the law.

"Oh, well, I was in the area and remembered your truck was in the shop. Thought I'd give you a lift and catch up."

"Cool." Jackson chewed the inside of his cheek, a better option than retorting with a salty "Yeah, right." Given that Mrs. Keller lived a few miles out of their quaint coastal town of Heart's Hope Bay, at the end of a long private road that wound up into the coastal hills, the chances that his dad was coincidentally passing by was somewhere in the vicinity of no chance in hell.

The old man was up to something. Was he going to have to play twenty questions to figure out what?

"Yeah, I'm getting new tires put on. I'm going to be heading out of town for the weekend, so if you could give me a ride to pick it up, that would be great. I was going to catch a ride with the guys."

"Sounds like a plan. You should know, Mrs. Keller called." His dad turned the truck off. "And"—he held up a hand, bronzed from years of outdoor work—"before you get your boxers in a bunch, she had nothing but good things to say about you."

"That's good news, right?" Jackson glanced back at the big three-story gray-shingled house, but there was no sign of the owner, who was famously nit-picky and high maintenance.

"You've got a knack for customer service. The clients like how you interact, the way that you take your time and explain things. This isn't the first time I've had someone sing your praises."

"Okay, great, but..." Jackson hooked his hand around the back of his neck and kicked at a rock in the driveway. "I'll cut to the chase. Do you have something you wanna say?"

"Boss! Time to go. You need to get your truck, and it's beer o' clock!" Reggie, one of the newer members of the landscaping crew, barreled around the house, then abruptly pulled up short when he saw the company owner. "Oh, hey, Mr. Lowe...didn't know you were here." His nervous laugh hung in the air as the rest of the crew came to a halt behind him, all of them taking a sudden keen interest in the steel-toed tips of their work boots.

Jackson made it a point not to cringe, bow his head, or give any outward sign of embarrassment. He had nothing to apologize for. His crew busted their tails, and if they finished a bit early and got to get a head start on their weekend, who was it going to hurt?

Alan gave his employees a curt nod, and despite the sunshine, the air seemed to drop ten degrees. It's not that his dad was a jerk, but he never was easygoing with the crews. Things like banter, fun, or letting folks duck out of work a few hours early— that was how Jackson rolled. Life was too short to take too seriously. Having fun made everything better, so why do otherwise? While he knew his dad didn't love the idea of him letting the guys off early while keeping them on the clock, he didn't ever mention it. Out of sight, out of mind.

Except for today.

"Um…hey…Boss?" Reggie stood by the truck, kicking dirt with the tip of his boot. "Are you catching a ride with us?"

"That's okay. I'm going to take him back into town," Alan called out evenly, answering for Jackson. "We have some things to discuss. Business things."

"Of course, Mr. Lowe, no problem." Reggie's expression was unmistakable. Straight *oh crap*.

Jackson forced a small reassuring smile and ignored the knot in his stomach, the one that came from still getting treated like the kid who had camped out in the principal's office during middle school and who had never once earned one of those stupid MY STUDENT IS ON THE HONOR ROLL AT HEART'S HOPE BAY HIGH bumper stickers like his other siblings.

"Have a good time!" Jackson threw up his hand in farewell as he rounded his dad's cab to climb into the passenger side. "You guys worked hard this week and deserve it."

The fact that the last part of the comment was meant more for his dad did not go unnoticed. It took until they had driven down the tree-lined driveway and turned onto the narrow country road, before Alan eventually spoke.

"Those boys look up to you. And when you let them cut out of work and stay on the clock while drinking beer—what kind of message does that send about personal responsibility? And not only that, but is partying it up over pitchers of beer the best way for them to spend their hard-earned money? From what I hear, Reggie's been couch surfing for months all over town. Shouldn't he be saving for a rental deposit instead of buying another round for his friends?"

"I hear you." Jackson rolled down the window, letting the salt-infused air cool his heated cheeks. Dad might have a point, but he also had a knack of making things sound worse than they were. What his dad didn't know was that Reggie had found out that his stepdad had been diagnosed with colon cancer this week and was stressed out. Having a chance to blow off some steam and forget about the real world for a bit couldn't be all bad, right? But what was the point of trying to tell his father any of that?

Alan Lowe wasn't a guy who liked to listen; he lectured.

Jackson nodded during pauses, but he'd tuned his father out, directing his gaze to the glimpses of sparkling ocean appearing between dips in the hills. What he wouldn't have given to be out there right now. When catching a wave there is no past, no future, just the present.

"I want to see you step up and focus, get some goals and real direction. You'll understand one day. When you're a parent."

Jackson turned and gave him a look. The idea of

having a kid was as relatable as taking a vacation to Mars. Jackson appreciated how his younger sister, Savannah, worked magic with rug rats at the Sunshine Corner preschool, and hell, his closest female friend had a child. But the idea of losing sleep for what looked like forever? Not to mention being unable to go surfing on a whim? Having to make sure he was setting a responsible example? Vacuuming regularly? Making grocery lists?

No thanks.

Parenthood appeared to be a helluva noble job, and he respected it, but it just wasn't his scene.

"Let's be real, Dad." Jackson smirked. "It's probably best that I'm just the fun uncle, right?"

His father slammed the brakes so hard that Jackson lurched forward, the shoulder belt digging hard into his chest.

"Dude! What was that for?" He glanced over, incredulous.

"Dude? Jackson Lowe." His dad's knuckles tightened on the driver's wheel. "You're not a kid, no matter how much you want to pretend otherwise. You have potential, and I've had my fill of watching you squander it. I've been thinking this over, and look, I can't stay in as the boss forever. Your mom has been pestering me about retirement. She wants to get out and travel while we are still fit and healthy, and if anyone deserves to have the world laid at their feet, it's her."

"On that at least we agree." Jackson's irritation ebbed. Most people thought their own mom was the best, but he knew that he was lucky enough to have the greatest mother of all time. She was the only one in his family who seemed to love him for who he was, not despite it.

"But I'm not too keen on giving up a business that I've poured my whole life into, a business that provides a good income for a number of people. What do we have now? Three crews with five guys on each? Plus, Donna and Nancy in the office. You. Me. That's nineteen people right there."

Jackson nodded, brow furrowing. What the heck was going on? First, Dad showed up out of the blue, wagging his finger for letting the crew duck out early and enjoy an afternoon beer while being on the clock. Then he started talking about responsibility, and having a kid. Now he was saying he wants to retire.

What gives?

"I want you to step into my shoes and take over."

"Me?" The realization hit him like a bucket of ice water just as his dad started driving again. "Take over the business?"

"Yes. You."

"Wh-what if I don't want to?" The words were out before he could swallow them back.

"You'd rather stay being the crew leader? You'd really want me to sell Lowe's Landscaping? To someone who is not a Lowe?"

"It's not that." Jackson frowned. He didn't exactly like that idea either, but this had never been his dream job.

"Come on, Jack. You had to expect this was going to happen sooner rather than later."

"Honestly, I haven't given it any thought. I'm happy. You seemed happy. It's all good."

"All good. It's all good." His dad sighed. "Those are your three favorite words, huh? Look, I promised to fly your mother over to Paris for our fortieth wedding anniversary. And then I want to surprise her with a Mediterranean cruise after. It's something she'll never expect. But that means my clock is ticking. I'm going to have to make a move. So I need you to think seriously about your future...probably for the first time ever."

Jackson nodded slowly, his dad's words floating through his mind, but not really sinking in.

"I mean it—seriously think about it. Don't say yes to make *me* happy. It's more that...I want this for you. I want to give you the opportunity to step up and be the man that I think you can be, not the oversized kid you seem intent on pretending that you are."

"Jeez, Dad." Jackson mimed a wounded chest, even though the words hit him like a gut punch. "Tell me how you really feel."

"The truth hurts, son. Grow up and get used to it. I love my kids too much to see any of you being anything other than your best selves."

"Okay, okay. I'll think about the offer. I will. I promise." His phone buzzed with a text. He pulled it out and saw it was a message from Becca—a meme of an older woman saying "It's been 84 years."

Where are you? Don't be late!

He snorted, a kaleidoscope of butterflies stirring in his body's core, sending a wave of internal flutters through his limbs. This always happened whenever Becca popped up, whether it was on text, or over the phone, or at his front door. He had no idea where this particular picture was from, but the message was clear. His friend was getting impatient.

Key word: *friend.*

Those butterflies could go back into hibernation. He wasn't going to let them take flight, ever.

Three dots lit up. She was typing again.

I know you won't get the reference. It's from Titanic. You know, the greatest movie of all time? The one you've always refused to watch with me? Anyway…you better not be surfing. We need to hit the road soon.

Need to pick up my truck and shower. Give me an hour he typed back before glancing at his dad with a one-shouldered shrug, as he deleted any lingering impulse to catch a wave or two. "Sorry, it's Becca. I'm supposed to drive her and Sofia to her cousin's wedding. Carter and Abby were going to take them, but Abby had some sort of a blood pressure scare with the pregnancy and her doctor recommended that she stick close to home and rest. Of course, Carter won't leave her side. So, I offered to go so Becca didn't have to be alone."

His dad's craggy face was inscrutable. "I knew it was Becca before you told me. Wanna guess how?"

"Because I don't have many friends." Jackson

winked cheekily. The exact opposite was true. He knew everyone in this town, from the high schoolers who ran the old-timey ice cream shop to the senior book club that gathered at the library on Tuesdays, the newcomers who moved in from Portland for a sea change to the long-timers whose great-great-grandparents had migrated here from Europe. He couldn't walk a block in Heart's Hope without having someone engage him in chitchat or honking as they passed by.

"No one else makes you smile that way." His dad's huffed laughter was amused. "Rebecca Hayes, the one who got away, hey?"

Jackson jerked his head. Oh God, there he went again.

"Dad, look. For the hundred thousandth time. Me and Becca. We are friends. *Just* friends. Capital *F* friends. Always have been. Always will be." If he said it enough, to his family, to his friends, to himself, eventually it might be true.

A flash of her wide grinning mouth appeared in his mind, those full lips darkened by the red lipstick she wore on occasion. A mouth he thought about sometimes when he shouldn't.

A mouth that he wasn't going to think about at all right now. Especially with his dad a foot away.

"But if I'm late to get her she's going to kick my ass, so let's try to at least drive the speed limit so I can get home to shower."

"That Rebecca Hayes," his dad repeated as he pulled up in front of the auto shop, clearly intent on ignoring Jackson's plea and maybe even enjoying watching him squirm a little. "She's got spunk. And made her own way, just like her brother."

Jackson bit the inside of his cheek. Spunk wasn't the half of it. Becca was an incredible woman: funny, smart, and about as good of a person as they come. She'd overcome so much, including a deadbeat dad, to carve out success for herself and her daughter. She deserved nothing but the best.

Which you're certainly not, the unhelpful little voice in his head reminded him in no uncertain terms.

"I respect someone who calls their own shots and makes their own way." His dad had a far-off look. "I like her a lot."

"Yeah. I like her too. Emphasis on *like*. As in she's an old buddy." He jumped out of the truck before his dad could embarrass him further.

"Hey."

He glanced back, ears burning. If Dad said another word about him and Becca then—

"That was a serious offer I made you before. I need you to think about if you are ready for the next step."

"I said I will." Jackson's smile faded. The idea of taking over Lowe's Landscaping felt like a rock in his gut, a burden he didn't want to carry. But his old man was making an offer in good faith, and the least he could do was consider it. "I'll think hard on it. And when I say I'm gonna do something, I do it, don't I?"

His dad's cryptic shrug could mean a dozen things, but Jackson didn't have time to analyze the inner workings of Alan Lowe's brain. He had to get his truck, get showered, and get his ass over to Becca's, or he'd be out of the frying pan and straight into his type-A best friend's fire.

* * *

Jackson wasn't late. Yet.

Becca rechecked the oven clock. He still had two minutes to make it by four.

"When are we going, Mama?" Her four-year-old daughter, Sofia, glanced up from the iPad Becca was letting her watch as she tidied up the house.

Becca resisted the term *clean freak*. Because there was nothing freakish about enjoying everything being put in the right spot, and if she'd used this year's tax return to treat herself to a Dyson, well...at twenty-eight she might as well admit that she'd rather vacuum the house than get pedicures or go to yoga classes. She'd swear on a stack of Bibles that her Dyson was better than meditation.

"Not yet, honey. Soon. We're just waiting for Jackson." Becca gave the counter a vigorous swipe, sending a few scattered sourdough crumbs from Sofia's peanut butter and jelly sandwich onto the floor. She bit back a muttered curse. Why was she so on edge? It was silly to be stressed about a weekend away—especially when it was for a destination wedding, of all things. The next few days were going to be about fun, family, friends, and delicious food.

But travel made her anxious. Home was her nest. She'd rather cook, or bake, or watch Netflix than go out. Here, she had Sofia on a strict bedtime schedule that guaranteed her a few hours of precious me time after dark, plus she had a well-stocked medicine cabinet and snack cupboard prepared to handle everything from a fever to a sudden fit of hangry. There were drawers of clean underwear. Her bed with six fantastic pillows.

Home, she could control. Home, she was always in charge. Home, well, it was a known entity.

God, she sounded so…*boring*. She grabbed the vacuum and sucked up the crumbs.

Ugh. Had she always been this boring?

The answer was no. She used to put herself out there. Go on dates. Get kissed. Get more than kissed.

Now it was just her and cobwebs, both in her house and in other unmentionable places.

But soon all that was going to change. Last night, after a second glass of wine, she'd gone and made an online dating profile. But since she'd activated it, she'd been too scared to go back on to look. What if no one had swiped on her? That would be such an ego blow. But what if someone had? That could be worse. Heart's Hope Bay wasn't big. People she *knew* might see her. Like the cute cop who let her off with a warning last week or the green-eyed owner of the new home goods store in town. That would be so awkward.

Sofia's giggle cut over the drone of the vacuum.

Becca glanced up, realizing she'd been standing in place in the kitchen, sucking the same patch of hardwood, lost in thought. "What's so funny, baby?"

A pair of big warm hands clamped down over her eyes, and before she could shriek in protest, she was jerked back against a body—a big hard body.

Two thoughts hit at the exact same time.

One was that someday she was going to be the one to sneak up and startle Jackson Lowe. The other was that he smelled good, really good, like shampoo, toothpaste, and something intangible and fresh, like cut grass.

"If you don't let go, I'm going to stomp on your toe," she snapped, getting her equilibrium back. Jackson was a looker, no doubt about that. But while that body might be all man, he was a big kid in so many ways. She found it charming...mostly. But he'd definitely be more of a catch if he'd just grow up a little.

"Big talk." His chuckle was slow and easy. "Coming from you, Fun Size, it's hardly a threat."

"Don't tempt me." She ducked out of his grasp and held her arms up in a martial arts stance. "I have a green belt in karate, remember?"

He reached out a big arm and petted her on the head, ruffling her hair. "Yes, yes. And I dropped out with only my orange, and you'll never let me forget it."

"Never." She eyed his shaggy blond mop, the ends of the tendrils still wet. "Let me take a wild guess, you were out surfing." If he wasn't working or at the Last Chance, he was usually down at Heart's Hope Bay Main Beach. She'd always joked that he kept office hours there.

"Sadly, no." His grin was uncharacteristically muted, his eyes looking more like a shade of slate gray than the usual twinkling indigo. "Just took a shower. My dad showed up at our site today as a surprise and wanted to 'talk.'" He made air quotes with his fingers.

"About what?" The Lowe family was a loving pack, but she knew sometimes Jackson felt like the black sheep.

"Eh. I'll fill you in later." He turned toward her daughter. "For now, what do you say, Princess Sofia-Bo-Bee-A," he said, using one of his pet nicknames for her. "Is it time to head off to the ball in your chariot?"

Her daughter squealed with delight as he scooped her up and out of her seat. "And I'm on time. You know what your mom would do if I was late, right?"

"She'd say no iPad for the rest of the day?" Sofia lisped her ultimate punishment.

"That would be horrible." Jackson nodded with exaggerated solemnity while tugging one of her daughter's braided pigtails. "No cartoons."

"Horrible," Sofia agreed, except her *r*'s sounded a lot like *w*'s.

Becca turned her head to hide her smile. It always warmed her from the inside out to see Sofia's love for her big, burly friend. "Our bag is by the door. Let me grab my phone and then we can head out."

"This phone right here?" He held it out, teasing, just as her phone buzzed with a notification. He glanced at the screen and did a double-take. "Uh. Okay. Um. You've got mail."

He thrust the phone at her, and there on her screen was a notification of an email from the dating app that read: "Congratulations! Someone has matched with you!"

"Oh. Right. Ha. Ha." Heat rushed to her cheeks as she struggled for nonchalance, plucking the device from his hands. "Thanks for that." Hopefully, her tone gave the impression that this was a regular thing for her, and not the first time she'd tried to get mixed up with the opposite sex in over five years, since her fling in Seattle with Graham—the very charming Brit who'd worked in the office next door, who had a witty sense of humor, wore fantastic cologne, and left her knocked up after a whirlwind romance before heading back across the pond to accept his dream job in London. "Now, does anyone need to pee before we hit the road? Sofia Kenani— I'm mostly talking to you."

"Dating app, huh?" To his credit, Jackson waited until Sofia had scooted off to the powder room before folding his arms. "Sounds like you've got some things to fill me in on during the car ride."

"Shhhhhh. It's nothing," she whispered. "I don't

want Sofia to hear anything. I'm just putting myself out there, all right?"

"Settle down. I'm not judging." He held up his hands in a defensive gesture. "I'm just surprised."

"Well, you shouldn't be. It might shock you to realize, but your old friend Becca isn't just a mom. She's a grown-up lady...and has grown-up lady needs. Got it?" And with that she ducked her head and booked toward her suitcase without waiting to see how he reacted. Why was her heart beating so fast? Were her hands trembling? And why did it feel so stupidly awkward for Jackson to know she wanted to put herself out there?

God, at this rate, dating was already for the birds.

Chapter Two

Becca's words echoed in Jackson's mind for the entire drive, like the hook to one of Sofia's catchy Disney earworm songs that's impossible to shake.

Your old friend Becca isn't just a mom. She's a grown-up lady...and has grown-up lady needs. Got it?

Oh, he got the message all right. Loud and clear. It was sounding off in his mind like the tsunami alarm at the beach that was tested on the first Friday of every month. The trouble was how was he supposed to keep casual with that newsflash circulating through his system? For the entire three-hour drive to Hood River, he listened to Becca's indie folk rock playlists without a single complaint about all the wailing, chatted about new TV shows, tuned in to random news of the weird variety, and ignored the frantic squawking from Sofia's iPad game in the back seat—all the while replaying those words in his head.

While he didn't dare bring the dating app up again, he knew with the same certainty that the sun sets in the west, that Becca was simmering with embarrassment. She still had the same nervous tics from when they'd met in band when she was a freshman and he was a junior.

Evidence 1: Hair playing—check. She'd been absently twirling fingers through her thick black locks all throughout the ride.

Evidence 2: Forced merriment—check. Her laugh went up a few pitches—nearing the level of a dolphin squeak—and over things that weren't particularly funny.

Evidence 3: Compulsive finger snapping—check. When she wasn't playing with her hair, she was snapping her fingers on her lap, a subtle repetitive gesture.

He knew her so well that he could often size up her mood with just a glance. It was tempting to try to get her to talk more about her plan. Like why now and what had changed to put her back in the game? But he also wanted to honor her request not to bring up any probing questions in front of Sofia.

He respected her instinct not to confuse her daughter, who already was dealing with the fact that she had to grow up with a dad she saw only once a year. A guy who had always seemed nice enough, if paler and skinnier than he'd expected Becca's type to be. Graham King was ginger-haired and tall, seemed to only wear V-neck sweaters and checkered collared shirts, and blinked three times faster than normal.

In short, Becca's fling-turned-unexpected-baby-daddy wasn't some horrible toad of a human, but he could never quite decipher how *that* was the guy Becca had gone for. Sure, he had money and made sure to provide ample support for Sofia as well as invest in her college fund, but besides being successful, he just never seemed like her type. Not that Jackson really knew what type Becca preferred. But it likely was a banker who did CrossFit and crosswords and organized his boxer briefs by the days of the week. Certainly not a six-foot-two surfer who worked for his dad's landscaping business and had never moved out of his hometown.

An infusion of jealousy shot through his veins, making his stomach go a little sour.

He did have a healthy ego, and most women in Heart's Hope Bay had made a play for him at one point or another. He had earned a sterling reputation for being fun in bed, respectful, and up front about not looking for a commitment. But Becca Hayes had never given him one single inkling that she thought of him as anything other than a pal.

He'd let that fact keep him in the friend zone for so long it was if he lived there now. But the idea of standing aside while another man got to step in and shoot his shot? If he did that, he'd likely build a time machine in the future and come back and kick his own dumb ass.

"Don't worry. We're going to make it right on time," he assured her as they passed through the outskirts of the Portland city limits. He tried to keep his tone casual, like he wasn't debating making a serious attempt on her panties.

"What? Me, worry?" She made a scoffing sound. "Who says I'm worried? I'm going to a wedding where my aunt has offered to watch Sofia so I can have my first kid-free night in years. How can you possibly think that I'm anything but relaxed to the max?"

"Uh...a common shared history." He arched one incredulous brow. "I've never taken you anywhere without you being stressed out about being on time. Even if the event is something like the annual town anniversary where boring city council speeches last over an hour before any music starts."

"Okay, fine. Maybe I'm just a little *aware* of the time." She sniffed. "But can I remind you, this is a wedding. If we're late, we'll miss it."

"So, guess it's a good thing we won't be late." He signaled and maneuvered around a semi pulling a trailer loaded high with logs. "Who gets married this late in the day anyway?"

"My cousin wanted a sunset wedding. I think it's going to be gorgeous. And with Mount Hood in the background? It sounds picture-perfect." She reached out and gave his arm a soft squeeze. "Hey. Thank you, both for putting up with my neuroticism and also giving us a ride. I know I should have sucked it up, but I really do get nervous driving too far with just me and Sofia. And then when I got offered a night by myself it sounded too good to be true, but I would feel dumb if I didn't have a date."

Date? His ears grew warm. Is that what she considered him? The spot on his arm where she'd touched him still tingled. He cleared his throat.

Keep it casual, bro. Don't screw this up by being some damn eager beaver.

"Happy to come. You know me. Never miss a chance for free beer."

"I know, I know." She snorted. "Don't forget, I know every single thing about you, Jackson Lowe."

But here's the thing. She didn't.

For example, as smart as she was, she had never ever gotten a clue that he'd harbored a secret crush on her in high school. That he'd liked her so much that he could never get the balls up to actually *tell* her. It was hard enough to admit the truth to himself, and a hell of a lot easier to hook up with the girls that came on to him than to pursue the quiet, sensitive dark-haired girl with the sad eyes who always seemed to relax a little when he was around. He'd quickly gathered enough of a clue that her home life was rough and her widowed dad had become a hot mess. She needed hugs, not a hornball, and he never wanted her to think he was trying to take advantage of her.

It turned out the friend zone wasn't so bad as long as he could keep being around Becca. It wasn't like he'd been a monk. He lived his life. She lived hers. It's just that…he knew he put her up on a pedestal, one that no other woman he'd ever dated had come close to toppling.

She was his opposite in every way. Short to his tall. Quiet to his gregariousness. Detailed to his laid back. Type A to his type B. And yet, they could make each other laugh, and they seemed to be able to communicate without even speaking. He didn't know anyone else in his life who just got him so implicitly.

It was a horrible idea to risk screwing up their friendship for a fling. Besides, she probably never even thought of him that way. He was just her good buddy Jackson. Always up to watch a movie or run around the park with Sofia.

Just a big kid. She called him that enough.

He kept calculating his deficits. He wasn't like that preppy debate captain in high school, the dude whose name she'd doodled in her notebooks and drawn hearts around. Or the Portland hipster from her college years who majored in creative writing and played bass in a band and never shut up about being a vegan. And he certainly wasn't anything like Graham King, who spoke with that posh accent like he was goddam royalty and drank tea unironically.

He was just Jackson Lowe. The guy who never went to college, who didn't have a stock portfolio or own a tie. But hey, he did have eight surfboards and a collection of flip-flops. And if he ever got lonely, he could find a local or a cute tourist to keep him company. He wasn't the guy that women got serious with; he was the guy women had fun with.

But then again...that didn't mean he never wondered what it was like to have Becca's hot mouth on his skin. The thought sent goose bumps racing up his spine.

He was a guy. He was built from flesh and blood, not stone. Thoughts like that happened sometimes. He didn't seek them out, but they would occasionally flash through his brain or sashay nebulously into his dreams, leaving him waking up sweaty, with a hard-on and a belly full of desire.

"I forgot to ask. Did you bring a tie?" she asked out of the blue.

"A tie? Like for a suit?" He glanced over with a snort. "That's cute."

"What?"

"That you think I actually own anything like that." He shuddered.

"Right." She swallowed a small laugh under her breath. "I mean, it's fine. You look fine."

"Fine?" He glanced down at his white long-sleeved button-down shirt. What the heck was wrong with how he looked? He even wore his best shoes. "I thought I cleaned up okay. Never heard any complaints before."

"Sorry. You do, you do." She patted his head. "But that's the same shirt you've worn for any semiformal event in the last ten years. And those khakis. Don't forget the khakis. Are those the same ones that you got for high school graduation? You have a real uniform."

"Hey, those are fighting words. And no, for your information, they are not the same. These are my fancy pants. I know how to dress up for a wedding."

"God, you're such a man-child. Fancy pants." She shook her head, but the smile tugging her lips was genuine. "And whatever, leaving the top two buttons unbuttoned really works on you."

"You think so?" God, did he have to sound so insecure? He was fine. He was who he was—a surfer from a small town. No frills. No fuss.

"I just think it's funny." She shook her head, pushing a lock of hair behind her ear. "I swear you're never going to grow up. You're like the Peter Pan of Heart's Hope Bay." Her teasing tone let him know she didn't really mean anything by it.

"Hey, if you remember, I'm older and wiser than you. So have some respect."

"Riiiiiight," she drawled. "You were what? Two grades ahead of me. I always forget because you were in my math class."

"So, it wasn't my strongest subject. But I was great at math puns, remember?"

"Great?" Becca cringed, chuckling. "That's not quite the word I was looking for."

"Do you like math? No? Me neither. In fact, the only number I care about is yours."

"That's terrible," she yelped. "I want to cringe on your behalf."

"Come on now, that's genius. Are you a forty-five degree angle? Because, baby...you're perfect."

Her groan came from her soul. "How did we ever become friends?"

"I think you took pity on me," he said.

"Yeah, right. Pretty sure it was the other way around."

He glanced over, but she looked dead serious.

"Jackson, you might have had the worst pick-up lines in the school, but you were a king there. Everyone loved you. And you saved me, the weird new girl, from social ruin by being nice to me."

"Weird? You're not weird, Fun Size." He cleared his throat. "I mean, you're not *that* weird. I mean...I *like* your brand of weirdness."

"I can get you a shovel if you want."

"I'm serious, though. I like it. I like you, Fun Size."

"Thanks, Big Buddy." She slugged his shoulder, using her nickname for him. "And thanks for not bringing up...you know..." She lifted up her phone from the cupholder. "I was going to tell you this weekend. I didn't want you to find out like that."

"Hey, it's no big deal." It was weird how he was having to force his enthusiasm over the concept of her dating. It wasn't like *he* wanted to date Becca; he just liked what they had. Two friends. Neither in a relationship where a significant other would get jealous. Just good companionship. Good vibes.

"Okay good. I just..." She glanced back at Sofia, who wasn't paying them any attention. "I've been starting to feel like if I don't use it I'm going to lose it." She gave a rueful chuckle.

"I get it." Jackson swallowed hard, refusing to let his gaze train on her bare knees, those great legs poking out from beneath her short emerald dress. Her skin was a deep rich brown, a testament to her Native Hawaiian ancestors, and her hair was so black that sometimes it appeared blue in the light. "You know me. Life's about having fun. So just do it."

"Literally."

Her deadpan comment ripped an honest chuckle from him.

"Who knows. Maybe I'll get lucky at the reception. My cousin works for a timber company. There is bound to be lots of manly men."

"Except you'll already be with the manliest of them all," Jackson quipped, thrusting out his chest.

When she didn't laugh, he glanced over and found her staring thoughtfully at his pecs. When she caught him noticing, a flush crept up the hollow of her neck, making her deep red lips look even more vibrant.

"Ha," she said, her voice a bit tight before she waved a hand as if to physically clear the air. "I don't know what's wrong with me lately. I'm just weird."

"Well, weirdo"—he pointed at the road sign—"we're only ten miles from the wedding venue, and we still have thirty minutes until the ceremony, so we're going to make it with time to spare."

"Thanks for taking such good care of me."

"Always." He winked. "It's what I do best."

"I'm serious." She picked up her purse and began to rifle through the contents, plucking out a tube of lipstick and lowering the car visor to pop open the mirror. He kept his hands at ten and two, and ninety percent of his attention was fixed on the road, but he'd be a liar if he didn't admit he snuck a few looks over.

There was just something about how Becca applied her lipstick. The way her mouth parted and her brown eyes hooded, the confident movements of her hand, expertly spreading the vibrant cover. And then best of all, when she'd finished, rubbing her lips together and opening them again with an audible *pop* before giving them a purse, almost a kiss, to admire her handiwork.

The sight never failed to hit him with the same warmth as a beam of July sunlight. What would it be like to press his lips to hers? How did she taste?

She turned her head to look at him, and he immediately focused on the light traffic, swallowing heavily. "I know we joke a lot, but really, you didn't have to come up for this wedding with strangers. I just want you to know how much I appreciate you, even if I don't always tell you."

"It's no problem. It's not like there was going to be good surfing this weekend." A lie. It was going to be awesome for the next few days. He didn't even know why he said it; the words just automatically popped out, giving him space, not letting any weird feelings press up too close.

She shook her head. "Well, since I've got you all to myself, I know exactly what I need from you."

A record scratched in his brain. His throat thickened. "Huh?"

"You know." She leaned in so close he could smell the rose from the face cream she liked to use. "If I'm going to try dating again."

He swallowed. Hard.

"You can give me advice. Tell me who looks like a creep. Be my wingman. Poke around the eligible bachelors and help me find someone to practice flirting with, get my kinks out, you know? But don't worry, I will try not to cramp your style. Obviously you are going to be chasing one of the bridesmaids, right?"

"Heh. Dunno. Guess we'll see." He slowed down to stop at a red light and blinked a few times to clear his vision. *Dude, get a grip.* She wasn't talking about dating him. Of course not. That would be a no-good, terrible, horrible idea. What was he even doing letting the idea take shape?

"My cousin is stunning. I'd be willing to bet her bridal party is . . . not ugly."

"Don't worry about me. I can take care of myself. But for real, if this is something that you want, then I've got you," he said. "You can trust me to find you the right person."

And it would be someone smart, successful, and self-disciplined. There would likely be a few business types at the reception, men who could talk about finance and whatever else Becca was into.

Someone who made six figures and had his life goals clearly mapped out.

That was the type who deserved a woman like Becca. A guy who could be her equal.

Someone who was nothing like him.

* * *

The wedding was a lovely and simple affair in a winery along the Columbia River with Mount Hood serving as the perfect snow-capped backdrop. It was short and sweet, and Becca was relieved that Sofia didn't make a peep throughout the ceremony. It wasn't that Sofia wasn't a wonderful kid, but she was four. Not to mention she had just sat through a long car ride, and that was a stretch for any kid. But she didn't so much as wiggle her booty on the church bench. Or stage-whisper a single complaint about being hungry. Instead, she seemed just as enchanted by the entire ceremony, from the beautiful dress, to the music, to the flowers, to the true loves' kiss, as Becca.

Jackson had known without her even asking to pass over a Kleenex during the vows. She'd never watched a romantic movie where she didn't choke up during the big confessions or grand gesture.

"Ohhhhhhh! Aloha, Becca! Aloha, Sofia." Her mom's younger sister, Kalani, appeared at the end of the ceremony in a silky long pink dress, her thick black hair coiled up and studded with flowers. "Mahalo for coming and oh…" She pressed a hand to her heart. "My, how this little one has grown like a weed. And isn't she the image of your mother?"

"I know—isn't it something?" Becca blinked back a fresh surge of tears. Thank goodness she'd put on waterproof mascara today. Her aunt's words were nothing but the truth. Sometimes, Becca would see Sofia's profile and she looked so much like her mom that the world felt like it was spinning off its axis. It had been so long since her mom died, but there was never a day she didn't miss her. It was like a bruise that had faded but was still sore.

Sofia tugged on Becca's skirt, and she glanced down right as Kalani seemed to notice Jackson, standing a few feet back as if he didn't want to intrude.

"Oh my, is this little Jack Jack? Although I guess you have never been little, have you? But look how you've filled out. So many muscles. So handsome."

"Mama," Sofia whispered. "Is Auntie Kalani who I'm going with?"

The reception was adults-only, and her aunt Kalani had volunteered to host Sofia at her Airbnb so Becca could blow off some steam with a rare night out.

"Yeah, baby." Despite her heels, Becca dipped into a low squat so that she could look her little girl square in the eye. "Does that still sound fun?"

Sofia's dad only visited once a year. As a single mom, she had been the center of her daughter's universe, and while yes, she did want a night for herself, if her child needed her to stick close by, it wasn't even a choice. Sofia always came first. End of story.

Sofia glanced up at Kalani, who was still doting on Jackson in her warm accent that still held a lilt from the Hawaiian Islands. "Yeah. She is nice."

"She is really nice, baby." Becca's shoulders released a little. "When I was a little girl, I used to have sleepovers with Auntie too."

"Really?"

Becca nodded. Her aunt had moved from Kauai to Portland after finishing community college, and her mom had let her go up to the city in middle school for slumber parties. Now she realized it was probably to give her space when she was having chemo treatments, but at the time it felt like a party.

"Hey, baby girl, do you know what I have at my rental place?" Kalani shook a manicured finger.

Sofia's eyes widened. "What?"

"A hot tub. With lights that turn on under the water! You know what else?"

Sofia shook her head, even as her grin deepened, revealing her two perfect dimples.

"Ice cream. Chocolate *and* marshmallow fluff. How about you come party with me and leave your mama to go to her boring old party."

"Okay." Sofia giggled. "Bye, Mom!" She threw her arm up in a casual wave as if she did this all the time and strolled over to Kalani, slipping her small hand into her great-aunt's.

For half a second, something ached in Becca. No

one had ever told her that even after having a baby and the umbilical cord was cut, they would still be connected forever and always.

But then she realized it was just a growing pain—a *good* growing pain—because her little girl was getting bigger and opening herself to new people and expanding her world.

And as she stood up and smoothed out her skirt, she glanced over at her best friend, who looked vaguely like Thor with his shaggy blond hair, thick arms, and trim waist. He flashed her an impish wink that had made him easily the most popular guy back in their Heart's Hope High School days. A thrill shot through her. Not because he looked this good and was her date—no. She shifted her weight. It wasn't that she was *attracted* to Jackson, but she had 20/20 vision and was well aware that her best friend *was* a good-looking dude. And so, for just tonight, she wasn't going to be a mom, home in her Seattle University sweatshirt and stretched-out yoga pants, cajoling a child to eat one bite of peas and one fish stick.

Nope. She had on her cute dress, her Chanel lipstick, and her dancing shoes.

Come hell or high water, she was going to remember what it was like to be a woman.

* * *

Jackson held the door open and gestured for Becca to enter. "Milady," he murmured, and it didn't feel ironic either, given the surroundings. The wedding reception was being held in a building designed to look like a medieval French château.

"Wow, this looks incredible," Becca murmured, her heels clicking across the marble floor in the direction of the event space down the hall.

"It does indeed." Jackson took advantage of the view, walking slowly behind, hoping he wasn't going to hell. Becca had always had curves, but since giving birth to Sofia, it was like they went into overdrive. Her narrow waist dipped in that snug dress and made it very obvious she had an hourglass shape.

The thought sprang up that friends aren't meant to check friends out, but he waved it away. Hey, he was a guy. He looked. That was allowed.

Touching—now that was a whole other ball of wax.

"When was the last time we hung out together?" Becca was saying.

"I see you once a week." He ate dinner at her place every Sunday night. Microwave bagel bites and carrot sticks. Not that he ever minded the menu.

"I don't mean that. I mean go out. And not with Sofia. Just us, like we used to."

"No clue." He forced a grin. "Been forever."

A white lie.

He knew exactly when. She had come back into town for Christmas five years ago. They'd gone to the Last Call for a pitcher of beer and halfway through the first pint he'd realized just how much he'd missed her since she'd left for college and then work. And how pretty she looked in the dim bar light. And that was right when she shared that she was seeing someone. A guy from England who worked across the hall from her and always made her tea.

Tea.

But that was ancient history, and tonight he was going to have fun with his friend. They deserved it.

She hesitated at the door to the reception. A jazz band was playing on the stage, and the tables were covered with white linen tablecloths topped by round glass vases of garden roses and lilies of the valley.

A well-dressed younger crowd congregated near the bar, sipping cocktails, as older guests picked their way around a buffet table laden with hot appetizers.

"Okay, so I meant what I said earlier," she said thoughtfully, tapping a finger against her lower lip. "About practicing."

"Huh?"

"Practice." She turned and saw his blank expression. "Sorry, I don't mean to be cryptic. I just feel sort of dumb here. It's making me feel awkward. What I'm trying to say is that this could be a good place to get some experience flirting again. It's been so long I feel rustier than the Tin Man in *The Wizard of Oz*."

"Right. Right. Yeah. Cool." He ground his molars

but tried to keep his features relaxed, pretending they were discussing the weather, not some random dude potentially biting her perfect tan skin. "Sounds good. And I'll be your wingman."

Maybe he should walk into a door. That would be more fun.

"Thanks, Big Buddy." She blew him a kiss.

For once he hated that nickname.

He knew she was responsible and laden with a need for control. But he couldn't shake this urge to see what would happen if she didn't make a plan for once, if she just went out and waded into life and took a chance, acted on instinct. Maybe even . . . with him? He might be just a friend. But he knew her. He knew all her buttons. And he'd be willing to bet he knew exactly how to push them.

God, and he'd also bet that she'd love it.

They walked in and said a brief hello to the wedding party. The bride was one of Becca's cousins, or maybe a second cousin—he had known her forever and still got confused about who was who in her extended family. After that was over, Jackson steered her toward the bar.

"Manhattan on the rocks," he ordered. "And an IPA, please."

"What if I didn't want that?" she asked.

"It's what you always order."

"I'm not that predictable, am I?" She put a hand on one hip and shot him a mock threatening glare.

Before he could fumble out an answer, she was laughing. "Relax, Big Buddy. You should see your face. Of course I was going to order a Manhattan. What else would I get?"

A guy in a velvet suit jacket and a pair of aviators turned around and gave her a lazy grin. "Maybe a sloe comfortable screw," he said.

Jackson tried to pretend that his legs were encased in concrete. Otherwise, he was going to step up and tell this bougie bro to back off. But he should have known Becca would have it in hand.

"Slow, huh? That doesn't sound like it gets your blood pumping," Becca replied.

"The night is still young." The guy's cologne clogged Jackson's nostrils.

"Thanks, but I'll stick to my cocktail of choice." Her tepid shrug invited no opportunities for a debate. It was a shutdown so simple and effective that Jackson was almost tempted to give a chef's kiss.

"You didn't want a fling with that guy?" he asked once the man drifted away.

"No thanks. He'd probably want to talk about Woody Allen movies for foreplay."

"That would be a buzzkill."

"Indeed. Besides, I still taste his cologne." Her drink arrived and she clinked her glass with his, taking a slow sip as she scanned the surroundings.

He watched her surveilling the room, and for a moment it was as if he was seeing her for the first time, a strong and beautiful woman who could bring any man to his knees with a simple smile.

He felt weak.

Maybe he was just hungry.

"Want to grab some food?" he asked.

"Now that sounds sexy." Her brows went up. "This dress might be tight, but who cares, I'm starving."

As they lined up at the food table, Becca *ooh*ed and *aah*ed at the spread, plucking up small meat pies, shrimp cocktail, fancy cheeses, and dried fruit until there was a mound on her plate.

They hadn't even gotten to a table before she popped an olive into her mouth and issued a husky moan.

"You know what?"

"Chicken butt."

He grinned at their old joke. "I never get sick of watching you eat."

"It is my favorite thing to do. Well…" She winked. "My second favorite thing."

He glanced around uneasily, but no one else had heard her innuendo. Good, because if any of the men here had a clue, they would line up, and soon that line would wrap around the block.

But then again…he was meant to be her wingman tonight, and wasn't a fun no-strings hookup just what his best friend deserved?

Hell, maybe it was time to step out of the friend zone and into the game.

What was the harm in two old friends getting friendlier?

Chapter Three

Becca had only drunk two glasses of champagne, but that's not what made her feel buzzed as she crossed the dance floor doing the Electric Slide. It was the fact that for the first time in years she was acting her age—a late twentysomething who had nothing better to do than tear it up on the dance floor. As much as she loved being a mom, it was undeniable that she needed this night to kick up her heels.

And while she had been more than half serious about trying to get her flirt on today with a handsome and anonymous stranger, it turned out that she was having way more fun just hanging out with Jackson. While the bridesmaids were as gorgeous as she had promised, and at least two had cast lingering appreciative glances at him, Jackson seemed more than content just acting silly with her—shaking his booty with exaggerated hip jerks during "Gangnam Style" in a way that never failed to send her doubling over into gasping fits of laughter.

"Stop!" She waved her hands as tears streamed down her cheeks. "I'm going to pee myself."

That only encouraged him, and it was only due to her rigorous regime of morning Kegels that she didn't make good on her threat.

When the song ended, the DJ shifted to a slow, romantic R&B croon, and that was her cue. "I need to stop for a water break," she said, panting.

"I'll join you," he said, just as one of the bridesmaids, a petite curvy blonde in a form-fitting rose gold cocktail dress stepped in. "Mind if I have this dance?" she said, a bright flush creeping across her cheeks that made her look innocent and somehow even more sexy.

It was as if a spell broke, and Becca suddenly remembered she wasn't easy and breezy; she was old beyond her years with a laundry list of responsibilities. Not only that, but she had a couple of stretch marks on her stomach, a C-section scar, and boobs that seemed to be answering the call of gravity unless she hoicked them into an expensive bra.

"That's cool, right?" She glanced back at Becca with a questioning expression. "I know he's your date, but I heard you weren't...together or anything."

"What?" Becca forced out a chuckle that came

with a little too much gusto. "We aren't together at all. Not even a little. We're like brother and sister." And that was more or less the truth. Jackson had never looked at her as anything even remotely romantic. He'd dated half of Heart's Hope Bay and had never so much as tried to make a move on her, even when drunk, even when bored.

"Brother and sister! That's so cute," the bridesmaid gushed. "Well, thanks so much. I promise to return him after."

He caught Becca's gaze and arched a brow at the bridesmaid's words. "You sure?"

Becca plastered on a smile and waved him off. She kept that smile all the way to the champagne punch bowl, where she got another cup and then slipped outside.

The evening air chilled her heated skin. She pressed her back to the brick building's façade and took a long sip of her drink, letting the bubbles tickle her throat.

Inside she could hear the sultry music, a woman crooning how at last her love had come along. Maybe she should have put herself out there more tonight. Knowing her luck, Jackson would go back to his hotel room with that gorgeous blonde, and she would be crawling into bed in her plaid pajama pants to watch *Desperate Housewives*.

She sighed and closed her eyes, as if to block out the sight. But that just made it worse, because now all she could do was picture Jackson swaying, his arms wrapped around that girl, his eyes hooded as she whispered naughty things into his ear about how she wanted to...

"Are you okay? Aren't you cold out here?"

Becca's eyes flew open, and there was Jackson, not inside getting his groove on, but standing a few feet away, looking at her with a worried expression.

"I'm fine," she said automatically—a rote response designed to deflect.

"Becca..." He gave her a searching look, one that seemed to see too much.

She took another drink.

"What just happened? We were having fun. Next thing I know I see you go outside and then not come back in."

She furrowed her brow. "Are you telling me you got worried?"

"Obviously." He threw up his hands in exasperation. "I always worry about you. If you are getting enough sleep. Eating more than the leftovers Sofia doesn't finish. Or...or...if you'll get hurt doing all sorts of odd jobs like changing a lightbulb, or cleaning the gutters."

She stiffened. "You don't have to worry about me. I don't want to be a burden. Please, just go inside and have fun. I'll join you for the next dance."

"I want to go inside and have fun. But with you."

"What about banging a hot bridesmaid?"

He looked at her as if she had three heads and they were all speaking different languages. "Huh?"

"You have a chance to hook up. Don't let me stop you from having a good time."

"For being so smart, I don't know what goes on in your head sometimes—because right now you sound silly. I want to be with you."

"You do?" God. She hated how pathetic that one little squeal sounded. Thank goodness there was no moon tonight, so at least she had a measure of privacy out here in the dark.

"I've been looking forward to this. Me. You. A few drinks. Some laughs. I don't need anyone else. I don't *want* anyone else." The intense way he was suddenly looking at her made her stomach jump.

"Careful, Jackson. You wouldn't want a girl to get any ideas. Just kidding—I know you don't see me that way." She let out an awkward laugh, then pushed off the wall and walked toward the balcony railing. Maybe she could just jump off and roll into the river and away from what was drifting close to a dangerous conversation.

He gripped the railing on either side of her, his chest against her back. As he leaned in she could feel the thud of his heartbeat against her spine. Before she could react, his lips were against her ear.

"You're my best friend, but if you think I have never noticed you are a woman, then you haven't been paying attention."

His breath on her sensitive skin made her shiver. She pushed a lock of hair back. "What on earth are you talking about? You've never so much as made a pass at me."

"A pass..." He was quiet for a moment, reflecting on her words. "Is that what you wanted?"

She kept her eyes on the sky, too nervous to turn and meet his gaze. The night sky was magical, a thick belt of stars from the Milky Way spilled across the sky and seeped into the horizon. Somewhere not far away an owl hooted low and cautiously, as if testing for danger.

"No. I don't know. Maybe." Was she really going to say this out loud? She licked her dry lips. "Sometimes . . . I think I've wondered why you didn't try. I mean, you're one of the most eligible bachelors in town. It might be nice to know that occasionally you saw me differently, something other than just as a single mom, or your friend, or the type-A person who likes to sort her closet by color."

"And what if it made everything weird?"

"I know." She gave her head a small shake. "It would be so weird, huh."

"Except . . ." When Jackson spoke again his words were thoughtful. "Maybe it would be fine. I mean we know each other so well."

"Right." Emboldened, she turned around so they stood face-to-face. Maybe it was the third champagne that made her feel giddy, but she'd been pacing herself pretty well. "Do you know how long it's been since I've had sex?"

He blinked. "I'm not sure."

"I think you know."

"Since having Sofia?"

"Bingo. We are talking about a five-year drought. And if I'm going to hop back on the horse, so to speak, I'm sort of afraid that . . ."

His mouth curled up at the corner. "You've forgotten how to ride."

"Something like that. And the idea of a casual hookup and trying to navigate that all for the first time...it's daunting."

"Becca..." He broke off and cleared his throat. "Are you asking what I think you are asking?"

Maybe it was the dark or the stars, but this moment didn't feel real. It was like she hovered outside herself. "That depends. What do you think I'm asking?"

"Are you going to make me say it?"

She nodded.

"Are you asking me to sleep with you?"

The words hung between them. She could make a joke, and the moment would float away. Or she could grab it with both hands.

"Just once," she said quickly. "Like we do it, and then *boom* it's done, and I sort of remember how it all works and blow off the cobwebs."

Guess she was grabbing.

He choked back a surprised laugh. "I'm not sure if I'm flattered or offended. I'm not a Dustbuster."

"No. You aren't. But you have more experience, and I...I just want to be with someone that I trust, Jackson. And not have it be a risk."

"A risk of falling for me?"

"Exactly." She spoke quickly now, not entirely sure what she was saying. Her brain felt like it was flatlining. "I mean, we've been such good friends for so long. This is just an extension of the friendship."

"A long hug."

"Yes!"

He paused. "Without clothes."

"Uh, well." Thank God it was dark and he couldn't see that she was likely blushing to the tips of her nose.

"And with condoms."

"Oh, right." Her thighs trembled. "Condoms. I forgot about condoms."

"I have condoms."

Was it her imagination, or was his face closer to hers?

"Right here?"

"Jesus." His laugh was genuine. "What do you take me for? No, Becca, not right here. In my suit-case. I keep a box in my toiletry case."

She forced a laugh. She could totally do this, be casual and witty. No big deal. Just discussing sexual protection with her best friend. "How responsible of you."

"I was an Eagle Scout. Like to be prepared."

"So, we could hypothetically go back to your hotel room, where there is a box of condoms, and we could...do the horizontal mambo or whatever."

"Never in a million years."

She blinked. *Wait, what?* Had she been misread-ing the whole situation? "Oh, sorry, I thought we were being serious."

"I am. And what I would do to you is nothing like

a horizontal mambo. For starters we aren't members of AARP. It's sex. I would have sex with you."

"Yes. Sex. Me." Her breathing was getting increasingly ragged.

"Such a little cavewoman. I had no idea. But I have a few rules if we do this."

"Go ahead."

"One, I get to kiss you. This isn't going to be me just deep-cleaning cobwebs. It's been a long time, so if I do this, I do it right."

"Kissing. Yes. Okay. Kissing. Great."

"I mean I can kiss you anywhere." His voice took on a little gravel.

There was no shooting star. No asteroid skimming the atmosphere. That crackling sound was coming from the nerves in her body.

"Anywhere?"

"Consider it a point of pride. This is you. This is me. I feel like I might need to show off a little."

She let go of the railing and placed her hands on her cheeks. "Is this for real?"

"I don't know." The uncertainty that passed over his face made him look more boyish than normal. It was like they were playing chicken. "That's up to you. What do you want to do?"

There was an edge to his breath too, one that matched hers. This wasn't some funny hypothetical joking-around conversation. It had shifted, and the enormity of what they might be about to do pressed into her chest like a boulder.

"We could...kiss and see."

"See what?"

"If it felt okay. I mean, you did call me your brother earlier."

"Gross." She smacked his chest. "I didn't mean it literally."

"Well, that's a relief."

"It's just that I don't want this to change anything. And I feel like this could do all sorts of changing. Throughout everything, you've been my one constant."

"Here is what I know. You're thinking that I never thought about you like that. You are wrong. I have. More than once. More than twice. More than I might want to say."

"Are you joking?"

"Not about this. You are smart, but also so oblivious sometimes. You have no idea how gorgeous you are. Trust me, every guy who talks to you thinks about it. I'm just being a pal and letting you in on the truth."

She searched his face, but there was no hidden joke to his words.

"Okay then, kiss me," she said, pushing back her shoulders. "Kiss me, and let's see if we even have chemistry."

"You are really asking me to kiss you. Right now. Right here."

"Are you really going to make me ask again—"

But he'd already fisted her hair with one hand while using the other to press into the small of her back, lurching her toward him as he slanted his

mouth on hers. It wasn't tentative. He didn't leave
room for her to have doubt. Good lord, he didn't
leave room for her to form a coherent thought. His
mouth was warm and firm, yet soft, coaxing, urging
her to open to him, and when she did it was a shock
that nearly sent her boneless.

Jackson's tongue slid across hers, stroking with a
soft but urgent pressure that demanded a response.
She had no choice but to reach up and grip his broad
shoulders and hang on for dear life.

When she kissed him back he made a low moan
of appreciation, pulling her closer still. Their teeth
clicked together, and then his hands were dropping
from her waist to the bottom of her butt, scooping
her off her feet and cradling her against him.

She had no idea kissing could be like this, so
intimate, so consuming—a slow dance that had a
rhythm all its own. It had always felt like a pleasant
exchange, something that a guy engaged in to move
on to the next parts. But Jackson kissed in a way that
was lazy and yet hungry, as if he couldn't imagine
doing anything else but was also starving and this
was the fuel he needed to keep going.

The strangest part was how this didn't feel awkward. She *knew* Jackson. She trusted him. And yet
this was getting to see a whole other side, a shared
intimacy that was unlike anything else that had ever
passed between them.

He teased her with the tip of his tongue, tasting
like oranges and hops. He didn't shove it in but
invited her to play, to explore, to feel everything

until her body felt like it was wound up tight, clenched with anticipation and aching in the best ways. Right when she wasn't sure if she would be able to breathe, he pulled away, nibbling up her jaw until he got to the shell of her ear.

"That wasn't so bad, was it?" He eased her back down to standing. When he set his shoulders it was easy to see the rise and fall of his wide chest, his breath coming in ragged pants, letting her know he was just as affected.

God. She was so spun around she couldn't even begin to think about holding his gaze. "I'd say I have had worse."

"Will anyone miss you here?"

She frowned, uncertain of his meaning.

"If I take you out of here. Do you need to say goodbye?"

The idea of walking around a room trying to engage in polite chitchat and casual farewells with her thighs literally quivering from desire was not high on her to-do list.

"I think we can make a quiet exit. To be honest, I don't think anyone will notice."

"My room or yours?"

"Yours." She rose up on her toes and bit his lower lip. Tonight, this beautiful man wasn't going to be her friend. He was going to be her lover. "You have the condoms, remember?"

And with that he took her hand and led her out into the night, neither one of them looking back.

Chapter Four

Becca had only run a mile before slowing to a walk. That was weird. She frowned, checking her heart rate monitor. She'd barely pushed herself, and yet she felt exhausted. Not only that, but her head hurt a little and her stomach was cramping. Hopefully she was just a little overworked and not coming down with something. Sofia hadn't been sick, so fingers crossed.

A horn beeped, and she glanced over to see Jackson pulling up to the curb, surfboards of various lengths piled in the back of his truck, loud guitar riffs blasting through the windows. He turned down the volume and shot her a lopsided grin.

"Well, well, well, if it isn't Rebecca Gump. Fancy seeing you here, stranger."

She couldn't make out his eyes with the sunglasses on—just her own face reflected back, hair tucked under a thick elastic band and eyes tired.

"Hey! Work was long today. I'm sneaking in some exercise before I grab Sofia from school."

"Enjoy your run. I'll be over by six, and remember, I'll bring pizza, so no need to cook for her."

"Thanks again for offering to babysit."

"Anytime."

She shifted her weight. "I know Savannah probably strong-armed you into it."

Jackson had texted out of the blue last night offering to watch Sofia while her sister-in-law Abby hosted a girls' night in, complete with face masks and mocktails. Her friend was fully embracing the second trimester and that brief period between feeling like you want to vomit and feeling as if you can barely move.

"She might have mentioned that it would be very kind of me to come over and help, and you know me, I never miss a chance to be a giver."

The memory of exactly how giving Jackson could be flashed in her mind. His tousled blond curls between her legs, the way he didn't quit until he made sure she was satisfied three times over.

She cleared her throat, and tried to keep her face as friendly and normal as his. He had kept to his word and treated her no differently after their one—fantastic—night together. No jokes. No innuendos. No gossip from others. It was like nothing had ever happened. Which was a huge relief and also strangely...disappointing?

They had a one-night stand and then went back to being friends like nothing ever happened. Just like Jackson had promised. Exactly like she had wanted. Right?

Right.

"Oh! Don't forget Sofia is boycotting pepperoni now."

He chuckled. "I'll make sure to get pesto and cheese."

"Thank you. I really appreciate getting to see the girls."

"No thanks needed. Sofia and I are going to watch *The Muppets*. It's time I introduce her to Fozzie Bear."

"Sounds perfect. Okay, I don't want to keep you. Have fun in the water. Be safe."

"Will do." He gave her a salute and was back on the road.

He didn't look back.

Not that she wanted him to.

They were friends. Friendly good friends.

Real good buddies.

* * *

Later that night, Becca pulled up in front of Sunshine Corner, the preschool Abby owned and managed and lived above. Her auburn-haired friend answered the door in royal blue silk pajamas that made her look like a goddess. As Becca followed Abby inside, she noted that she was the last to arrive. Their friend Gia was already there, chatting with Tori and Savannah, both of whom worked at the preschool. Hilde, Abby's awesome grandma, tipped a glass toward her in greeting. Soon they were all nestled on the comfy overstuffed couches in the living room with minty mocktails and Korean sheet masks.

"It's so good to finally have everyone together," Savannah said, twisting her long blond tresses into a messy bun before sprawling out. "It feels like it's been forever."

"Tell me about it." Gia adjusted a pillow behind her back, her movements as quick and sharp as a little bird's. "I feel like my body is just starting to not feel like it was hit by a bus. Promise me if my nipples start randomly leaking that no one will judge."

"Never!" Tori giggled. "But can I say, I'm proud of how you and Marco are handling the transition to parenthood. I know there have been bumps, but you are both taking it like champs."

"Hopefully you can fill me in on all the tips and tricks." Abby rubbed her swelling belly in a slow circular motion, a habitual gesture Becca remembered from her pregnancy with Sofia. "You too, Becs."

"Me?" Becca shook her head, the corner of her mouth curling into a rueful smile. "I know it sounds hard to believe, but I honestly can't even remember the newborn stage. If I didn't have pictures to prove it, I'd probably wonder if it ever really happened." She'd been a single mom, and sleep had been elusive. It took two years before life felt even halfway normal. "I'll tell you the one thing I remember, though. How grateful I was to get a catheter in the hospital after my C-section. The last few weeks before having Sofia, I swear to God I had to pee every five minutes. She treated my bladder like her own personal soccer ball." She pushed herself up to standing. "On that note, do you mind if I use your bathroom?"

"Go ahead. I just got Carter to install a new faucet. Took him *hours*." Abby rolled her eyes even though she grinned. "Your brother might be able to design me a dream living room, but handyman jobs are *so not* his forte."

"I think he can be forgiven, as this looks like something out of a social media post." Becca waved her arm around the open living room that was designed in a more minimalist style—lots of warm light wood and crisp white walls that reflected light from the big picture windows.

"I suppose." Abby giggled. "I mean he can't be perfect. Just pretty damn close."

As Becca walked to the bathroom, her stomach roiled. It wasn't jealousy. She was genuinely happy for her friends finding luck in love. And she was grateful to the moon and back that Carter and Abby had made their way back to each other after years spent apart. Just because she hadn't been able to be fortunate in the romance department didn't mean that she wanted the people she cared about in life to be alone.

She wanted the people she loved to be supremely happy. She just wouldn't mind getting a little of that love for herself.

Six weeks into this dating plan, and all she had to show for it was sleeping with her best friend at a wedding and engaging in a few casual conversations on the dating app that hadn't even led to coffee.

She didn't think she was picky, but for the love of Pete, she couldn't swipe on a guy who posted a fishing selfie or a shot flexing in the gym. Plus, it didn't help that for some reason she kept comparing everyone to Jackson, and at the end of the day, they simply didn't measure up.

The brief bout of nausea went away as fast as it came. Hmm...there was a reasonable explanation for it, she was certain. Probably nothing more sinister than the fact that she ate something weird. She had bought fresh fish yesterday from the new shop near the marina. Maybe it hadn't been the catch of the day as promised.

After going to the bathroom, she went to Abby's kitchen to get a glass of water. Savannah was in there, setting up a charcuterie board.

"That looks good," Becca said even as the idea of soft cheeses, olives, and smoked meat sent a fresh round of woozy curling through her.

Maybe she needed to just call it a night. What if she was getting sick? It would be horrible to pass it to everyone else.

"Thanks! I've been getting really into charcuterie. Noah and I keep trying to outdo each other with boards every night. Right now I have him beat." She winked. "Also..." Her voice was carefully neutral. "I just needed a tiny break from the baby talk. It can be a lot, and you know me—I love babies. And Rosie is the best—literally my favorite person on earth, except for her dad."

Noah and his daughter, Rosie, had fit into Savannah's life like the perfect set.

"I get it." Becca nodded in understanding. "You get a bunch of us together who have a shared experience like motherhood, and it's hard for it not to dominate the conversation. No one intends to leave anyone out, and yet it happens. It's hard to balance sometimes—being a woman versus being a mama."

Savannah gave her a relieved nod, grateful to be understood and not judged.

"Well...moving on...I'm really hoping to persuade you to take that trip next winter. Now that Sofia is comfortable staying with your auntie Kalani, maybe we really can go to Italy. Picture it! You. Me. A Tuscan villa. Romance novels. Vespas. Food and drinks we don't have to make."

"Gelato and espresso." Becca sighed. "Sounds like the most amazing thing ever. I haven't had a vacation anywhere since Sofia. I need one badly."

They clinked glasses.

"Do you think you'll ever have another?" Savannah asked just as Abby's grandmother, Hilde, wandered in, her silver hair covered up by a mauve headscarf adorned in intricate golden stitching.

"I don't need to consult a Magic 8 Ball to tell me that particular outcome is not likely," Becca said ruefully. "I need a man before I can even begin to think about that."

Hilde swung her head to face her straight on, her gold hoop earring winking in the light. "Oh?" was all she said.

"Oh?" Becca suddenly was gripped by an uncomfortable sensation similar to how being a specimen under a microscope must feel. "What kind of *oh* are you talking about? Uh-oh? Or yay-oh?"

"Hmmmm. I suppose that is all up to you." Abby's wise grandmother had that look about her, the one she always got when she sensed something . . . big.

"No freaking way." Savannah gasped, the whites of her eyes showing. "Are you saying that Rebecca is—"

"Thanksgiving," Hilde interrupted with an authoritative nod. "Yes. That's the due date."

"Due date?" Savannah and Becca exchanged meaningful glances before slowly turning to face her.

"I'm sorry." Becca forced a laugh. "Whose due date?"

"Why, yours, of course!" Hilde turned to give her another once-over. "I'd say you are six to seven weeks along. Suspected it the minute you walked in the door."

"What!" Savannah clapped a hand over her mouth.

"You have a bun in the oven? Girl, why didn't you tell me?"

"Uh, because I don't?" Becca glanced between the shocked face of her friend and the knowing gaze of the older woman. "Stop looking at me like that. I am *not* pregnant, that's impossible..."

The protests trailed away as she thought about her increasing nausea and need to pee.

Six weeks ago...she had slept with Jackson during their one unexpected, and unexpectedly amazing, encounter.

But he wore a condom. She knew. Heck, she'd put it on.

Her stomach twisted into a hot pool of apprehension.

But condoms aren't 100 percent effective.

"No way," she said, sinking into a chair, wishing she had a blanket to throw on top of her head. "No, I can't be, that's crazy."

"What's crazy?" Abby walked in with Tori and Gia in her wake. "And why are you all hidden away in here? I was wondering where the party went."

"It's nothing," Becca said at the exact same moment Hilde announced, "She's pregnant."

"Are you serious? Oh my God! You're pregnant!" Gia squealed, stepping forward to hug Savannah. "Welcome to the club!"

"Whoa, Nelly, eager breeder. I have my hands full with Noah and Rosie, and that's fine by me." Savannah held up her hands, warding her off. "Take a seat. It's not me. It's her."

Everyone pivoted to stare at Becca.

"You? But...who is the dad?" Tori's puzzled voice shared what everyone was clearly wondering.

"What's all this about? Who says I'm pregnant?" Becca said weakly, leaning against the wood-backed chair.

"Girl, get it together." Savannah's tone was matter-of-fact. "When the great baby whisperer of Heart's Hope Bay speaks up, you for sure have a hot cross bun in the oven. We don't make the rules."

"I wanna know what guy has been in your oven, sis." Tori was like a dog with a bone.

"Savannah's right. You know when Grandma gets the feeling, she's never wrong. Oh wait, I have an extra pregnancy test." Abby held up a finger. "It's in the hall closet. I was wondering if I should throw it out the other day but never got around to it. Wanna take it?"

"What? No, come on, y'all. I'm not pregnant." She rubbed her temples. "I'm almost positive that I'm not pregnant."

"Almost." Gia put a hand on her narrow hip. "So, you're saying there's a chance."

"Oh my gosh, you sly dog." Savannah looked half annoyed and half impressed. "You slept with someone and didn't tell us. I didn't know you were so secretive."

Panic burbled up in Becca. What was she supposed to say? She got down with Savannah's big brother? That it was by far the best night she'd ever spent with a guy? That it had left her waking up every morning since panting from dreams that were incredibly sexy?

"Oh God, okay, hold on, I'm going to be sick." She bolted to the bathroom and fell to her knees, hitting the bowl just in the nick of time.

After she cleaned up and splashed some water on her face, she opened the door. Abby was there with a glass of water and a pregnancy test.

"Grandma is never wrong, you know that." Her friend's blue eyes were gentle, but her voice was firm. "If you're really pregnant again, then you are going to need a plan."

"If I'm really pregnant I'm going to need a lot more than that." Her eyes began to burn. "A single mom of *two* kids with *two* different dads?"

"You mean an awesome mom who is raising a fantastic little girl." Abby patted her shoulder. "Just find out first. You can worry about the rest later."

Becca took the test and froze. "Wait. Shoot. I can't do this."

"Sure you can. I know it's hard. But you should at least know for sure."

"No." A hysterical giggle ripped from Becca. "I mean I peed a couple of minutes ago. I don't need to pee again."

"Ah, gotcha." Abby joined in the laughter before handing over the glass of water. "Bottoms up."

Becca was chugging the water as the other women appeared, each holding a water glass. Apparently everyone had overheard and was there to help ensure she quickly reached the stage of peak saturation.

"Operation Fill the Bladder, reporting for duty." Savannah collected the empty glass and handed Becca a new one.

"I cannot chug five glasses of water at once. I will definitely throw up again."

"But think of how great your skin will look," Gia said.

That sent them into a round of hysterics.

"Okay, okay." Becca held up her hand, feeling a small but urgent pressure build. "I think I can do it. Hang on."

She retreated into the bathroom. "Can you all go in the other room, though? I'll get performance anxiety if you all stand out there listening."

"Come now, girls." Hilde pushed everyone away like a mother hen before closing the door behind her with a wink.

Once alone, Becca sat down and used her teeth to tear the test open. "Ok. Here goes nothing." In just a few minutes she'd learn if her life was about to change.

Except the moment she set the test on the counter the second line was already pink and bright and very clearly announcing *hellllooo, you are pregnant.*

"What the hell." Becca stumbled back. She hadn't even flushed, let alone washed her hands and already the answer was . . . positive.

She cleaned up in a numb haze. It was as if her brain had switched off and she was on autopilot. Inside her was a baby? A baby she made with Jackson?

She walked into the living room. The gang took in her stricken expression and a hush fell over the space.

"So ... congratulations?" Gia said hesitantly, looking as if she wanted to burst into applause but was waiting to read the room.

"Grandma!" Abby shook her head, her long red hair sweeping over her shoulders. "You did it again."

Savannah leapt up and pulled Becca into a big hug. "Breathe, just breathe okay? You look as white as a sheet. Sit down."

Tori brought over an ottoman and Becca sank onto it, wrapping her arms around herself as if that could keep her together. "I'm pregnant." Her whisper confirmed what everyone had already surmised.

Savannah sank to her knees beside her. "We didn't even know you had been hooking up with anyone."

"I wasn't," Becca said dully. "It was just one person, one time."

"Six weeks ago?" Savannah furrowed her brow before her eyes opened wide. "Wait. Oh. My. God. Wasn't that when you went to that wedding in Hood River?"

Becca nodded slowly, slowly raising her gaze to meet her friend. Her vocal cords seemed to have gone on strike. "Yes," she whispered.

"So you hooked up with someone at the wedding?" she continued. "But didn't Jackson—" Savannah froze. "Okay, okay, wait. Jackson went with you as your plus-one. But it couldn't have been... Oh my God, was it?

Becca nodded again.

"Holy crap. So are you saying he... you... this baby..." Savannah went as pale as Becca felt. "This is Jackson's baby. My big brother Jackson? That's your baby daddy? I'm the aunt of this baby?"

"Whoa," Tori said. "This night isn't going at all like I'd expected."

"What am I going to do?" Becca directed her question to Savannah, who was already pacing.

"Jackson as a father. Oh my God! How does that even look?" Her friend's face scrunched up as she thought out loud to herself. "I mean, he is a child. Obviously not technically, but the guy's favorite food is chicken tenders and Sprite. His biggest priority is the daily surf report. He still watches Cartoon Network!"

"Let's dial it down a little." Abby forced a laugh, nudging Savannah hard in the ribs. "And Becca, to confirm, Jackson really is the father?"

"I've slept with one person just one time since having Sofia. So, unless we're talking about some sort of miraculous conception, then yeah, it was him."

"What are the odds?" Gia whistled. "Pregnant on your first one-night stand in years? That's some bad luck."

"Or good luck." Tori swatted her friend. "I mean look, Jackson is a kid at heart, but is that so bad?

I mean, he is great with Sofia. Isn't he babysitting her tonight?"

"He's wonderful with Sofia." Becca massaged her temples as blood thumped through her ears. "But that doesn't mean he wants to have his own child." She looked down. Through her shirt she could see the pounding of her heart. She took a deep breath to calm herself, but it was impossible—her lungs were too shallow. "Oh my God, this is going to be like Graham all over again. Except instead of a fling with a guy who moved back to a whole other country, it's my friend who lives in my town, and I'm friends with his family, and when this doesn't work out— and it's not going to work out—everything is going to be ruined."

"Well, there is only one way to find out," Hilde said gravely. "You need to tell him."

Chapter Five

After Jackson bumped into Becca during her jog earlier, he couldn't shake the unsettled feeling he had all the way to the beach.

He knew she'd enjoyed their night together and that he'd made her feel good. But it was also more than that...It hadn't just been sex. The fact that they had a shared history, that it was *them*—Jackson and Becca—that made it more than just a random one-night stand. In truth, it was easily the most incredible evening of his life. Maybe because they knew and trusted each other so much, that was why the whole thing just worked.

And now? He had promised her it wouldn't be weird afterward, and he was doing his darndest to make it so. But when he ran into her without having a chance to brace himself, it was like his stomach was encased with a whole lot of butterflies.

He parked his truck up on a bluff that had a good view of the surf break below. His older brother, Aaron, was already there, sitting on the hood of his SUV and drinking a soda.

"You're late," Aaron said in lieu of a proper greeting.

"Sorry, man. I saw Becca on my way over and stopped to chat."

"Ah, Becca," his brother said with a fake breathy tone. He loved to give Jackson shit about being so close with a woman he never dated. "And how is the lovely Rebecca?"

"Great. I'm babysitting for her tonight so she can hang with her girls." He ripped off his shirt and fished his wet suit out of the cab.

"Man, why don't you just admit that you love her and get married and have a dozen babies?"

"Dude. I could tell you it's not like that, but why waste the oxygen. We have been having this conversation for over ten years. Unlike some Neanderthals, I believe men can be friends with women with no strings attached."

Aaron flashed an okay sign with his fingers. "Sure, Jan," he said, impersonating Marcia from *The Brady Brunch*.

"Do you want to sit here busting my balls or get in the water?" The lineup was already crowded on account of the good weather.

His brother jumped up and pulled the back zipper

cord up, adjusting the wet suit around his neck. "Let's do this."

They were both expert surfers. After they each caught a few rides, they paddled back to share the waves with the growing crowd—mostly teens— who looked like they were here on vacation. Heart's Hope Bay was a bustling tourist destination, which meant that on the weekends, the main beaches filled up. Some people complained or picked fights trying to claim local privileges on the waves, but that was never Jackson's scene. He came here almost every day, so why not share it—wouldn't kill anyone.

"So…I heard a rumor," Aaron said. "And it was about you."

"I swear to God, if you start with Becca again…"

"No, not about her. I came around for dinner last night to see the folks. Heard the old man complaining to Mom that he asked you to step up and take over the big chair, be the top lawn mower, a few weeks ago, but you still haven't given him an answer."

Jackson snorted. "Maybe I should have gone to law school like you did." Jackson sat up on his board, rolling his neck. "I feel like it's an offer I can't refuse, you know."

"But is it what you want to do? Does it align with your goals and shit?"

"Dude. Goals? My only goal is to get to this beach as many times as I can in a year. If that works out, everything else is gravy."

"But *dude*, you are over thirty. Surely you have some goals."

"And what if I don't? Can't it be enough to be healthy and happy? I can pay rent. I can put gas in my truck. I have good friends and a pretty decent family."

"Hey now." Aaron gave him a warning splash. "But this is serious. I'm being serious for once. Do you want to do it?"

Jackson dropped his shoulders. "I don't know. I feel like I don't really have a choice." He was staring off toward the horizon when he heard frantic shouting. "Tyler. Tyler!"

The brothers glanced over to see a younger boy, maybe thirteen, caught in a rip. He was paddling so hard his face was red with strain, but he kept getting pulled out.

"Hey." Jackson cupped his hands around his mouth to be heard over the crashing waves. "Kid! Swim this way."

The boy glanced over, his eyes wide with panic.

"I said, come this way. You'll get too tired if you try to fight it. Come right."

The boy was frozen in fear. This wasn't a dangerous situation yet, but people had drowned on the beach before, usually folks from inland who weren't aware of the laws of the ocean—number one being don't try to fight a rip current. It's a battle you never win. The only chance to escape is to exit on the side.

The kid made a feeble attempt to follow his directions.

"Shit. I'm going to get him." Jackson was paddling before Aaron could respond. He got to the kid quickly.

"You gotta go parallel to shore, bud."

"I'm too far out. Gotta go closer to shore."

"Nope, in this rip you aren't doing squat. It will keep pulling you out. Think of it as a river of water. A river is narrow, though, right?"

The boy nodded, hesitant, almost in tears.

"If you come with me this way we will get out of the current. Then you can paddle back into shore. Got it?"

The boy swiped his eyes. "Okay."

"Your name is Tyler, right?"

"Yeah. Tyler."

"Hey, Tyler, I'm Jackson. I've been coming to this beach since I learned how to walk, and you are gonna be just fine. We are going to do this together, all right?"

Within two minutes, Jackson had the kid out of the rip and back on shore, where he hugged his mom, finally breaking into tears.

"Christ! That happened so fast," the dad said, shaking Jackson's hand. "I feel like an idiot. We are from Bend, so we don't get a lot of ocean time. The boys wanted to try surfing, but there wasn't a surf school or anything, so we were just winging it."

"Oh right, yeah. There used to be a place—Go Ride a Wave—but it closed down after the owner retired and moved."

"That's a shame. Seems like a place this popular could use some surf instructors."

"I used to teach at the surf school back in the day. If you want, I can let Tyler go back out with me and give him some pointers."

"Seriously, man? That would be great. You obviously know what you are doing. We'd be happy to pay."

"No, no." Jackson waved him off with a laugh. "It will be fun. I love surfing, and it's great to get someone else stoked about it too."

For the next few hours, he helped Tyler get used to watching the waves, sitting or lying prone while being balanced and centered, as well as some paddling techniques.

"Remember that with the pop-up, you wait until you feel the board catch the wave. Then it's a quick push up."

"I get it, but I keep flipping."

"That's fine. You're learning. Here's a little secret to take with you into life: You got to suck at something before you're good at it."

Tyler chuckled before looking serious. "Okay, I think this is my wave."

Jackson did a quick scout. It was the right speed and height for a beginner and on the inside, away from where the more experienced lineup was positioned.

"Yep, you got this."

The kid paddled hard, and this time, when he popped up, he kept his balance. Sure, it was a little wobbly and his arms flailed like two windmills, but he was riding the wave. And when he turned around, his grin was wide.

Jackson laughed, recognizing the blissed-out expression. This kid was going to be surfing the rest of his life.

He was still thinking about how much fun he had out there in the water that evening after getting Sofia to bed and sitting on Becca's couch to wait for her to come home. It *was* weird that no one else had ever opened up another surf shop after Go Ride a Wave had closed.

Could there be something there?

Headlights shone through the window. Becca must be home. He straightened up the pillows around him and restacked her magazines before rising to greet her.

But she didn't come in.

He walked to the window and glanced between the curtains. He could see her silhouette in the driver's seat. Why was she just sitting in the dark?

He was about to go and check on her when she climbed out and walked slowly, head down, up her walkway.

"Hey," he said as she opened the door. "Is everything okay?"

She popped her head up like it was on a spring. "Huh?"

He frowned. Wow, she was really out of it.

"Is something wrong?"

"Well…" She licked her lips, brow furrowed. "I guess that depends on your definition of wrong."

And with that she burst into hysterical giggles.

Jackson rocked on his heels, unsure if he should take a few steps back or go give her a hug. Before he could make a firm decision, she collapsed to the ground and put her head between her legs, hyperventilating.

He moved quickly to the kitchen and got her a drink of water, then came back and sat next to her. She took the glass and drank deeply. He reached out and rubbed her shoulder, noting that the muscle was rock-hard with tension.

"It's okay. If you can't tell me, I get it, I'm here for you no matter what."

She dropped her head between her legs again, quiet a moment before saying "The thing is…I have to tell you."

"Okay. I mean, what are friends for?"

"This is beyond the normal bonds of friendship. Look…" She pushed up to her feet and began to pace. "I'm just going to tell you. On the count of three. But I need you to stay calm. Promise."

"Unless you just killed someone, I promise."

That earned him a smile. "No murder."

"Then lay it on me."

"Okay, here we go…one…two…"

She broke off—silent.

"Three," he said, equal parts bewildered and curious. He'd never seen his friend so rattled. She was always so together and organized.

"I'm pregnant. Six weeks pregnant."

"Oh." He blinked. Out of all the things in the world he'd expected her to say, that was the last one.

He almost asked "Who is the father," and then he realized what happened six weeks ago. And while Becca was within her rights to do whatever with whoever, he also was willing to bet she hadn't.

"Did you hear what I just said?" she whispered.

"We're going to have a baby." As he said the words, he realized that his first reaction wasn't panic; it was wonder. "Becca, whoa."

"*Whoa* is right. And thank you for saying *we*. I...I feel really overwhelmed right now. I don't even know how it happened."

"Well, we did, you know..."

"I'm aware of that." Her cheeks flushed as she glanced away. "But we used protection."

"We did. But I dunno. I guess the condoms hadn't gotten much use lately. Maybe they expired."

"And here I thought you were such a ladies' man."

"Hey. Ouch. There is a big difference between flirting with someone and sleeping with them. I'm not just having sex all the time."

"I never really asked. I just assumed."

"It had been a long time for me too," he said simply.

And it had. He wasn't just some guy in his twenties looking to take someone home. At this point in his life, he was looking for quality, not quantity. And no one could hold a candle to the woman standing in front of him.

"I wasn't sure if you'd freak out."

"Becs. Hey. It's me. I mean...I'm surprised. And I'm not sure it's really sunk in. But I'm not upset. Whatever you need, I'm right here." He stood.

Her whole body seemed to sag as if the relief of his words left her exhausted.

"Are you serious?"

"You are the coolest person I know. You and Sofia are already family for me. So, this is just...making us even closer."

"I'm not trying to trap you into a relationship here."

"Get over here, kid." He reached out and pulled her into a bear hug. "Stop talking nonsense. No matter what happens, I'm in this with you, okay? Promise. Every step of the way."

She melted into his embrace. He breathed deeply, inhaling the faint scent of rosewater. But deeper than that was her own scent—impossible to pin down, but something that reminded him of sea breezes, fresh bread, and a sun-dappled afternoon. It always gave him a feeling of calm and comfort.

He'd hugged this woman hundreds of times, but since the night they shared, he hadn't touched her again—partly out of nervousness but also because he was afraid to *want*. Because he had tasted her once, and he might as well admit that it wasn't enough, it would never be enough. But he had made a promise that it was a onetime thing, and he didn't want to mess up what he had with her.

But now, inside her, was a child, *their* child, and

the idea sent a surge of protection through him. He couldn't afford to screw this up. Even though he knew deep down that what he felt for Becca went beyond friendship, this was serious, this was a life that he helped create, a destiny set in motion, and so the best thing he could do was just be there to help, to support as best as he could, and not destroy the best relationship he had in his life.

"How is this going to work?" Becca mumbled into his shirt, her face buried into his chest.

"I don't know, but it will." It had to.

"Your sister already knows," she added. "I'm sorry. I got sick at Abby's and then took a pregnancy test. But she promised she wouldn't tell anyone in your family."

Right. His family. What would his dad say? His chest tightened, but that wasn't important right now. All that mattered was giving comfort to the woman trembling in his arms.

"That's all right. Savannah won't blab to them. She'll let me tell them when I'm—sorry, *we* are ready."

"You know, you are a really good guy, Jackson. Like the best guy."

"Don't forget it," he teased, gently tugging a lick of her hair. "I should record you saying it just to play back whenever you're pissed at me."

"Do I ever get mad at you? Like seriously mad?"

He thought about it. "No. Not seriously."

"Well, I guess that is a good thing if we are having a baby. I just can't believe you are being so calm.

Graham freaked out when I told him about Sofia. Which also is fair...I mean she wasn't planned at all, and we were in our early twenties. God, I can't believe this has happened to me twice. The town is going to have a field day."

"What's there to gossip about? You have a beautiful little girl, and you are raising her up right. And now you will have another baby, and this time it's mine. And if anyone has anything to say, they can take it up with me."

Becca stared up at him with so much hope that it was all he could do not to bend down, slant his mouth over hers, and kiss her until he could taste her sweetness.

Friends, dude. Just friends.

Jackson dropped his arms from around her and took a few quick steps back.

"Are you absolutely serious, you want to be a part of this?"

"I'm as serious as a heart attack." He was glad his words came out even, because deep down he knew his dad was going to risk a very real attack when he heard the news.

Chapter Six

One more bite," Becca pleaded as Sofia glared at the piece of sourdough toast in her hand, smeared with huckleberry jam and peanut butter. "Seriously, what's not to like?"

"I want a Pop-Tart."

Becca braced her hand on the top of her sedan and prayed for Jesus to take the wheel. The morning already had felt like an entire day. She'd decided to delete the dating app off her phone while drinking her first cup of coffee for the day. She figured it probably wasn't wise to start a relationship when she was going to have a baby in a few months. And then Sofia came in to announce the toilet had overflowed. That had been a fun twenty minutes, and now she had a meeting with her boss at the bank in thirty minutes and couldn't in good conscience send Sofia to preschool for a day on nothing more substantial than her four-year-old stubbornness and a few gulps of air.

"You have had a Pop-Tart exactly once in your life. And that was with Jackson. This is a healthy choice for breakfast and will give your body energy to play with friends until lunch. In our family we make smart choices."

"Hey! How's it going?" Abby came out of the school, dusting her hands on her apron. "We were just making some play dough inside. Sofia, aren't you going to come join us?"

"Don't want toast. It's yucky." Sofia burrowed into her car seat, shaking her head so hard that her pigtails whipped back and forth across her face.

Becca mouthed *Help me*, and Abby flashed an okay sign.

"Ah, so you don't want to finish your breakfast. What do you want to do instead?"

"Go play."

"Yeah, you want to come inside and hang out with all your friends. Try the new play dough. It's all nice and warm right now, too. It feels good on your hands."

Sofia bit her lip.

"But remember, snack time isn't until after arts and crafts, song circle, *and* recess. That's a long time. Your tummy will get so hungry if you don't eat now."

"Fine!" With an air of resignation, Sofia took a

bite of toast, chewing it thoughtfully. She licked her lips before taking another.

Becca quickly unbuckled her from the seat and handed her the little Disney princess backpack. "Have a fun day, honey, okay?"

"Okay." Sofia shoved the rest of her toast in her mouth. "Love you, Mama." With a quick hug and kiss, she bounded inside.

"I swear to God, I don't know how you do it," Becca said to her friend. "I'd rather negotiate diplomacy at the United Nations than try to logic battle with a preschooler."

Abby giggled as Savannah and Hilde slipped outside, brows furrowed in concern even as they regarded her with kind, gentle expressions.

"How did he take it?" Savannah said, no need to specify the *he* in question.

"Surprisingly well." Becca shook her head. "Not that I expected him to be a jerk or anything like that. But I was bracing for a lot more shock and panic. He seemed...relaxed."

"That's good though, right?" Abby frowned. "Why am I getting the sense you aren't sure if that is good?"

"Having a baby is a lot of work. Sofia completely changed my life. Obviously I'm not complaining, but my world before and after having a child doesn't compare. Jackson likes his me time. He sleeps in late. He runs to the beach every moment he can. He has no idea what is coming, and I'm honestly worried he doesn't fully get it."

"Does anyone, though?" Hilde asked sagely. "Of course he doesn't get it, but that doesn't mean he won't rise to the occasion."

"Right." Savannah rocked on her heels, staring thoughtfully into the distance. "But still...Jackson has some growing up to do, and there is a ticking clock. It's now or never."

"I know, I know." Becca put her hands over her lower belly. "We just have to see how it goes. But no matter what, I'll be okay. My job pays well, I can keep doing it remotely, and I've been building up savings. Plus, Sofia's dad helps out."

"Jackson will have to help too." Savannah was adamant. "My parents will probably pitch in as well."

"It's not about the money right now. I'm super fortunate with that. It's just...kids need routine and structure to feel stable. What am I saying?" She gave a short laugh. "I'm preaching to the choir telling this to preschool teachers."

"One day at a time." Hilde stepped forward and rubbed her upper back. "Remember, everything will work out in the end, and if it's not all right, it's not the end."

Becca blinked. "That's so wise."

"Isn't it?" Hilde's giggle was girlish. "It was on the tag of my teabag this morning. Seemed like good advice."

"You are all the best." Becca's throat felt like it had swelled a few sizes as tears threatened. "Hey, I'm going to get going before the waterworks turn on. With all the hormones in my body, I could flood the school."

She was driving toward the bank when a red Subaru pulled up behind her and flashed its lights three times. It was her big brother, Carter. She checked the clock. She had just enough time for a quick conversation so she pulled over.

"Sis!" He jogged up to the driver's side window. "Glad I caught you. Heading to get your workday started?"

She nodded.

"I'm going to the office too, but I wanted to say congrats. Abby told me the news, even though it's all hush-hush. You know how much I love being an uncle. Way I see it, more kids means more love, right?"

"Thanks, bro." She might still feel anxious about the whole situation, but she was glad to have his support. "And yeah, we're keeping it quiet for now."

Carter nodded, then grimaced. "Are you going to tell Dad?"

"Not anytime soon. He was a total jerk about Sofia." Becca gripped the steering wheel.

"I'm not sure if it was about Sofia or just that he *is* a total jerk."

She nodded with a frown. "True story."

They were both quiet a moment, thinking the same thing.

"I wish Mom was here," she said at last, a catch in her voice.

"Me too. Every day. She'd know all the right

things to say. She loved kids. She'd have been the best grandma in the world. It's so unfair she has to miss all of this."

"I hate that she isn't here. And I really hate that Dad was so horrible the last time I told him I was pregnant. Did you know he called me a loser?"

"Damn it." Carter's hands balled into two tight fists. "That's rich. Considering you paid your way through college and make more in a year than he has probably earned in a decade. Let me give you one piece of advice. It's not easy, but I try to remember it. Don't care about what the old man says. Let it slide like water off a duck's back. Keep paddling and ignore him. He's nothing but a bitter old snapping turtle."

"Oh my God." An image of her father's sour face popped into her mind, and she laughed despite everything. "You are right. He looks exactly like a snapping turtle."

"Once you see it, the truth cannot be unseen." Carter looked relieved to see her mood lighten. "Hey, I won't keep you any longer, but let's get together for dinner soon. I'll barbecue."

"Thanks. You're a pretty darn good brother."

"What can I say? I was born this way." He gave her a mock salute before turning away with a mumbled "Love ya" that warmed her to her toes.

Thank goodness she had such a great brother. It almost made up for having one of the worst fathers. Despite everything Carter said, she knew her dad always found a way to cut her with words. She'd have to try her best to keep her protective armor up when she told him, but it didn't change the fact that she was nervous.

* * *

Jackson hung up the phone with the insurance company. He had decided on a whim to renew the insurance he used to carry when working for Go Ride a Wave. After helping Tyler for the day, the family had hired him for the rest of the weekend and then referred him to other families they'd run into while out hitting the local tourist hot spots.

His next lesson was in an hour. It was his day off with landscaping, but teaching surfing never felt like work. He enjoyed helping kids bring up their confidence, and he loved seeing the joy beam from their faces when they first got up and enjoyed the feeling of being pulled along by forces far greater than themselves. It was humbling and exhilarating all at once. Plus, the pay was pretty great. The family was leaving soon, but their referrals had grown his unofficial new side hustle 300 percent.

After making a quick peanut butter and jelly sandwich, he decided to head out early and catch a few waves before the lesson. Thirty minutes later, as he was paddling out, the sun warm on his face, a welcome contrast to the cold Pacific Northwest water, he was grateful he had made that decision. This was his favorite spot to think, and he had a lot on his mind.

He hadn't spent much time with pregnant women. His mom had five kids, but he was the second youngest and couldn't remember anything from her pregnancy with Savannah. And when Becca got pregnant with Sofia, she wasn't in town. She'd returned after she had the baby.

A wave rolled up and almost crashed down over him before he noticed and did a quick duck dive.

"Hey, man, thought you were about to eat it." Jackson swiped the saltwater off his face and turned to see his buddy Ben paddling over with a wide grin.

"Me too." Jackson chuckled wryly. "That one snuck up on me."

"Whatcha contemplating? Your favorite tree? How to prune faster? And, uh…" Ben sat up on his board and wrinkled his brow, trying to come up with more landscaping tasks. "I dunno, man—how to best mow grass?"

"How'd you guess? I was out here thinking… hmmm… what's the optimal length to cut grass? Do I play it conservative and go with two and a half inches or let it have some personality and go all the way to three." Jackson glanced over his shoulder and saw the next set coming. That beauty cresting up was his wave. "Mine," he called as he paddled hard, getting his speed up to match the wave, and there it was… the rush from the drop-in, the roar, and then he bounced up and was flying. He rode all the way in and enjoyed the paddle back, the feeling of his shoulders and arms working together to propel him through the water.

Surfing was straightforward. You waited. You watched. Some waves were yours. Some you let go by.

But fatherhood? His stomach seemed to roll with his board over the next set. He meant every word he said to Becca. He would figure out how to support her and the baby *and* Sofia. He *had* to. And the idea that he and that amazing woman created life? That in a little over seven months that life would be out in the world, blinking at the sun, feeling the wind on its little face, needing to be kept safe, protected, and loved?

He couldn't screw this up.

He wouldn't screw this up.

But that little voice in the back of his head whispered in a cold, soft voice: *But you will.*

"Damn, Jacks, you planning your funeral over there?" Ben was looking at him with an expression that was equal parts amused and concerned.

"Thinking about fatherhood."

Ben snorted. "Your old man is a lot. No offense, he works hard and keeps his word, but the way he looks at you? There is a lot of pressure in that gaze."

"Nah. I'm not thinking about my dad. I was thinking about how I'll be as a dad."

"You?" Now Ben was laughing. "That's a scary thought."

Jackson's smile faded. "You really think so?"

"Jackson Lowe as a father? Where do I even begin? One . . . you sleep until noon unless the surf is good or you gotta be at work. Two . . . you play video games like it's a second job. You'd forget your ass if it wasn't attached, so you'd totally forget your kid in a shopping cart or leave it at school. And anyway, why are you even thinking about that? Right now you are in your prime. Single. Ready to mingle." Ben shook his head as if trying to clear away the unbelievable idea. "You, a dad. I can't even imagine it. But hey. Kid would be a surfer, right? At least you could teach 'em that."

The worst part was that Jackson knew his friend wasn't even trying to be mean. Sure, he was talking crap, but that's what they did with one another. And since Ben had no idea what was happening, this was his unvarnished opinion.

Wait. Jackson frowned. That wasn't the worst part. The *worst* part was wondering if deep down, Becca felt the same. Did she wish she could take back their night? Or that it could have been someone else—preferably someone with a stock portfolio who worked nine to five in an office and golfed once a month? The idea of letting her down, of letting *them* down, constricted his throat so tight that black shadows grew at the edge of his vision.

If he wanted Becca to believe he was up for the job, he needed to believe in himself. The trouble was, he didn't have the first clue how.

Chapter Seven

"Fair warning, if we get pulled over because you're driving twenty miles under the speed limit, I'm going to fake sleeping to avoid embarrassment." Becca gestured at the 45 MPH sign Jackson crept past. She had her first maternal care appointment in ten minutes, and at this rate she might be an hour late.

"Go on, laugh at me all you want. I'm secure while living my best *Driving Miss Daisy* life. I just want to be careful, precious cargo and all." Jackson didn't take his eyes off the road. His hands were at two and ten, and he refused to even let her turn on the radio, saying he needed to focus.

"Please don't tell me you are going to get one of those BABY ON BOARD car stickers once it is born."

"Actually, that's a great idea," Jackson shot her some side eye and winked. "But also, we can't keep call the baby *it*. We need a nickname."

"A nickname?" Becca pursed her lips. "I never did that with Sofia."

"What did you call her while you were pregnant?"

"Sofia. I had some tests done at thirteen weeks and found out she was a girl. I'd always wanted to name my first child Sofia, so that was it."

"Ah, well, I don't want to know the baby's sex."

"What?" Becca clapped a hand over her mouth trying to process his words. "But how do we know what to buy? The color scheme? If I don't know, I can't plan, and you know me. I need to know my homework assignment."

"Whoa, Becs. First up, take a breath. Second, at the end of the day, all of this is your call. You want to learn the baby's sex? You learn the baby's sex. Although I would rather you didn't tell me. I like surprises."

"You don't think we've had enough surprises for a lifetime?"

He was quiet for a moment. "I guess…it's like this, right? There is this little being inside of you. And we don't know anything about them. But I do know I want them to have the world. And I want them to be loved no matter what, just for existing, no other reason. They have a whole life ahead of them to be put into boxes. To be categorized. Right now, this is the only time they will have to just be, and still be loved."

"What the hell, Jackson Lowe." Tears prickled Becca's eyes, and she blinked them away, laughing in amazement. "How do you just sometimes come out with the most beautiful things to say? When you put it like that, you win. I guess it will be another surprise for us."

"Bolt," Jackson said out of the blue, turning into the clinic's parking lot, then angling them into the space closest to the front door. "Like Thunderbolt. That's the baby's nickname."

"Bolt." Becca tried it out. "Bolt. It's different." Her grin was sudden, but genuine. "But I like it. It's cute."

He held the door for her as she walked into the clinic, following as she went up to reception and gave her name.

She briefly scanned the waiting room, hoping that she didn't see anyone she knew, since most of the town was very unaware that the two longtime friends were having a baby together. Small-town life had its charms, like free parking and neighbors who looked out for each other. But there were also people who were nosy and wanted to know—and share—everyone's secrets. She'd always thought she was an open book, but she was feeling more than a little protective of her pregnancy because she knew this was going to be hot town gossip once it got out, and she didn't want to get burned.

Luckily there was no one there. They took seats next to each other, and Jackson reached out and grabbed a magazine off the table, some celebrity gossip rag.

She watched him open it up and calmly flip through the pages. "I didn't realize that was your preferred reading material."

"Well..." He studied a page as if he were a scientist trying to decipher a long-lost culture. "I'm just skimming. And now I'm wondering who wore it better?" He angled the page with the same question plastered across the top showing different actresses caught out by paparazzi wearing the same outfits.

"Becca Hayes?" A young nurse in pink scrubs and blue Crocs stepped into the waiting room, holding a clipboard.

"Hello!" Becca gave a shy wave. "That's me."

"Phew. Saved from being faced with the hard choices," Jackson said, tossing the magazine back before rising beside her and gesturing with a "ladies first" arm sweep.

"Hello," the nurse greeted them as they walked past. "Let's get your height and weight first."

Ew. Becca had blocked this part of the pregnancy journey out. The incessant focus on weight gain. She never used scales at home and had an allergy to anything that promoted toxic beauty standards for women, but she wasn't made out of stone. The regular checkups and inevitable slow uptick of the number on the scale always left her with a vague dread.

But as she stepped on, the nurse turned to

Jackson and said, "And you're the husband? What's your name?"

"Jackson," he answered at the exact same time that she stammered, "Oh, h-h-he's not my husband."

"Oh. Of course. Sorry. I didn't mean to imply anything." The nurse's cheeks could match fire engines. "I'm just tired and it came out automatically."

"It's fine. We aren't together. But I am the baby daddy." The way Jackson said it, so relaxed and matter-of-fact, like he was discussing how he wanted his coffee made or what the weather was going to be on the weekend . . . it shifted something in Becca's heart. He'd jumped in to take that hit for her, put himself out there with the truth because he knew she'd stumble a bit and hated being awkward.

"I see, ha-ha. Cool. And uh, congrats?" The nurse was obviously flustered. She quickly finished recording Becca's details and got them into a room. "The doctor will be with you shortly."

As soon as the door shut, Becca spun to Jackson. "Baby daddy," she hissed, half mortified and half laughing. "We aren't together. Oh God, we sound like we are auditioning to be on a daytime talk show."

"Come on, Fun Size, it was funny. And true." Jackson prowled the small room. "Look. Gloves. I want a few."

"For what?"

"I don't know. Stuff comes in handy. Be prepared. That's the Boy Scout motto."

"I suppose old habits die hard." This was the same guy who always took extra ketchup packets too.

"Whoa, check this." He paused in front of a poster that equated the size of the baby to food. "So right now, Bolt is the size of a kidney bean." He scanned down the list making audible gasps as he went. "Nah. Nah. Nah. Is this a joke?"

"What?"

"It says here that in the end, at forty weeks, the baby is the size of a watermelon."

"But like...a small watermelon." Becca made the approximate size with her hands. "Picture something about the girth of a mini seedless."

It was like he was a statue. She wasn't even sure if he was breathing. "Get outta here."

"I'm serious." She half-giggled, but was also aghast at his confusion. "Sofia was eight pounds."

"So..." He licked his lips, raking a hand through his hair. "How does eight pounds of person come out of you?"

She cocked her head. "Please tell me you have some idea." He hadn't been the best student in the world, but surely he must know how to get a baby out.

"Look, I know about childbirth. I mean I think I know as much as someone who hasn't been through it or whatever. I've seen movies and stuff. But I've never really thought about it that hard. Women are just pregnant, and then *poof*, there is a baby."

"It sounds like you have steps one and three down." Becca jerked at the sound of an amused voice. "But let's just say there's a whole lot more to the *poof* part."

The doctor looked about her age, with short hair tipped in hot pink spikes, and she peered at them both through funky horn-rimmed glasses.

"But might I suggest visiting YouTube to learn a little more on how babies come out," she continued dryly. "Best to set some expectations." She stepped forward and shook Becca's hand. "Hi there, I'm Dr. Fridley. I'm new to the practice, and to Heart's Hope, only been here a few weeks. Excited to meet you and congratulations to you both." She glanced over to Jackson as she washed her hands, drying them briskly on a paper towel before dropping it into the bin. "And you are the, ahem, baby daddy, I take it?"

"That's right, Doc. And yeah, I have a lot to learn. But here's the thing. I'm ready and willing. Whatever you need, or whatever Becca needs, I'm your man."

"I'm glad to hear it. We'll hold you to that." She turned to Becca and winked. "Can you lie back on the table? I'm going to do an ultrasound to see how everything looks."

Becca eased herself back, hearing the thin sheet of paper beneath her crinkle and crackle from her weight. "Do you want me to pull up my shirt?"

"If you could tuck it up to your bra, that would be great. And look, you're wearing these cute yoga pants so that will make this a cinch."

The doctor positioned the ultrasound machine

next to the bed and grabbed a bottle of gel. The clear
jelly was cold on Becca's skin. She had been doing
fine up until that point, but now a small creeping
sense of worry began to set in.

What if something was wrong? The pregnancy
was in the very early days, and as much as she
hadn't planned on this baby and her level of surprise
was still quite high, there was no doubt in any part
of her body that she wanted to have this child.

"What's that for?" Jackson looked like a curious
kid on a field trip, and Becca couldn't help but grin,
grateful for the distraction.

"I'm doing the first ultrasound today. Ultrasound
sound waves are not very efficient if they are travel-
ing by air. So, we use gel because it reduces the air
between the patient and the transducer and allows
for less acoustic impedance and a crisper image to
be produced." Dr. Fridley turned on the machine
and began moving the transducer slowly across
her belly.

Becca's attention was pulled away by the fuzzy
image beginning to appear on the screen.

The doctor watched the screen closely as she
glided the wand around. "Okay, let's see. Let's
move a little this way and—bingo! There we are!
There's your baby."

The image was grainy, and it was hard to know
what exactly was what, but the small, twitchy little
bundle on the screen was unmistakable. Then came
the sound...whoosh, whoosh, whoosh.

"The heartbeat." Becca covered a hand over her

mouth as tears threatened. "Jackson, look. That's the heartbeat."

"It sounds like horses racing," Jackson said with such awe. "Is that really it?"

"That's really it." Dr. Fridley put some more gel on her stomach. "I'm going to take a few measurements."

Jackson moved closer to Becca and squatted down next to her. "That kidney bean is going to become a seedless watermelon?"

Dr. Fridley glanced at the poster. "I have mixed feelings about that. On one hand it gives a good approximate size, but on the flip side, it makes you think about eating, and maybe being hungry, and I'm not sure we want people starting to think about eating babies." She glanced at their serious expressions.

"I kid, I kid. Anyway, everything looks good size wise, right on track. Talk to me about any symptoms you are having."

"I'm starting to feel woozy in the morning, not throwing up, just feeling off. And I have had a little cramping."

"Let me reassure you about that. It's very normal to cramp. You'll want to call us if they ever get so severe that you can't talk through them or if you notice blood, but otherwise, it's fine. Any cravings? Talk to me about those."

"Nothing yet," Becca said. "But it's still early days." With Sofia, one night she had fried pickles and had eaten them with peanut butter. But she would never *ever* admit to that.

"And when those days come, baby daddy, are you going to make sure that she has her heart's desire...in the food department, I mean."

"That's something I can do. Between the two of us, I'm the one who can actually use a kitchen, not just use it as a place to watch spinach slowly wilt in the crisper."

"Hey! I feel seen," Becca protested. "And judged."

Dr. Fridley laughed. "Well, the heartbeat and gestational size are both great. Barring any issues, I'd like to see you back in a month. Here's a picture to keep, and it was so nice to meet you both."

As the door clicked shut, Becca looked down at the grainy black-and-white photo from the ultrasound. There was no warning. No slow build. The tears came with the force of a fire hydrant being whacked open with a mallet.

"Whoa, whoa, whoa." Jackson approached, arms out, hands open. "Hey, what's going on? You heard the doc. She said Bolt was fine."

"It's real." Becca held up the image. "This is a real baby."

"I know. That's why we are here right? Because we knew this?" Jackson hooked a hand around the back of his neck and gave her a searching look as if she was a complicated riddle that he could solve if he just concentrated with enough intensity.

"Of course, yes. But knowing and *knowing* are two different things, you know."

"Yeah, totally." It was clear from his earnest but blank face that he had no clue what she was talking about, but it was also obvious that he cared deeply about what she was saying and that counted for something. In fact, that counted for everything. A fresh round of tears engulfed her. At this rate she was going to dehydrate herself into a little raisin.

"I think this is the h-h-h-h-h-hormones," she wheezed before pointing at her dripping nose. "Tissue, please." Jackson was one of her oldest friends, and he'd seen her naked, but that didn't mean he needed to also bear witness to a snot river cascading down her chin. She might be a single mom knocked up for round two, but she still had her pride.

"Fun Size, get over here." Before Becca could do anything, Jackson had her wrapped in a bear hug. His cotton shirt was soft against her face and smelled of laundry detergent, and the warm scent of his body that reminded her of sunlight and soil. And, even as the last random sobs shook through her body, it was impossible to ignore how hard the muscles were in his stomach. The night they'd spent together she'd been too shy to pay them the attention they deserved. Truly those abs could not only wash prairie women's petticoats, but they could also ruin her sanity. Those muscles had first appeared the last year of high school and the V-line had only gotten stronger and more defined as his body filled out from that of a boy to one of a man.

Of course, she'd been aware Jackson Lowe had a six-pack. He wasn't modest and often strutted around without a shirt. It was a simple fact. But that also didn't mean she wanted him to know that she had noticed those carved muscles from time to time, or that on more than a few occasions, when she'd been alone in her lonely bed, she'd imagined licking drops of sea water off that sun-bronzed skin.

She pulled back, shaky from the unexpected sob fest and now turned on to the point that it was taking every ounce of her reserve not to rub up against him like a cat.

"That was all hormones."

"All hormones," she confirmed. "Please don't freak out."

"Not at all. I just want to make sure you don't shut me out now. Like you usually do."

"What does that mean?" Becca stood up and reached for her purse. "Let's walk and talk, because I'm sure they'll need the room."

As they exited the building, Jackson took her wrist and urged her to stop. "Don't take this the wrong way, but you have a default setting when you get upset. And it's to push people away. To say you are fine. To sit there even with a face full of tears and act like it's all normal."

"I know I got emotional, but really, I am fine. I promise."

Jackson put his hands on her shoulders. She knew he wanted her to look up, but the idea of having him this close, knowing that he was all in to support her, was too much. She was a woman who made small compartments for each of her feelings, kept them as neat and separate as the bento boxes she packed for Sofia's preschool lunches. If she met his gaze, she'd start to spill over within herself. And then it would be a complete mess.

"You challenge me," he said softly. "You challenge the hell out of me. But I'm not going to let you do the thing where you shut down and keep all the hard things for yourself. In this situation, you gotta share some of that. I'm a big guy. I can take some of the load."

"Thank you," she said softly, focusing on the concrete between their shoes. "I mean it." And she did. Every word. "I like that you care."

And she liked how he had held her in the doctor's office. Her body was still warm in the places that he touched. But she wasn't going to tell him any of that. Those were feelings she would load into her mental elevator and send to the basement, where she kept all her darkest secrets. She'd given in to the temptation once, just one time, and now look. She didn't regret the child, but it was an undeniable consequence. If she considered what it would mean to let Jackson be more than her good friend, she knew there would be more consequences.

It was enough for him to try to get it together and be a co-parent. He was willing, but he wasn't in the trenches. Like being up at three a.m. with a feverish baby and wearing clothes stained with spit-up.

The best thing for everyone was to keep pretending like all she felt was friendship and to focus on the most important thing: hoping he'd continue to embrace the idea of being a dad.

Chapter Eight

I'm sorry, you want me to do what?" Becca hissed to Savannah, staring in abject horror at the pile of disposable diapers and candy bars on the kitchen table.

"Shush, don't be so dramatic." Savannah choked back a giggle. "It's a game. It's supposed to be fun."

"So let me get this straight. I'm supposed to take those candy bars and microwave them *inside* the diaper, and then we're going to go out there and invite people to sniff or lick pretend *poop*. And this is meant to be a good time."

Savannah nodded. "It's a tradition. My family always does this at baby showers."

"I could have lived my whole life and happily not known anything about this game." Becca swallowed, a faint twinge of nausea roiling through her middle. Hopefully it was the prenatal vitamin she'd taken an hour ago and not a sign that morning sickness was here to stay. She'd suffered for four months with Sofia, and it wasn't just morning sickness. It was afternoon and evening sickness too.

"Are you okay? Do you need water? A chair? Am I pushing you too hard?" Savannah tucked a lock of hair behind her ear and leveled a worried look at her.

"I'm fine. Just grossed out, but happy to play along." Becca ripped open a chocolate and peanut butter candy bar, broke it in half, and shoved it resolutely into the diaper. "Let's nuke this sucker."

As she waited for the microwave to ding, she watched Savannah arranging the cupcakes. Each one was frosted in pale peach, yellow, or cream to look like roses.

"You really outdid yourself organizing the shower."

"You think Abby's happy?" Savannah adjusted the last cupcake, ensuring the whole tray was just so.

"Considering she hasn't stopped beaming since she got here, I'd say mission accomplished. Especially once she gets to try one of those cupcakes. I'm tempted to steal one right now."

Savannah looked up, a mock glare on her face. "Don't you dare or I'll…I'll…" Her eyes lit up as the microwave dinged. "Chase you with a fake poopy diaper."

It turned out Savannah's diaper game was a hit. Ten minutes later, the living room was filled with hoots and screams as the seven diapers were passed around. Most guests were tentative, taking a small sniff, but a few dug right in, scooping out a nibble and trying to guess the variety.

"I remember how much I *loved* changing diapers in the hospital," Gia said, leaning back into the couch with a contented sigh. "I know it sounds weird, but it was so quiet, and it was just me and the baby, and I could lean down and give tummy kisses. There is nothing, and I mean nothing, better than newborn kisses."

Abby took a sip of the sparkling apple juice in her champagne flute and mulled it over. "That's promising. I can't say that late-night diaper changing was on my radar as a happy experience."

"Just remember, if you have a C-section, you won't be getting up at night. At least not for the first night at the hospital anyway," Becca said. "It took me two days to be able to even hobble to the bathroom. I had to take tiny steps and hold a pillow to my stomach so it didn't open up and then..." She slammed her mouth closed when she realized that she was about to say "all my insides would fall out." But the implied meaning was clear.

"Of course, who knows what will happen. I'm just saying don't set any expectations for the birth. I had this whole plan to labor drug-free, do hypnosis, use essential oils, and then Sofia got the cord wrapped around her neck, and it was off to the operating room for an emergency C-section."

Abby blinked. "You know, I know all of this,

and yet these stories feel more *real* now that I'm closer to it."

"Birth is birth," Hilde said gently. "And however your sweet spirit chooses to come into this world is going to be absolutely perfect."

Becca was tempted to add "but don't forget to ask for an epidural," but she didn't think it was the moment to be brutally honest.

"I don't even remember the pain of giving birth," Gia said with wonder. "It's just a blur until I was holding this beautiful perfect little person. Of course, I had Marco there holding my hand the entire time, so that probably had a lot to do with it. He was so supportive, and I know Carter will be too."

Becca felt a twinge of unease and maybe even a touch of sadness. Gia was so blissed out in new-mom world that she didn't quite remember that Becca didn't have a beloved partner. And when it came to the birth, she'd had a C-section with Sofia. Would she try for a VBAC this time? If she did...would Jackson hold her hand as she pushed? Massage her lower back as it spasmed? Stay calm even if things came up unexpectedly? Becca had been alone with Sofia. Graham had planned to be there for her due date, but Sofia was so eager to be out in the world, she came three weeks early. Becca squeezed her eyes shut, trying to picture Jackson in the delivery room. But she couldn't get the mental picture to materialize. Maybe that was an omen.

She opened her eyes and blinked.

Abby was looking at her, probably hoping for some reassuring words about her big brother.

"Oh yeah." Becca waved her hand as if to brush away any doubt. "Of course, Carter is going to be amazing. Look at how he puts all his attention into everything he does. If I know my brother, the question isn't if he's going to be supportive as a birth partner, it's more like will he try to push the doctor out of the way and deliver the baby himself after reading a couple of obstetrics books. Let's be real here. You know you can see it, right?"

"Duh." Abby's eyes glowed. "That man applies himself to any task one hundred and ten percent."

"Clearly," Gia teased, gesturing at Abby's belly and wiggling her eyebrows up and down as everyone laughed. Even Becca, who stuck her fingers in her ears.

"What? I can't hear you. La la la la."

"Okay, we won't torture you." Gia passed over a cupcake. "Although I do just want to flag that for whatever reason, sex while pregnant was not... unpleasant. Maybe it was the hormones, or because I had to be on top, but wow."

"Honestly..." Abby gave Becca a sidelong glance. "I wouldn't know. I've been falling asleep at the dinner table every night."

"Just wait," Gia said. "You'll be surprised."

"The only thing I wanted to make love to the last half of my pregnancy was a tub of cookies and cream ice cream," Becca said quickly. Maybe it was TMI but she also felt like Gia was selling an overly glamorized view of pregnancy. If she had amazing third trimester sex and a perfect postnatal life, that was absolutely fantastic. But that hadn't been her road, and she didn't want Abby to feel like she was coming up short if her experience was different.

"Of course, of course," Gia said quickly, catching on finally. "It's different for everyone. All that matters is that you are happy and making choices that are right for you."

"Does that mean I can go to sleep for three months and wake up with the baby here, preferably all cute and washed and perfectly swaddled? Because let me tell you, I seriously suck when it comes to swaddle practice. I've been trying in birth class, and it's reminding me how I never have been good at origami."

"I wouldn't worry about it too much," Hilde said matter-of-factly. "You don't know if this baby will even want to be swaddled. Save yourself the effort. But you'll be a great mom, and whatever the baby likes or doesn't like? You'll handle it with flying colors."

"Well, then." Abby rubbed her belly with a rueful grin. "I'm not sure if I should cheer or worry. But I guess I can always call on the baby whisperer if I need some backup. Good thing I have an inside connection."

"Any time." Hilde's smile was broad.

Abby lifted up her empty champagne flute. "I think I need a refill of my sparkling apple juice, stat. Make it a double."

"On it." Becca grabbed the flute and took it to

the kitchen. When she was away from the others, she set the glass down on the island and leaned against the fridge, splaying her hands over her still flat stomach.

Who was in there?

She'd been thinking so much about the external part of the pregnancy that she'd forgotten that there was a whole person in there—or at least a whole potential person. Would they get along with Sofia, have a relationship like the one she'd developed with her brother? Or would they be locking horns, constantly driving each other wild? She had a little family with her and Sofia; they were small but mighty. The idea of expanding it to include a new person—would she have room in her heart for more love? It seemed like a silly question, but a trace of worry lingered.

And then there was the matter of Jackson. He'd always been there, but with a little more distance, friend but not family.

That was changing now too.

She didn't have a clear sense of how her new family would be, how it would look or feel. And that made her very anxious.

* * *

"What'll you have today, good sir?" Ben asked from behind the tap.

"I love how we have this conversation every time I come," Jackson joked.

"Well, someday you might change your mind, so who am I to assume?"

"IPA going once, twice, and that's it. That's the order." Jackson glanced over at his friend Noah on the barstool next to him. "Sound good?"

"Nah, I just can't get into IPAs." Noah shrugged. "A pilsner is fine." He reached into the peanut dish and cracked a nut, eating the middle before tossing the shells on the floor.

The Last Chance was a dive bar, but purposefully so.

The weathered floorboards had seen years of folks coming in to belly up to the bar, and every day they gained another dusting of peanut shells. The walls were lined with a mishmash of old surfing photos, newspaper articles from local fishing competitions, and animal heads all centered around a painted piece of driftwood that said NO WHINING.

Ben's personal motto.

The crowd was light at the moment, part of the reason Jackson had chosen to come in. The after-work gang was clearing out, and the night drinking hadn't gotten going yet. He liked being there when Ben had some time to hang out between orders.

"You want to play pool? Darts?" Noah asked.

"Nah. All good. Just wanted to hang with my boys. Enjoy a beer and shoot the shit."

"Cheers to that." Ben set the two pints in front of them, and Jackson and Noah clinked glasses before talking a long drink.

"That hits the spot." Noah wiped his mouth and

gave a contented sigh. "I had three night shifts this week. I'm dragging."

"Has it been busy?" Jackson couldn't help but admire his friend, whose day job working on an ambulance as a first responder often required him to confront people at their worst moments.

"It was actually quiet, which is hard in its own way. Sometimes the adrenaline on the job makes the time pass quicker. But Memorial Day is just around the corner. So, we can expect it to pick up soon." He reached out and knocked on the bar top. "Not that I'm saying I'm hoping for accidents or anything."

"Just a heart attack or two." Jackson arched a brow, loving to get a ribbing in.

"Always a wise guy." Noah rolled his eyes. "I think I want to quit nights altogether though. I used to like that schedule, but my night owl days are done. Living with a four-year-old has a way of forcing you to be an early bird."

"Better you than me." Ben shuddered. "Right, Jackson?" He jerked his thumb at Jackson while turning to Noah. "Imagine this guy having to wake up and get breakfast at six in the morning."

"How about braiding hair," Noah said with mock seriousness. "Pigtails are very important business. Especially at seven o'clock in the morning."

"God, can you imagine?" Ben nudged his chin in Jackson's direction while shaking his head. "Hilarious."

Jackson finished half his beer rather than spill the beans. He knew Becca had told her girlfriends, but she had also sworn them to secrecy. She wanted to wait to make the announcement, and he understood.

Even though the waiting also twisted his gut a little.

Was she waiting because she was embarrassed of him?

"Okay, we'll quit busting your chops, man." Noah grabbed another peanut. "How's the job going this week?"

"Which one?" Jackson shot back, a little more terse than he'd intended.

"My guy is hustling surf lessons down at the beach," Ben said quickly, obviously looking to smooth over the tension.

"For real? That's a great idea. We need lessons in town. Too many folks come here from Portland and Seattle and have no idea how to be in the water." Noah mulled it over. "I bet you're a damn good teacher too."

"I thought it was a joke seeing me with kids."

"Nah, we took it too far." Noah punched his arm. "And look, you might be a big kid, but you're also the best surfer in town. I can see you inspiring that passion in people."

"Inspire—ha! Go tell my dad that one." Jackson waved a hand at the tap. "I'll take one more." He glanced back to Noah. "And that's it, dude. I don't drink and drive."

Noah flashed him a thumbs-up in approval.

"Here's the deal. There's a real opportunity to

start a surf school here. But I've never had such a huge responsibility like that before. Plus my dad is wanting me to step up and start running the landscaping business so he can retire."

"Well, you are good at landscaping." Noah seemed to choose his words carefully. "I hear about your dad's company a lot. But not going to lie…it's never seemed like a passion for you."

"Right. Not like how it is for you guys. You're a professional hero out there helping people day in and day out. And you"—Jackson gestured at Ben—"own the finest dive bar on the Oregon coast. You're good with people, and you like telling stories from behind the bar."

"I do indeed. Most of the time it doesn't even feel like working."

"Me? I just started working for dad after high school. Chased waves—"

"And women," Ben butted in.

"Sometimes. But I've hit thirty. What worked for me at twenty isn't the same anymore. What filled me up then doesn't do it for me now. Noah, you're making a family. Ben, you're building a business. And I'm just here ready for a change."

"Well, if that's the case, I do have another customer for your fledging surf business." Ben grabbed a rag and started wiping down the bar. "See those guys sitting to the right of the jukebox?"

Jackson glanced over to the three men in their early forties laughing around a table. They wore casual collared shirts that were dressy for Heart's

Hope Bay. They were clearly from the city. "I see 'em."

"When they were ordering, they were saying that it would be fun to surf. They are here for a buddy's bachelor party. You should go talk to them."

"I dunno." Jackson shifted on his barstool. "Wouldn't that be weird?"

"You miss a hundred percent of the shots you don't take," Ben said.

"Go on," Noah coaxed. "Unless you're a big ol' chicken."

"What are we? Ten?"

"Deep down, maybe more than we like."

"All right, all right, I'll go see if I can drum up some business." Jackson stood up, trying to pretend he didn't feel nervous. It's not that he minded talking to strangers. It's just that he'd never tried to build anything before, make something for himself by himself.

But, as he crossed the bar, a little voice piped up in his head. *You might want to try the same thing will Becca.*

Because like Ben said, you got to be in it to win it.

Chapter Nine

Becca frowned at her reflection in the bathroom mirror. She'd washed and blow-dried her hair, put on her fancy yoga pants, and was now contemplating makeup. All of this to stay in on a Monday night and watch a movie with Jackson. He'd texted her at four and asked if he could come over tonight and hang out, watch a movie. That was it. No other context.

In the past, that would've been normal enough. But these weren't normal times. These were the days of growing a baby and not knowing what she was going to do about everything. From revealing to the world she was pregnant again, to Jackson being the dad, to them not being together, to her not being entirely sure how she felt about him.

She shoved the makeup bag back in the top vanity drawer. That's it. No makeup. This wasn't a date. This was two friends who happened to create a new life together hanging out to watch a movie. As one does. Past her daughter's bedtime. When they'd be very much alone and unsupervised on a very snug loveseat.

Okay, no makeup. But she did grab a bottle of floral perfume and sprayed it down the front of her shirt before tossing it in the drawer and clasping a hand over her mouth to catch a nervous giggle.

She was acting like the biggest virgin ever. But in many ways it wasn't altogether wrong. Obviously, she'd done the deed before. But in the last five years she'd been completely celibate, and the one night with Jackson felt more like a dream than a reality.

She found herself reaching for lip gloss. It was clear. Totally didn't count, right? She popped her lips. "Right."

She heard tires on the gravel outside.

He was here.

Her heart fluttered. This was Jackson. Jackson Lowe. Her friend.

The man she had seen naked. And there was a lot to see.

Heat shot up her spine. Maybe Gia was right and pregnancy was making her frisky. That's all this was. Her hormones were out of control and surging through her body with the force of a mini tsunami.

She waited five seconds after hearing the knock

to start walking. Good. That way she wouldn't seem eager.

When she opened the door, Jackson was on the front porch with a bouquet of yellow tulips and a tub of cookies-and-cream ice cream, looking like a threat to her sanity. His worn surf shirt clung to the rise of his pectorals and stretched over the breadth of his broad shoulders while his faded denim jeans looked like they'd been designed to hug his trim waist. Worse—or better, depending on whether she listened to the angel or the devil on her shoulder—his thick blond hair was still damp from a recent shower, the ends curling up on the nape of his neck.

He glanced up uncertainly and extended the flowers. "I...I...picked them at a job site today. It's no big deal. I was just thinking about you and how to make you happy, and then I saw these and they made me happy and...yeah..."

"Aw, thank you." She reached out and took the flowers with a polite smile, trying not to play it cool and not to swoon. "I'll go find a vase. Come on in."

He followed her into the kitchen. "You're still liking ice cream?"

"It's not so much that I like it, more that I have a primal need to consume ice cream and it feels as if I might die if I don't."

He chuckled, his shoulders relaxing a bit. "So, you're telling me not to bother with getting you a bowl and spoon. Just hand over the carton."

"Tempting, but I should at least pretend to pace myself." She grabbed a large mason jar from a cupboard and filled it with water. "But I'll take a tablespoon. None of that teaspoon eating garbage."

"I'd be fine bringing you a shovel, no judgment here. Like I said…I want to make sure you're happy. That you have everything you need."

And just like that Becca's throat went tight.

There was nothing studied or rehearsed about Jackson. He was the kind of guy where what you saw was what you got. And what she saw was a good guy, a great guy. One who wanted to protect her, who had enough strength that she could lean into him for a minute and just be.

As she set the flowers on the counter, she suddenly realized the kitchen was a bit of a mess. Sofia's art projects were on the breakfast table, dishes were piled up in the sink, the garbage looked like it needed to take itself out, and the floor clearly hadn't been swept in…a while.

She froze. Normally she prided herself on keeping a neat and tidy home. When had she put on blinders? How had she stressed out about wearing makeup but not about washing the spaghetti pot?

"I'm sorry it's a mess." She ran a hand through her hair trying to decide what she should do first, to just make it a little less gross. "I'll just take out the garbage real fast."

"You won't do any such thing." He finished making her a bowl of ice cream, then took her arm and led her to the couch.

"I didn't realize how messy the house had gotten.

I must be in a brain fog. I can't relax if it looks like this."

"I know, I know." He spoke to her calmly, as if she were a skittish pony. "That's why I'm going to do it."

"No!" She tried to push herself up. "That's ridiculous. It's my responsibility."

He held her shoulders down, gently but firmly. "Your responsibility? Your only responsibility tonight is to put your feet up, grab that cozy blanket, pull it over yourself, and enjoy the ice cream. You're doing the most important job in the whole world, you're making life. The least I can do is load your dishwasher and take out the trash."

"Are you sure?"

"It would make me happy. Think of it like you're doing me a favor."

He had that stubborn set to his jaw that she knew better than to argue with, and besides, it felt so good to just collapse into the couch.

"Very well. Carry on," she said in a mock British accent, pretending to adjust her crown.

"As you wish." He winked.

It didn't take long for him to have the kitchen gleaming. As he bent down to sweep the dirt pile into a dust pan, she told herself that admiring his perfect butt was just the icing on the incredible service he provided. And better still, he whistled the whole time, seeming to genuinely not mind the chores. A far cry from her own father, who never lifted a finger in their house unless it was to . . .

No. She pulled the microfiber blanket tighter around her lap. She wouldn't ruin her night by thinking about her dad.

"Have you decided on a movie?" he asked, dusting his hands on his jeans.

"I actually just sat and ate and zoned out and didn't think of one," she admitted, cringing. "I'm sorry, this is so unlike me."

"That's fine." He sat on the couch by her feet. "We could do... I dunno... *The Princess Bride*?"

"Oh," she deadpanned. "That is my favorite movie."

"Is it?" He played along. "I couldn't tell, considering I've only seen it about thirty times with you."

"You know me. I can never turn down seeing men in tights."

"No more rhyming and I mean it." His fake Sicilian accent was three kinds of adorable.

"Anybody want a peanut?"

They both burst out laughing.

"As you wish," she said. "Wait. You quoted that to me earlier, right?"

"And it went right over your head."

"I just didn't realize you'd paid that much attention to what I like."

"Becca." He shook his head. "I pay attention to everything about you."

It's a good thing she was sitting down, otherwise she'd have risked sliding to the floor in a puddle of emotions. Who was this new, sweet Jackson? Had he always been like this and she'd never noticed?

He started the movie and for the next twenty minutes she was blissed out on Farm Boy Wesley and Buttercup. But then her head started to ache a bit. She rubbed the back of her neck but that didn't work. She drank some water. Still there. Nagging. Not enough to warrant a pain reliever, but enough to demand some attention.

"Hey, Squirmy." Jackson squeezed her foot. "What's up?"

"Just a little headache." She grimaced. "Because God forbid my body can just *be* for more than thirty minutes."

He shifted and patted his lap. "Come on over here."

She made a face even as her abdomen muscles reflexively tightened. "Why, what are you going to do to me?"

"I have magic hands." He wiggled his long fingers.

Thank God she wasn't drinking water when he spoke because she would have sprayed it all over the living room. Her skin tingled as her nerves remembered just how spellbinding his touch could be. But one glance at his face and she realized she was the only one gripped with a wave of inappropriate thoughts. He looked so sweet and innocent her teeth hurt.

"I'll rub your temples, Fun Size. I bet it will help."

How could she turn that down? So, she moved over and put her head on Jackson's thigh, trying and failing to ignore that it was rock hard. His hands sank into her hairline and his fingers began to rub the edges of her temples in slow circles. It didn't take long before her body started to go limp, the niggle of pain retreating, replaced by a catlike pleasure of getting petted. She closed her eyes. There was no agenda to his touch; maybe that's what made it so damn sexy. Jackson wasn't touching her to try to coax her into anything. He simply wanted her to feel better.

Her stomach warmed and she thought of the little being inside, growing in the darkness of her body. It wouldn't grow up with a father who would cause fear or use those big strong hands to hurt. She might have some reservations on Jackson's ability to step into the monotonous duties of fatherhood, but never over his ability to care and protect.

She glanced up and froze. His eyes were locked on hers, the irises as blue as a deep mountain lake up in the Cascades. Around the bridge of his nose was the lightest dusting of freckles. She knew every constellation they made, how the ones that crossed his left cheek looked like Orion's belt.

His expression wasn't suggestive; it was wistful, full of quiet longing, and maybe that's what gave her the courage to speak. "What are you thinking?"

His nostrils flared at his sudden inhalation. "About something I shouldn't do."

Her heart began to pound. "Do what you're thinking of." She pushed herself up and turned. "I mean it. Whatever you're thinking, just do it."

And just like that he was against her, his hand sliding around to cradle the back of her head, his

fingers tangled in her hair. Her next breath came
from inside his mouth as his lips pressed against
hers, soft but insistent. His uncertainty fading as
he coaxed his tongue into her mouth, teasing hers
with a soft stroke that made them both moan...and
then giggle.

When they pulled back, she knew she was as
wide-eyed as he was. Their ragged breath filled the
room while explosions from the fire swamp boomed
from the television.

"Are you sure about this?" he asked.

She fought for reason. She fought for logic. Her
body was screaming for her to lie back and let him
have his way with her, but her brain urged caution.
If they rushed into this, everything would get more
confusing, more muddled, and there were more
people to this equation who could be hurt than just
the two of them.

"Just kissing," she whispered. *Kissing couldn't
hurt, right?* "You okay with that?"

His brow went up. "Am I okay with kissing you?
I think I can suffer the experience a little more." He
leaned in, but she stopped him with a single finger to
his chest, feeling how hard his heart was beating.

"I mean it. I don't want to take this too fast. Mess
anything up."

"Same here." He reached out and cupped her
cheek. "Last thing I want is to make you pull away.
Tell me what you want, and I'll do it."

"Kiss me again," she whispered, closing her eyes.

* * *

She tasted sweet, like the ice cream she'd been eating, but her lips were warm. As Jackson moved his mouth against hers, it was as if his brain filled with static, short-circuiting his thinking. He'd tried so damn hard not to rehash his one amazing night with this woman, but now that she was here, soft and willing in his arms, he remembered every gasp, shudder, and stroke.

He let her take the lead, keeping his hands firmly on good behavior even as she began to tentatively stroke his body, first shyly, then with more open curiosity. Her palms moved against his chest and then down to his stomach, which flexed under her touch.

"Ticklish?" she breathed into him.

He pulled back and nipped softly at the delicate skin where her jaw met her throat, feeling a deep primal satisfaction when her lips made a perfect *O* and her eyes hooded.

Then she looked at him with such determination that all reason left him. She crawled up and straddled his lap, leaning down to fasten her lips on the side of his throat. He hissed her name like a plea, a prayer.

Everything blotted from his mind except for Becca. Goose bumps shot down his back. Heat pooled. Control slipped.

No!

He thought of Seahawk player stats, about song

lyrics, about playing puzzles with his grandma...but nothing worked. He was unable to distract himself from how Becca moved against him, how she made him feel. But he'd made a promise...only kissing. And he'd stick by it, even though he burned.

"Whoa." Becca rolled off him and pushed herself to the other end of the couch. "Wow. So that went from zero to a hundred."

"I let you in the driver's seat." He forced his shoulders to stay relaxed, grabbing a throw pillow and positioning it on his lap, hoping she wouldn't notice.

"You did." Her gaze was unsure, even as her kiss-swollen lips curled into a hesitant smile. "I just didn't think it was going to be like getting the keys to a Lamborghini."

"Is that a compliment?"

She covered her mouth with one hand and giggled. "I'd say so, yes. But...is it okay if we stop? I can't keep going and keep my sanity."

His cheeks flushed. "I told you, you call the shots here."

"Well, I don't want you to feel used."

The only sound in the room was the quiet, persistent tick from the grandfather clock against the far wall.

Finally, he cleared his throat. "Becca, have you ever taken a good look at yourself? What guy is going to turn down being used by you?"

Her gorgeous brown eyes went wide in surprise, the whites showing around her caramel irises.

And with just a few words, he'd gone and done it. Cast the dice, put out the first hint that he wasn't in this for a short time, or just a good time.

More silence. More of the quiet *tick. Tick. Tick.*

Her introspection was killing him. So was the fact that she wasn't in his arms.

"Do you know what's the weirdest part about… this?" She gestured at the space between them. "It's that it's not weird at all."

And that was just it: Being with Becca was comfortable and unfamiliar, strange yet secure. It was as if they'd stepped from firm friendship into a new, alien land…yet it still felt easy. And retreat suddenly felt unthinkable. The only problem was, where did this unexpected path lead, and would they get lost along the way?

Chapter Ten

So let me see." Dr. Fridley reviewed her chart. She'd moved on from hot pink hair in favor of a brilliant superman blue in the last few weeks, and her glasses were clear plastic. "Welcome to twelve weeks, Becca. Today we're going to do a nuchal translucency screening, which means we'll be checking for markers like Down syndrome, trisomy 13, and trisomy 18. We'll be doing a blood test and measuring the fluid on the back of baby's neck with an ultrasound."

Becca nodded from her perch on the examination room bed, noting that beneath his sun-kissed tan, Jackson was a little pale. "Will you be okay?" she said. "He hates needles and blood," she told the doctor.

"Blood's a problem for you?" Dr. Fridley leveled a stern stare at him. "Well, you'll want to work on that ahead of labor. Becca wants to try for a VBAC, which is a vaginal birth after a prior C-section. And frankly, I don't like it when dads go down in the delivery room."

"I'll be fine. But what do you mean by *down*?" Jackson tilted his head, clearly unsure of her meaning.

"Fainting," Dr. Fridley said. "Becca here is going to be working hard. She's the star of the show. You will need to figure out a way to keep it together so you don't come in like a scene stealer."

"No, of course not," Jackson said quickly, before grimacing. "How much blood are we talking though, Doc?

"It all depends. Usually there's the bloody show and then the..."

"B-b-bloody what?"

"It's the mucus plug. It comes out before labor starts and there's a bit of blood with it."

"Mucus?" Jackson was hushed.

"Mucus," Dr. Fridley confirmed. "It comes from the cervix."

"How about Jackson just agrees to step it up with some independent research on this," Becca butted in. She wasn't quite ready for her cervical mucus to be the subject of casual conversation.

"Yes. Of course. Good idea." Jackson shot her a look of pure relief.

"Don't let him off the hook though," Dr. Fridley

said as the nurse came in with the ultrasound equipment. "Six months seems like it's far off in the distant future, but it will be here before you know it, and you want to make sure that you've done everything in your power to be the best birth partner you can be."

Jackson nodded but still seemed rattled.

Becca's heart sank a fraction. Jackson was so great with everything fun...making her laugh and, lately, making her swoon, but would he be able to be there when she needed him, when her mind and body opened to the point of panic, when she'd need a rock to lean on?

And the uncomfortable truth was that she truly didn't know.

On one hand, she could picture his strong arms wrapped around her, holding her, encouraging her when the contractions bore down, but what if he let her down? Made an excuse? Nudged her girlfriends into the room so he could retreat out to places where he felt in control and understood?

Her mother had once told her that her dad had cried when she was born. Becca wasn't sure if she believed the story or not. She'd never seen her dad demonstrate much in the way of sweetness or sensitivity.

Jackson caught her gaze, and all she could think was *Please, please don't let me down*.

Fifteen minutes later, the ultrasound was done and her blood was drawn. This time Jackson didn't even flinch—a total surprise. And a little impressive.

"We'll have to wait on the lab results, but from everything I saw, it looks like you'll have a very healthy, very boring pregnancy." Dr. Fridley winked. "And boring is great. Now who wants to hear the heart?"

"Can't wait." Becca smiled, and as the Doppler passed over her belly, the whooshing sound filled the room.

"The baby sounds so strong," Jackson said. "It sounds good, doc, right?"

"Perfect." She let the sound continue, clearly seeing how much Becca and Jackson were enthralled.

"Good job, baby," Becca cheered.

"And now that you've entered the second trimester, if you've been holding off on telling people the good news, I think you're on safe ground to proceed."

Becca blinked rapidly. "Oh right. Of course." What was the big deal? Her closest girlfriends knew, even though she'd sworn them to secrecy, even from their partners. Carter knew. But that was it.

Telling the news would make this real, and right now that heartbeat felt like the realest thing in the whole world. She wasn't scared to talk about the baby. It was the Jackson part she was concerned about. What would people around town say? No one would believe Jackson Lowe was dad material, and would comments undermine his confidence, make him pull back? And what would his parents say?

What would her own dad say? She'd have to tell him eventually. And with Sofia he'd been so characteristically cruel. She recalled his words clearly. "You did this to yourself. Don't expect my help fixing your mess."

"It's a baby, Dad," Becca had shot back. "Not a mess."

She'd never let her dad meet Sofia. He didn't deserve to, and worse, he never asked to, and that pain was something she'd never fully shake.

But here was a new chance to bring light and hope forward. She listened to the heartbeat, clear and jubilant. *I'm here. I'm here. I'm here. I'm here.*

If she knew one thing, she'd never let her father dim her children's brightness.

After the appointment, they walked back to Jackson's truck.

"Do you want to grab some lunch? I could really go for a bean burrito at the taqueria."

"Sounds good to me," Jackson said, and then he slapped his forehead. "Oh no. Today's Tuesday, isn't it?"

"Yes."

"Damn. I forgot about my volunteer shift today. It starts in fifteen minutes."

"Hey, it's no big deal. Forget lunch. Do that."

"No way. If a pregnant lady wants a burrito, I'm buying. I just feel bad. A lot of the dogs don't get a walk if I don't take them."

Jackson never talked too much about his volunteer work at Heart's Hope Bay Animal Shelter. Becca knew he went, of course, but he wasn't the kind of man who was going to brag about his work to get a gold star. She had to admit, while she didn't

have a lot of pet experience, she was curious to
see this other side to him. The more she looked at
Jackson, the whole man behind her longtime friend,
the more she was impressed . . . and more than a little
infatuated.

"Actually, I'm not starving. I could wait a little
while. How long is your volunteer shift?"

"Usually two hours." He looked at her, considering. "But if you want to help me out, we could get
it all done in an hour."

"And then eat to a job well done! Let's do it." She
realized she was twirling her hair around one finger
and immediately dropped her hand. It was one thing
to be developing a serious crush on her best friend
since high school, but another thing entirely to act
as if she was back in high school.

He blinked. "Really? You'd come with me?"

"I'd like to see you in action, doing something
you're passionate about." And she meant it.

The shelter was on the edge of town. It had been
recently built after a capital campaign had been
generously supported by an anonymous donor. The
result was a modern building with mudbrick, natural
wood, and sleek modern designs surrounded by dog
parks and fenced-in patios.

They walked inside, and Jackson had a word with
the volunteer coordinator, who asked Becca to sign
a waiver before giving her a green vest with a paw
print on the front.

"Big or little?" Jackson asked as they started
walking toward the back.

"I...what?" She was distracted by the smell. The building's air was a mix of industrial-strength cleaner and the thousands of animals that had passed through its doors.

"Big dogs or little dogs? I have to walk one of the groups."

"Oh. Well. Let me see..." Becca was uncertain. "I've never walked any dog, so let's start small."

Jackson tripped and turned to stare at her. "Never walked any dog? In your whole life?"

"You know me. I never had a pet growing up. Nor have I ever pet sat."

"I guess I never really thought about it. But you never walked a dog, Becs? Wild." He shook his head before pushing open a door to a room filled with caged bays. Barking rose up, bouncing off the concrete.

"Is it always this loud?" she yelled, cupping her ears.

"You should see the big dogs. Sometimes I can't hear a thing. Don't worry, they'll settle down once they get used to us. Go grab some treats." He pointed to a stainless steel bowl on a card table filled with dry dog treats. "If you start passing those out, I'll check the charts and see who is due for a walk."

"Okay. Dog treats. Got it." Becca walked forward and grabbed a handful of treats. It seemed impossible, but she'd swear the barking got even louder. She turned around and there was a Chihuahua. "Hey, uh...Beowulf," she said, noting the name of the gate. "Big name for a little guy."

She offered the treat through the wire, and he took it in a quick movement, retreating to the back of his space before turning around to consume his prize.

Humph. "Very polite."

She went down the row, offering treats, trying not to be nervous about the ones that growled or glum for those that looked at her with baleful sad eyes. She'd never entertained the idea of having a dog, but these animals were tearing at her heart.

The last cage had a black terrier, with a sign on the front that read SHADOW.

"Really?" She crouched down to offer him a Milk-Bone. "We have Beowulf, Maxie, Kiwi, Zippy, Jekyll, Pugsley, and even an Underdog. And then you...Shadow." He cocked his head, his ears at attention. "But hey, you know your name."

"You want to walk this little guy?" Jackson asked, approaching her with a leash. "There is a path outside. I'll catch up. There's a corgi over there that might be sick. I don't want kennel cough going through the group, so I need to leave a message for the vet up front."

"Um..." She glanced at the leash and over to Shadow. He was so small, a little bundle of black fluff. What could go wrong? "Yeah, sure. Of course. You won't be long though, right?"

"Five minutes. Max." He handed her the leash and was gone.

She glanced into the kennel and opened the latch. "We can do this, right? Aaaaaaaaaaaah!"

For a little dog, he moved like lightning, and

he was through her legs in a flash. There was a cacophony of howls as the other dogs got wind of the jailbreak. Another volunteer opened the far door. "Everything okay?"

But Shadow was already outside.

"Oh no, that one is an escape artist," the volunteer moaned. He started to give chase but clearly had a bum leg.

"I've got him." Becca moved past him. She wasn't setting any track and field records, but she had a better chance. "Here, boy! Here, boy!" Shoot, she was going to have to sound a lot more convincing if she wanted to cajole the dog back. "Shadow!" The dog pulled up short, did an about face, and watched her, head cocked as she approached. For a moment, it felt like he was going to wait for her, but then he gave a loud yip that sounded a lot like *yeah, right*, and kept right on running, all four paws off the ground, living his best life.

Except the dog was so hung up on his unexpected jailbreak that he didn't seem to notice he was heading straight for the parking lot, and a delivery truck driver was just starting to back up.

"Oh no! Shadow. Halt! Whoa! Heel!"

"Hey, don't worry, I got him." Jackson bounded past, easily outpacing her. He was quick, and Shadow had no chance now, but as the terrier looked over one shoulder, he was missing the fact that he was headed right toward the truck's back left wheel.

And Jackson wasn't slowing either. He wasn't looking and the driver was backing up way too fast.

Becca stopped, in horror, seeing everything play out in her mind's eye as she shouted, "Jackson, wait. No!"

He bent and scooped the dog just as the truck rolled over the space where Shadow had been. Throwing himself out of the way, he hit the asphalt hard on one side and immediately rolled over and came up on his knees.

The truck slammed to a stop with screaming brakes.

The driver jumped out of the truck. "Man, you okay? You came outta nowhere."

"I'm fine. You didn't hit me." Jackson held up the dog. "I was chasing this troublemaker."

Shadow barked as if to acknowledge the statement, and the driver chuckled.

"Your arm." Becca approached him. "Oh my God, you're bleeding."

Jackson looked down and quickly glanced away. "Guess I am."

The color rapidly drained from his face as a steady trickle of blood flowed down his arm.

"Come with me," Becca said, walking forward to grab Shadow, who wiggled in protest. "You! Cool it."

Shadow, sensing she meant business, complied, relaxing into her hold. She held out her hand for Jackson.

"I'm okay."

"I'm glad. But let me help you for once."

He seemed to sense that it was best to comply

rather than argue. With a one-shouldered shrug, he pushed himself up and walked beside her back toward the shelter.

"Where's the first aid kit?" she asked.

"I'm not sure, probably the front desk."

"Then that's where we're going."

"I don't need first aid."

"Hush. And...don't look at it, all right?"

He caught her gaze and forced a smile. "Dr. Fridley would consider this cognitive behavioral therapy, huh?"

She allowed a tight smile, her heart still beating hard. "Absolutely. I'll make sure to tell her you were very brave. Also...I'm sorry. That was my fault. I didn't realize how fast this little guy was going to move."

"No, I shouldn't have left you alone. It's on me. I'm just glad he wasn't hurt."

But you were, she wanted to say.

As they entered the lobby, the front desk ladies jumped up at the sight of Jackson's bloody arm.

"Good heavens, what happened?" one cried out, coming around the desk, eyes wide behind her bifocal lenses.

Becca passed off a very subdued Shadow, who seemed to want to be invisible and not the source of all the recent drama. "Do you mind taking him and getting me the first aid kit?"

"Of course, of course. Dolores, the first aid box. Under the printer."

"On it." The wiry woman scooped up the plastic

kit emblazoned with a red square with a white cross. "You need any help?"

"No, we'll just clean it up. Which way is the bathroom?"

"There's a family bathroom down the hall there and to the right."

Becca carried the first aid kit, walking with what she hoped looked like authority and confidence. Inside, she was racking her brains trying to recall the first aid course that she'd taken almost a decade earlier. She'd had to do chest compressions on a dummy and practice packing a wound, although thankfully neither of those scenarios seemed to be required now.

As they were about to enter the restroom, she heard a little yip next to her. She looked down and grinned at the impish dog. "You really are an escape artist, aren't you? But no more funny business today."

The family bathroom had a faux leather lounge chair set up in the corner, presumably for nursing. "Take a seat." Becca knelt in front of him, setting the box on the ground and popping open the latches to inspect neatly bundled gauze, bandages, scissors, and antiseptic spray.

Great. She'd start there. She spritzed his arm, and he sucked on his teeth. "That stings."

She regarded him through narrowed eyes. "I bet it would sting a lot more if you'd gotten run over by that truck." As much as she hated it, her lower lip was threatening to quiver as the shock wore off.

But even though she was mad—and not even at him or the dog, just the universe for putting her person in danger—she wanted to make him feel better. Leaning forward, she gently blew on his wound. Glancing up, lips still pursed, she caught his gaze and realized what she had thought. *Her person.*

Her friend, yes.

Her lover, yes, that one time.

But person?

Two patches of color shone high on his cheeks. "Careful," he said after a minute. "If you're going to treat me this good, I'm going to be jumping in front of moving vehicles more often."

Shadow sat between them, his ears at attention, as if he was hanging on to every word.

"Poor little guy. He looks so lonely," she murmured.

"Yeah." Jackson's voice softened. "His owner passed away."

"Oh no." Becca glanced back down at the pooch. "That's terrible."

"I know. There was no next of kin, so the dog ended up here. It's a shame, because the way I hear it told, this dog was living quite the life of luxury. He even had his own bedroom!"

"What will happen to him?" She'd never had a dog, never *wanted* a dog. And with a preschooler and a baby on the way, the idea of voluntarily accepting more responsibility felt like a terrible idea... but that little face was making her feel all sorts of ways.

"I was tempted to take the little guy myself. I mean look at this face." Jackson slid out of the seat and dropped to one knee, scooping up Shadow and positioning him on his knee. Holding his two paws, Jackson began to imitate Shadow talking in a high-pitched voice. "I am such a good boy. Don't you want me?"

"I'm serious." Becca hugged herself. Maybe it was the hormones, but the idea of him staying here alone hurt her heart. "I'm worried about him."

"Well, first thing to know is that this is a no-kill shelter, so you can take any of those thoughts out of that pretty head. Second, Shadow's already found a forever home."

"He did?"

"Yeah, I heard about it earlier. There is an older couple in town looking for a lapdog." He glanced at her and did a double-take. "What's up? You almost look sad. You're not going to tell me you wanted to keep him, are you?"

"No! No." She shook her hands as if waving the crazy idea away. "Of course not, that makes no sense. It fits into none of my plans and is totally, absolutely not something that I should do."

"Except you wanted to?" Jackson's voice was a little quieter. "Do something that makes no sense?"

The air between them thickened. Tension pooled in her belly. Something had shifted. "You're not talking about Shadow anymore, are you?"

"Becca." A muscle ticked in his jaw. There was gravel in his voice when he'd said her name. "I—"

The bathroom door swung open. "And how are we doing here?" The front desk lady poked her head in and gave a toothy smile.

She looked so friendly and earnest that Becca felt bad for wanting to scream. Or maybe she was relieved. The conversation with Jackson had a dangerous, seductive pull, and it was probably better not risking finding out. Better to stay on the surface of things.

"We're great." Becca reached down and grabbed the first aid kit. "I'll go put this back where I got it. I think Mr. Lowe here has learned a good lesson: Remember to always look both ways before crossing the street. Right?" She shot him her brightest smile, pleading inside for him to go along with it, to understand that whatever was between them... that maybe it was better not to push it, to name it, to look at it straight on. The feelings were too fragile, too uncertain.

"All good. You're a regular nurse," he said, turning his attention to Shadow. "I'll go put the little rascal in his kennel. He goes to his new home tomorrow, right?"

"Yes, I'm so happy he's found his forever home. But I must say we'll miss him here. During these last few weeks, he's put a smile on all of our faces. He'd had a good life before and was probably a bit at a loss at the changes in his life, but sometimes good things come out of periods of uncertainty and stress."

"Isn't that the truth?" Becca refused to make eye

contact with Jackson. Better to get some distance and pretend that the universe wasn't trying to speak to her through a friendly shelter receptionist. Pretend that her world wasn't going off its axis. Pretend like nothing was changing when some moments it felt like everything was shifting like the earth had turned to quicksand underfoot.

And so that's just want she did, all through lunch, and the drive home. She pretended everything was the same...although she was beginning to suspect maybe that wasn't true. And even more confusing, she was starting to think that...maybe she wanted something different with Jackson. Maybe she wanted...more?

Chapter Eleven

"Can you throw the drinks in the cooler?" Alan Lowe asked, glancing up at Jackson from over the top of a long to-do list.

"Done. I finished while you were in the shower." Jackson picked up a clementine out of his mother's fruit bowl on the kitchen counter and plunged a thumbnail into the peel. A few citrus-smelling drops shot out, nearly hitting him in the eye.

"Whoa." He swiped at his face, grimacing at the citrus sting.

"Don't make a mess in here, or your mother will kill us both." It was Memorial Day and they were hosting a large backyard barbecue for the family and some friends. Jackson's big brother, Caleb, was coming back home from California with his wife, Issa.

"Who is making a mess in my kitchen?" Pauline Lowe appeared in the doorway as if called by a maternal sixth sense. "I mopped after breakfast. If anyone puts a mark on that floor, so help me by all that's holy...I'll be remopping with *you*."

"Whoa, whoa, whoa. I'm just trying to eat some fruit. Be healthy. You know, vitamin C?" Jackson filled his expression with mock innocence while holding up the clementine. "You want me to be healthy, don't you, Ma?"

"You're on thin ice." His mom made a *V* with her fingers and pointed to her eyes before turning them around to point at him.

They both burst out laughing as the doorbell rang.

"Oooh, are they here?" Pauline bustled toward the front door. Caleb and Issa were driving up from Sacramento, where they'd spent last night camping outside of Lake Shasta.

"You're going to have a full house." Jackson turned around to face his dad. "You want me to run the grill today?"

The pause took on weight as his father mulled over the offer.

"I'm not asking to manage your stock portfolio, just grill some burgers and dogs."

His dad folded his arms sizing him up. "It's a big job. You up for the responsibility?"

"You serious?" Jackson forced out a chuckle.

"I am. Given that you haven't been able to come

back with an answer about the business, I'm not sure if you wouldn't prefer spending the day with a six-pack and playing horseshoes."

Ouch.

"Jeez, okay." Jackson raked a hand through his hair. "Tell me how you really feel."

"What I want is for you to get your head screwed on tight and—"

"Look! Look everyone." Pauline came back in, her eyes bright with happy tears. "Caleb and Issa are here."

Pauline Lowe was a lawyer who had been serving on Heart's Hope Bay City Council ever since Savannah had graduated from high school. While her middle name was technically Frances, she often joked that it should be Organization. She had raised five kids after law school and worked almost full-time scheduling all their sports and lessons and events on a color-coded family calendar, keeping the whole family on track. But while she was no-nonsense when fighting with developers who wanted to violate city ordinances, when it came to her children she was as soft as a marshmallow, and they all loved her for it.

Jackson turned away from his dad, and the tension pulling tight between them eased a fraction as his big brother strode in, filling the room with his deep booming voice and infectious laugh. Following behind him was his wife, Issa, who bounded forward, arms outstretched.

"It's so good to see you," she exclaimed.

"You have a good drive?"

"Yeah, it took forever though, especially since I was carsick and we kept having to pull over. I think most of Northern California got to watch me lose first my breakfast and then my lunch."

"Oh dear. I just made some fresh lemonade. Let's get you a glass." Pauline didn't wait for a yes or no before heading to the cupboard and grabbing a pint glass.

"You been working out?" Caleb came up and slapped Jackson's bicep. "You're looking more jacked than usual, little bro."

"Just the usual," Jackson said with a shrug. "Surf every chance I get."

From behind him came the heavy sound of his dad's sigh. Jackson forced himself to ignore it. This was a day to reconnect with family and enjoy everyone being together, and he could see how much this meant to his mom. His dad had a single focus, and there was nothing he could do about it today expect ensure that he didn't burn the meat.

The doorbell rang again. This time it was Savannah, her long blond hair in loose curls over her shoulders, looking every inch the baby princess of the family. Noah was beside her with his six-year-old daughter, Rosie, behind them fussing on a small plastic device.

Jackson's jaw dropped. "Holy sh— ahem, heck, is that what I think it is?"

"My old Tamagotchi?" Savannah said primly. "It is indeed. No matter how much you and every other brother in this house tried to hide it from me, I always got it back. And now it's been passed on to the next generation."

Noah's gaze connected with Jackson's with an expression that clearly said *What are you going to do?*

Savannah was one of the easiest going, happy-go-lucky people he knew in life, but that Tamagotchi had made her seem like a close relative of the devil. She'd scream when she couldn't find it. Doors would slam. Tears would fall.

"Oh, Carter and Abby just pulled up." Issa pointed out the living room window. "And Becca's with them. Oooh, I love her haircut. And oh wow, is that little Sofia? She's so big now."

"Sofia's here?" That got Rosie's attention. "I got to go show her this, she's going to love it." And with that she was gone to find her friend.

It didn't take long for the house to fill up. Jackson grabbed the meat out of the fridge, stacking it high while grinning at the sounds of laughter and banter and teasing. He loved being part of a big family. These days he was finding his cottage to be quiet. Too quiet.

"What are you doing to your skin these days?" Issa was asking Becca. "Facials? Korean face masks? Retinol? Give me your secrets. Your skin is absolutely glowing."

"Uh…" Becca's gaze darted to Jackson as uncertainty flitted over her features. "Just drinking a lot of water, I guess."

"Oregon's water must hit differently." Issa laughed.

"Speaking of which, Pauline, this lemonade is really good. Thanks so much. I'm feeling more human again."

"Hey, Becs, you mind grabbing the door for me?" Jackson balanced his chin on top of the meat packages.

"Thanks," she whispered after they were outside, alone on the back deck. "I didn't expect to feel so guilty here."

"What do you mean?" Jackson glanced up at her as he lit the grill.

"That we haven't told your family. I mean, I know Savannah knows, but I am allergic to secrets. I don't want to let the cat out of the bag, but it feels like so much to keep under wraps."

"I get that." He reached out to tuck a lock of her beautiful black hair behind her ear and he caught his mom watching them curiously from the kitchen window.

He dropped his arm back to his side, clenching his fingers into a tight fist.

But from the way his mom was arching a brow at him, it was clear she had some questions. And she wasn't the only one. Becca had been watching him lately with an expression that made him hope for something he didn't quite believe was possible: That maybe he stood a chance with her. Not for a single night. But for a lifetime.

The thought both thrilled and terrified him. What if he wasn't enough for her? What if he couldn't be the man she deserved?

But what if he could?

The promise was sweet and enticing, like summer warm strawberries.

"Oh God, your mom just busted us." Becca was speaking without moving her lips, trying her best to look as if she was just smiling casually, but in reality looking slightly crazed.

"Look at that bird over there." Jackson pointed, so that she'd turn around.

"Huh? I don't see anything." She put her hand on the deck railing and peered out at the sizable yard.

He sighed and gave a slight chuckle. He was about to explain how he was trying to save her from herself when the doors flung open and everyone began to pile outside.

"So sorry, big brother, but I'm in charge of the playlist," Savannah sang out, plucking the wireless speaker out of Aaron's hands, then shrieking down the stairs as he began to give chase. "No one wants to listen to your couuuuuuuuntry," she squealed as she bolted across the grass.

"Some things never change." His brother Spencer cracked open a beer. "Including Savannah being a pest."

"She's not a pest!" Rosie shook her Tamagotchi at him in irritation. "She's the best, right, Dad?"

"Absolutely honey. The best...pest." Noah winked at the guys, but was clearly enjoying the show.

"Is that croquet?" Aaron asked excitedly from the lawn. "We haven't seen that set in forever."

"I asked your father to get it down from the garage. We haven't had a family playoff in a while." Pauline sounded wistful. "Over ten years."

"What's croquet?" Sofia asked, looking from one adult to another, clearly wanting an answer and quickly.

"Come on, friend." Abby took her hand, her red hair falling loosely over one shoulder in a fiery wave. "I'd love to teach you. It's an easy and super fun game to play with a stick called a mallet and a ball."

"You all go, enjoy yourselves." Jackson shook the stainless steel spatula. "I'll hold down the fort up here." Alan seemed to hesitate. "You too, Dad. Trust me, I got this."

"Look at little bro, stepping up." Spencer saluted him. "But don't burn the meat."

"Unless it's mine," Pauline butted in, finger waving. "You know I prefer well done. No pink."

Everyone left except for Carter.

"You don't like croquet?" Jackson asked. "My family used to treat it like a blood sport. Caleb has a scar on his knee from where Savannah threw a ball at him once after she'd lost because she swore he'd cheated."

"I like it fine. Looking forward to kicking your butt on a round later today. But for now, I figured I'd keep you company. Wanted to talk."

"Yeah? What about?"

"I think you know."

Becca had mentioned that Abby knew...and so

did her brother. He scrutinized Carter's face. He didn't look pissed. But he didn't look happy either.

Jackson grabbed his beer. "I got a good idea."

"I have to say, on my bingo card for this year, you knocking up my little sister was not one of my picks."

"You know, I have to agree with you. But I'm not sorry about it." That had to be said. If the truth was coming out, he was going to lay it all on the line here. The only person in this world who cared about Becca on the same level was her big brother.

"For real?" Carter didn't so much as bat an eyelash.

"I know everyone thinks that all I care about is having a good time, surfing, sleeping, gaming. But your sister deserves a hell of a lot more than that."

"I'm not arguing with that." Carter seemed to be sizing him up. "What's your plan to ensure she gets that?"

"I'm going to figure it out. Find out how to be the guy she wants."

Carter considered his words. "I don't think you need to do much in that department."

"Huh?" Jackson was expecting a lecture, but instead Carter's face had broken into a wide grin, his eyes open and friendly.

"You really are a dumbass sometimes, Lowe. My sister has been in love with you since high school."

The words hit him with the force of an invisible one-two punch. "She told you that?"

"Naw, man. She didn't have to. I have two eyes, I can see it, always have. I don't even know if Becca realizes the truth herself. Probably not—she has always protected her heart. I blame our dad for that. But you've always been there for my little sister, and I know you'll do the right thing by her. I'm not here to bust you or make threats. I just want to shake your hand and wish you both the absolute best." He held out his hand.

Jackson shook it firmly. "Guess I figured you didn't think I was good enough."

"My sister is a smart cookie. She knows what she is doing, and if she thinks you're worth taking a shot on, then I trust her judgment."

"She's been holding up so well." Jackson was quiet. "I don't know how she got that strong."

"When you grow up like we did..." Carter's features darkened. "You don't have a choice. It's sink or swim. Neither of us wanted to let our old man drag us down to his level, so we had to kick hard to the surface every day, fighting to keep our faces in the air."

"How do you think he's going to take the new—" A scream cut Jackson off. He and Carter both turned toward the large yard, where everyone was congregated.

"Issa!" Down in the yard, Caleb came running around the side of the house. His large body went rigid with tension as he scanned the area, locating his wife by the fenced in vegetable garden. She was running backward and windmilling her arms.

"Bee!" Abby was also retreating, bobbing and weaving like a boxer going up against an imaginary opponent.

"Shit." Caleb took off across the lawn.

Jackson and Carter exchanged concerned glances before bolting down the stairs.

"Dude, what's up?" Jackson called out, pumping his arms.

"She's allergic to bees," Caleb shouted over one shoulder, concern lacing his words.

"Crap," Carter muttered.

Jackson and Carter were fast, but Caleb left them in his dust, charging after his wife like her life depended on it, and maybe it did.

Issa stumbled into him and he scooped her up, sweeping her off her feet and scurrying backward.

"Baby! Are you okay? Did you get stung?" he asked, dropping down to one knee and positioning her on it, checking her over as if she were made of delicate glass.

"No, I'm okay," she said.

"I didn't realize you were allergic," Pauline said.

"I didn't know either!" Issa said. "I'd never gotten stung before. And then last fall, when we were apple picking at an orchard, one got me, and I had some swelling and started to wheeze. The urgent care doctor told me that I should keep an EpiPen on me."

"Well, heavens. I'm glad you're okay," Pauline said as she moved closer to her daughter-in-law and son.

Caleb looked up, eyes wide, clearly coming down from the panic. "I'm sorry I freaked out. I just didn't know what would happen to the baby if she was stung."

Issa dropped her hands into her face and started giggling. Caleb's jaw fell open, the realization of what he'd just shared spreading across his face as he turned red.

"B-baby?" Pauline turned to Alan. "Did I hear this right? Did our son just say *baby*?"

"We were going to tell you today, in a slightly less dramatic fashion." Issa stood up, smoothing down her shirt over her still flat abdomen. "We are thirteen weeks along."

"No way. So are we!" Jackson blurted, before realizing his monumental blunder. His fingers itched to grab the impulsive statement back and shove it into his mouth.

But this was real life. And as if in slow motion, the adults gathered slowly shifted their gaze to Jackson.

"We?" Pauline blinked. "I'm sorry, someone please explain this all to me. What is this about *we*?"

"Hoo boy." Carter coughed into a fist as Abby mumbled something about taking the girls inside to get Popsicles.

"Okay. Let me get this straight." Spencer pointed at Issa. "You are pregnant?"

Issa nodded shyly.

"That's fantastic, congratulations, sister from another mister." He stepped forward and gave her a bear hug before shaking Caleb's hand. "Hope it looks like her."

Caleb playfully slugged him in the bicep before Spencer whirled to Jackson. "But wait. Dude. You're not getting off without an explanation. Why did it sound like *you're* also having a baby?"

Everyone fell silent. In the distance a truck back-fired out on the road. Every gaze was fixed on him. *Shit.* He and his big mouth. He didn't mean to drop the news like this, and yet he couldn't lie without making a big mess. There was no choice right now except to face the music and answer as honestly as possible.

"Yeah, that's right." He rocked back on his heels. "I'm...having a baby too."

"Well, last time I checked you aren't a seahorse," Spencer said wryly. "I'm guessing you aren't carry-ing the kid."

Becca was behind him, just out of his field of sight but he could sense her presence. He wanted to turn, to hold her hand, but that wasn't where they were at...and now their sweet little secret had been blown wide open by his big mouth.

"I'm serious, people! Can someone please explain this to me?" Pauline's voice crept up an octave. "Jackson Lowe, you didn't go and get someone pregnant did you?"

He nodded as his dad blew out one of those long sighs that implied that while he should be surprised by his youngest's son's antics, he really wasn't.

"I did." Jackson heard those two words detonate

in the gathered group—gasps rang out, eyes went wide, and furtive whispering begun.

"Who?" Pauline gasped, stumbling back. "One of the waitresses at the pizza parlor? Oh no." Her hand flew up to cover her mouth. "It's not a tourist, is it?"

"Ma..." Jackson was exasperated. Did she really think that knocking up women on vacation was his modus operandi?

"Me." Becca's voice rose above the whispering, her tone soft but clear.

Jackson closed his eyes as he caught the light smell of roses. It was Becca's perfume. He knew without glancing over that she'd come to stand beside him. He hated that she needed to be party to this moment of scrutiny. He truly wished he didn't put her in this position. "I'm...uh...we're thirteen weeks pregnant too."

"You? Becca?" Pauline's hand dropped from her mouth down to press against her chest. "You're the one who is having the baby with Jackson?"

Chapter Twelve

"OMG, that's amazing." Issa pressed a hand to her heart. "Caleb, did you hear that?"

The pause lasted three...two...one and then all hell broke loose, the questions surrounding them like a storm.

"Since when have you been together?"

"How are you feeling?"

"Are you a couple?"

"Does Sofia know?"

"Hey, hey." Becca held up her hands. "Whoa. So, first things first. We aren't together. And I'm feeling okay, just really sick sometimes, and very hungry for ice cream. We aren't a couple, we're good friends. And most importantly, no, Sofia doesn't know, and

I am hoping that it can stay that way until I tell her the news myself."

"Two grandbabies." Pauline burst into tears. "I'm so happy that I don't know what to say. What a day. What a beautiful surprise."

She went and enfolded both Issa and Becca into her arms.

Caleb nudged Jackson in the ribs. "Just friends?"

Jackson nodded.

"Pretty damn good friends then, huh?" Aaron quipped as Spencer tried to cover up his barking laugh with a cough that failed to fool anyone.

"Um... hey everyone? I need a little help up here," Abby shouted from the balcony. "Something is burning on the grill."

"Oh no." Jackson slapped his forehead. "The burgers."

He jogged back to the grill to find the patties charred. Swearing under his breath, he looked over at the sausages and breathed a small sigh of relief. At least there would be enough of those to go around and keep everyone fed now that the burgers were a bust.

"Looks like you didn't have it handled," Alan said by way of greeting, coming up the stairs.

"Got distracted by Issa's emergency. But we have enough food to be okay."

"Thanks to your mother." Alan's tone was pointed.

Jackson winced, knowing he wasn't getting off the hook.

"You're going to be a father."

"I am."

"Do you have even the slightest clue of the responsibility you are taking on?"

Jackson slammed back his shoulders. "You know what, Dad? I don't. I can imagine, but until I'm in it, no, I don't think I can truly comprehend it."

"You're going to have to take on the company. That's it. No more dithering. This is bigger than me and you now. This is about providing for the next generation. This is for the future."

"Dad, I hear you." Jackson held up one hand. "But I need you to back off a little. Trust me when I say I know I have to figure stuff out."

"I trusted you to not burn our lunch, and look what happened." Alan nodded at the pile of burned meat. "It's not that you can't do these things, Jackson. Don't get me wrong. I know you can. But you aren't willing to stand up and take responsibility. To do the hard thing instead of the fun thing. But you're a man now, not a boy, and you're going to be a father, not just a son. I know you think I'm here just busting your chops, but it's not for my personal entertainment. I want—no, I *need* to see you be the man that I know you are deep down inside. But you need to believe he is there first."

And as much as his dad's words drove him crazy, Jackson couldn't move, couldn't blink, couldn't even draw a breath, because while his dad might not get all the things about him, nevertheless he was able to find the perfect words to cut through Jackson's armor and pierce his core.

Because it was one thing to want to have what it takes to be a provider and a father, but a whole other thing to actually make it happen.

Becca had been let down so many times in her life. He couldn't—he wouldn't—be another disappointment that she had to bear.

* * *

"Oh my God," Issa grabbed Becca's hand and tugged. "What if our babies are born on the same day? This is so wild. I can't believe you are going through this all with me."

Becca turned to look over one shoulder and saw Jackson and his father deep in conversation up on the deck. He was busy, which meant she had to hold down the fort here.

"I know you guys probably have a few questions."

"Maybe one or two," Spencer quipped.

"But the most important thing right now is that you know we are here for you." Pauline stepped forward and rubbed a hand over her arm. "Whatever you need, you have our entire family to fall back on. It's what we do. Who we are. You're family now."

Don't cry. Don't cry. Don't cry, Becca repeated in her head like a mantra. She had Carter; she'd always had her big brother. And she had Sofia.

But a big supportive family always felt like something for television or for other people. Not for her.

While the idea filled her with warmth, it made

her dizzy too. She'd been so used to being an island, of living a small contained life where her business was hers, and her decisions affected only her, and it was safe. Protected. Fortified.

"I'm sorry," she blurted, hoping to shake the attention, to direct it back toward Issa, where this had all begun. "Really, this is Issa's day, her news. I'm sorry that we somehow slipped into the spotlight."

"Never!" Issa was practically jumping up and down. "Just think. we can do a joint baby shower. Joint birthday parties. You'll have to come down to San Francisco. I know this amazing photographer and we can do a whole mommy and me photo shoot at the Presidio with the Golden Gate Bridge behind us and put them in matching outfits. Oh, and we can also…" She trailed off as a horrified expression came over her. "I'm so sorry. I went full Momzilla. I don't even know where that came from! I'm excited of course. But a photo shoot? My hormones are making me crazy."

"Just as long as you're the one saying it," Caleb quipped.

"I should go check on Sofia," Becca said, half to excuse herself and half because she did want to make sure her daughter hadn't overheard anything and wasn't off stewing with a million questions.

"I'll walk with you." Pauline slung her arm through Becca's.

"I'm sorry the news came out so unexpectedly," Becca said again, as they began to walk toward the house.

"If you say sorry one more time, I'm not going to let you have any of my chocolate cake for dessert." Pauline wagged a threatening finger. "And I used the salted caramel frosting."

"Okay, okay," Becca said with a small smile.

Pauline squeezed Becca's arm gently. "You know, I love all my children equally. I know it's hard for some people to believe that. They always think that certainly there must be one child who you connect to on a different level, one that you feel a little closer to, root a little harder for."

Becca tried to smile but it was hard. "I'm nervous about this actually. I love Sofia so much that I'm worried about not loving the new baby as much. Or what if I get so wrapped up in the new baby that Sofia and I grow apart. Our relationship is so special that I can't bear the thought."

"I felt the exact same way after having Spencer. Like how was I ever going to top the love I feel for this being? But with every new child my heart grew a little more. Now it's as if I have five extra hearts in my body. One is for Spencer. One is for Caleb. Then Aaron. Then Jackson. And then Savannah. And something tells me you will be the same way."

"I hope so. You're such a good mother. Your family is so great."

"We are." Pauline nodded, but her eyes were distant. "But we aren't too. We have our issues, just like every family."

"I know Jackson sometimes has a hard time with your husband."

"Yes." A small furrow appeared between the older woman's brows. "Alan is a good man, and he has done so much for this family. He is kindhearted but also pigheaded. Sometimes he makes it his way or the highway. It's not coming from a malicious place; the poor guy thinks he is helping. But ever since Jackson was born he has marched to his own tune. Spencer was the easy baby. Caleb and Aaron? They had their moments. But Jackson. Good grief, Jackson! He started walking at nine months old, can you believe it? I've never seen anything like it. The boy didn't even crawl. He was so determined to chase after his brothers. And he could never sit still. He had so many broken bones when he was younger that I was half afraid the emergency room was going to call the authorities on me. Then there was that darn senior prank."

"When he put a steer in the school gym?"

"Yes, the numbnut. He thought it was funny. The joke was on him when he was banned from graduation."

"Not his finest moment."

"Indeed not. But he is so happy-go-lucky you just can't help but say to yourself..."

"Oh, Jackson," they both said in unison before looking at each other in delighted surprise.

"You are so good for him. So stable and grounded. I'm not saying that you need to be his mother, but I see you as a strong foundation for him. I know he could build a wonderful life with you."

"I appreciate that. It's just...I know it's weird

with me being pregnant and all, but we aren't a couple. We're just friends."

"I'm friends with Alan too." Pauline offered a small smile. "Friendship is a necessary part of happily-ever-after. But I know my son, and when he looks at you? It's as if he's just found the end of the rainbow. It's always been like that."

"I'm not so sure," Becca protested. "We've known each other since high school, and he's never even asked me on a date. And he isn't exactly what anyone would call shy."

"No. No indeed. But he doesn't think as highly of himself as he could. Behind that sunny smile is someone who isn't sure they deserve someone like you. Alan thinks the best way to ramp up his self-confidence is to put him in charge of the landscaping company. But I keep trying to tell him…Jackson is the sort who makes his own path. My husband worries, but I have always known that someday Jackson is going to figure out his place in the world, and all the things I love about my boy will grow and become magnified. And maybe then, that's when he will finally feel like he deserves someone like you."

"But I'm so far from perfect. I know you know enough about my childhood. How after my mom died my dad shattered, and he was never able to put himself back together again. And since he was so broken…well, he wanted to break me and my brother too."

"But he couldn't, could he?"

Becca bit her lip, softly shaking her head. "I guess not. But sometimes I wish I knew what it was like to come from a family that's happy, that's whole."

"You know much more than you give yourself credit for, just like that brother of yours. All I ask, as a mother, is that while you're busy growing that second heart for the new baby, do me a favor." Pauline reached out a hand.

Becca took it and squeezed it. "Anything." And she meant it.

Pauline stared deep into her eyes, with an intensity that made Becca want to blink. "Search your own heart, and see if there is room in there for a man who loves you."

Loves? Becca shook her head and withdrew her hand. "No. I meant what I said earlier. Jackson and I aren't together. We're just friends."

"I know my son." Pauline gave her arm a squeeze. "And you've never been just a friend to him. Even back in high school, I saw the way he looked at you, and that has never changed."

"I d-d-don't understand," Becca stammered.

"Really?" Pauline arched a skeptical brow. "Honey, you're a smart girl. You never saw the signs?"

"No." Becca shook her head weakly. "I don't think so... I don't know. I'm... I'm not sure." But if she were really, *truly* being honest with herself, in her heart of hearts, hadn't she had some sort of inkling that there was something there between them? But any time her mind went in that direction, she shut it down. And it was easy for her to believe he wasn't interested in her since he never once asked her out in all these years.

Her friendship with Jackson had always been one of her greatest joys. She knew that finding someone she could share her heart with, someone who understood, accepted, and even appreciated her, just the way she was, was priceless. But she also knew that relationships could end in a way a friendship didn't feel likely to. She wasn't a risk-taker by nature, and she didn't want to ever live without Jackson by her side. Better they keep on firm and familiar footing, especially as they stepped into uncharted territory as co-parents.

And yet, for some reason, the expression in Pauline's face made Becca doubt herself. Pauline looked so certain that it was impossible not to ask herself if maybe she'd been telling herself a comfortable lie for so long that it felt like the truth.

"You're it for him." Pauline's no-nonsense tone let Becca know she wasn't getting off the hook easily. "And that's a fact."

Chapter Thirteen

So much for June gloom," Savannah announced, plucking her sun hat off the tropical patterned beach blanket and placing it on top of her sun-kissed head. "How hot do you think it is today?"

"My phone says eighty-seven degrees." Becca reached for her zinc sunscreen and rubbed another handful onto her skin. Her Hawaiian genes blessed her with darker melanin, but she could still cook like a lobster in direct sun. "Sofia, baby. Come get your hat."

Sofia glanced over before turning back to the sandcastle she was making on the beach with Rosie.

"Oh ho." Hilde glanced up from the paperback she was engrossed in under the blue and red striped umbrella. "Looks as if someone has come down with a case of selective hearing."

"Sofia Kenani . . . I'm going to count to three. One. Two. Two and a half. Two and three-quarters."

"Fine!" Sofia threw the shovel down with a huff and ran over to where Becca was sitting with her girlfriends enjoying an unseasonably warm day. Often Oregon coastal summers had a bit of a chill, the heat concentrating more inland, but today was perfect. If she closed her eyes she could imagine they were in Maui, back when they would spend summers visiting with her mom.

After Sofia was safely coated in a fresh layer of zinc, Becca wiped her hands on her upper thighs and stared off into the water, where Jackson's blond mop was easy to pick out in the lineup. Also, he was one of the only guys out there not in a full wet suit. His bare arms and legs were bronzed, and she caught herself drooling when she'd glimpsed the muscles bunching and flexing as he maneuvered himself deftly around the lineup.

Around him were out-of-town folks he'd rented boards to for the day. He'd set up his truck in the parking lot before breakfast on a whim and put out a stack of his old boards. It appears his big idea was a positive investment, because he'd been booked and busy all day.

He caught her staring, and before she could glance away, his grin split his face and he threw up a hand.

She ducked her chin shyly but not before wiggling her fingers back in greeting.

"You two need to get a room," Gia said, before rolling over and toasting her backside. "Although I guess you've been there, done that, am I right?"

Becca gave her a *what the heck* expression and gestured at Savannah, who was currently trying to lick a rapidly melting Drumstick she'd bought when an ice cream truck had come by.

"Becca," Savannah said flatly. "You've got a bun in the oven from my brother. And I know how you got it in there. As much as I don't want to think about you doing the deed with Jackson, you don't have to pretend it didn't happen."

"But has it happened again?" Tori asked.

Abby leaned back before grimacing. "I just can't get comfortable today. Sorry, Becca, but you have to dish on your love life. I need the distraction."

"Well..."

"It's fine," Savannah said, shoving the rest of her cone into her mouth and speaking through it. "Just don't go into the gory details."

"We've kissed. Once."

"That's it?" Gia said, one eye shooting up into her bangs. "Jackson Lowe got you pregnant, and since then all you've done is kiss him...one time."

"Why is that weird?"

"Because look at the man." Gia waved her hand. "He's a whole meal, and you know what you do when you have a snack right? You nibble it. You don't kiss it once."

"Okay, on second thought..." Savannah rose to her feet. "I love you, Becca. And I love my annoying brother. But I'm going to go take a quick dip in the water, because otherwise I might need to drown myself if I hear more."

"I'm sorry," Becca called out as Abby nudged her with her bare foot.

"Gurl, don't be sorry. All I've been able to do for a month is sleep. I'm excited to hear more about someone with an actual, nontheoretical love life, even if it is G-rated."

"Well, that's all fine and good, except that this is now making me remember that you're pregnant because of *my* brother." Becca burst out laughing. "This is a real problem for girl talk."

"Small towns," Hilde interjected with a knowing expression. "Everyone is in everyone's business."

"And sleeping with everyone's brother!" Tori quipped.

"And besides, I'm not sure if it's a good idea to do more right now." Becca tried to be her best pragmatic self. "This isn't all about fun and games. Someone has to be a responsible grown-up who remembers to eat vegetables, take her daughter to soccer practice, play outside with her, and take her to the farmers market."

"But all mom life and no sex life makes for a dull Becca," Gia interjected.

"You don't think being physical will get in the way of Jackson and me connecting? He really wants to try to figure out this whole fatherhood thing."

"It could bring you closer together," Abby offered. "Do you have feelings for him?"

All of her friends perked up, clearly interested in her answer.

"Define *feelings*," Becca said at last.

"Those pesky emotions that...you darn well know what we're getting at, Miss Ninja Evader."

Becca took a breath. She hadn't yet vocalized all her internal thoughts, hadn't even spent much time inspecting them, but if she couldn't be honest to her best girlfriends, who could she be honest with?

"Jackson and I have good chemistry. That's... well, that's not a problem." Her cheeks heated, but she kept going. "We also have been friends for so long. It's comfortable. We know so much about each other, but here's the real issue. We know what it's like to be together when everything is fun, when we want to be hanging out. We watch movies. We joke around. We laugh. And...I've heard smarter people than me say how friendship is a necessary foundation for a long-term relationship. And I see how it makes sense..."

"I am sensing a *but* buried in here," Hilde said.

"Right." Becca pushed up her glasses and ground her fists into her eyes so hard that she saw a cascade of bright spots. "The *but*. Life isn't just about fun, you know? I don't even feel that old yet, but adulting isn't fun. Paying taxes isn't fun. Grocery shopping on a Monday night after work because you don't have milk or bread for the next day isn't fun. Mopping the floor on a Sunday morning isn't fun.

Trying to find missing socks. Not fun. Balancing bank accounts. Satisfying? Yes. Fun, no. Jackson is great at the fun stuff. But I know that life isn't just about that. Does that mean that he'll just avoid those other things, and I'll have to be an adult for both of us? Or will he do it and resent me, and eventually what's good between us gets poisoned as we slowly drive each other crazy?"

The sun passed behind a cloud and the temperature dropped slightly, sending goose bumps up her arms.

"Oh, honey," Abby said. "I hear what you're saying. And honestly, that's all totally valid."

"Right." Gia leaned back on her elbows. "You have so much on your plate, and soon you're going to have more. So I do understand if you don't want to get involved with a guy who will essentially just be another child, albeit with facial hair. But aren't you also—and don't take this the wrong way, I just don't know how else to say it—stuck with him now? I mean, you're having a baby with him."

"I am. And I have no doubt he'll be a great dad. I'm sure he'll take the baby out to the park. Teach it to swim. Go fishing. Play games." Her heart fluttered as she mentally pictured Jackson doing all of those things. "But he can be a great dad without being my partner."

"That's the word, isn't it?" Hilde crossed her legs, considering. "Partner. Partnership. Have you spoken to Jackson about these concerns?"

"Honestly? I've barely spoken to myself about them."

"I've been around the sun longer than the rest of you," Hilde said. "Here's my two cents, and you can take it or leave it. Don't rule him out. But don't count him all the way in. Give him a chance. See what happens. You might be happily surprised. You might not. But at least you'll know and never wonder."

"What if I take a chance and get hurt?"

"Will it hurt to always wonder?" Hilde was frank, not pulling punches.

"I guess so. Yeah."

"Well then, that's the answer."

Becca looked back out to the ocean. Jackson was there with nothing but the horizon behind him. She watched as he picked out a wave and lay on the board, arms expertly paddling faster and faster, bringing him up to a matching speed. With a fluid grace, he launched himself to standing, aggressively shifting his weight so that the board cut into the side of the cresting wave, before squatting down low and letting the force propel him to shore. The athletic artistry was powerful, and she felt the same pride she always did when watching him in the water, as well as a new feeling churning underneath. Possessiveness.

She wasn't alone in admiring him.

Two women in small bikinis stood by the water's edge, clearly admiring more than the scenery.

She might be confused about what she wanted,

but there was one truth that was clear and bright. The days of her being able to overlook other women admiring him seemed to be ending.

Interesting.

"You're right. I'll keep going, see where it takes us."

"Whoa," Abby said.

"I know. Imagine me focusing on the journey and not the destination." Becca turned and gave her friend a self-conscious smile.

Abby was staring at her with a confused expression. "Whoa," she repeated, her big eyes growing even wider. "Whoa. Whoa. Whoa."

That's when Becca registered that Abby's hand was splayed over her round belly. And that she was at full term.

Hilde sprang into action, moving like a lightning bolt, dropping to her knees next to Abby. "Is there pressure?"

"Mm-mph." Abby nodded, squeezing her eyes closed.

"Just keep breathing," Hilde said, drawing back her granddaughter's long red hair off her shoulders. "Keep breathing. It will fade in a moment."

Abby's shoulders began to relax, and she opened her eyes, looking around. "I think...I think something might be happening."

Becca reached into her beach bag and whipped out her cell phone. "I'll call Carter."

The next ten minutes passed in a blur. Abby had three more sets of contractions, fast and furious.

Savannah and Gia packed up the beach gear as
Becca rounded up Sofia and Rosie and waved
Jackson in to explain the situation. He helped carry
Abby up to the parking lot, and Carter pulled in as
if he'd been in a Formula 1 race, his skin pale but
his jaw set with more determination than Becca had
ever seen.

Abby and Hilde loaded into the car and they were
off. The world seemingly returned back to normal,
and yet, Becca realized, everything was about to
change. Carter was becoming a father. She remembered the profound transformation that Sofia's birth
had wrought on her heart, growing her capacity
for love in ways she didn't know was possible.
It seemed impossible that the same phenomenon
could happen again when this new baby was born.
And yet, somehow she sensed she would. It was the
magic of love.

* * *

While the onset of Abby's labor had come fast, time
now seemed to have slowed. Becca had been in the
hospital waiting room with Sofia for three hours,
adjusting her weight in the hard plastic chair and
letting her daughter burn out her retinas watching
cartoons on her smartphone.

Hilde had left moments ago, saying she'd be
back with some things for Abby and the baby. Jackson had suggested that they also wait back at her
house, but Becca had refused. She might not be in

the delivery room, but she wanted—needed—to be close to her big brother as his life shifted. Growing up, he'd always put his career first. He craved the same order and stability she did, the same traits that their household lacked as her father stumbled from one binge to another, leaving emotional devastation in his wake.

But Carter had finally decided to be brave, to push beyond his comfort zone and to love another person with his whole heart. Becca knew how hard-won that journey had been and admired him for it. It was always fantastic when the good guys won, and Carter was definitely one of the good guys.

"It's not much to taste, but it's hot." She glanced up to see Jackson in front of her with a paper cup of coffee. "I found a coffee machine down the hall. They said it's a cappuccino, but it looks more like water that has a memory of caffeine."

"Thanks," she said, cupping the thin paper. She wasn't thirsty, but she appreciated his gesture.

"Any updates?" He'd left to stretch his legs a half hour ago, too antsy to sit still for long.

"Nothing. I hope that means that everything is moving ahead normally."

"Of course it is." Jackson took her hand and gave it a squeeze. "This is a great hospital, and if there is one thing I know in this world, it's that Carter isn't ever going to let anything happen to either Abby or that baby."

"You're right." Becca gave his hand a grateful

squeeze, appreciating the pep talk. "I'm so excited to be an auntie."

"She's here!" Carter barged into the waiting room. "She's here! Ava Olivia Hayes is here!"

"Ava!" Becca jumped to her feet and crossed the room, wrapping her arms around her big brother's waist. "Ava Olivia. I love that name."

"Is that my new cousin?" Sofia was right there too, not willing to miss a moment of the action. She'd been so excited for Aunt Abby to have the baby.

"She's seven pounds, four ounces, and I forget how long, but she's perfect. And she has red hair. Come meet her."

"Are you sure?" Becca hesitated. "We just wanted to be here to support you. I don't want to interrupt your family time. We can come back tomorrow."

"Interrupt family time?" Carter laughed. "Sis, you *are* family. Now follow me and come meet your new niece." He glanced at Jackson lurking in the back. "You too, man. Come on."

"Are you sure?" Jackson whispered in her ear as they walked down the hospital corridor, Carter speeding to get back to Abby and his new daughter.

"If Carter is okay with it, then I am too. Have you ever seen a brand-new baby?" Becca whispered.

"Nope."

"Well take this as a teachable moment."

Chapter Fourteen

Jackson had been inside the Heart's Hope Bay Community Hospital more times than he could count. A childhood of breaking ankles, wrists, fingers, his clavicle, and his nose, not to mention concussions and needing half a dozen stitches, meant that he'd been on a first-name basis with the emergency room docs and nurses.

But he'd never been here in the area where people were admitted. And certainly he'd never been down this wing, through the coded door with the word *Maternity* on it.

The first thing he noticed when he entered the ward was the quiet.

He wasn't sure why—probably Hollywood—but

he half expected to hear the sounds of screams and swearing intermingled with babies crying.

The walls were covered with tons of small 4×6 paper cards with tiny footprints dipped in colorful paint. The names of the feet drawn with care and sometimes light-hearted doodles.

Maxwell.

William.

Adam.

McKenna.

Gina.

It almost took his breath away to realize that in a matter of months, there would be a new set of footprints up here, and a name. He hadn't even considered what to call the baby. He and Becca would decide what the child was going to be named—that responsibility felt big, awesome even. But nothing prepared him for the shock of going into the last door on the right. Carter opened it, practically crawling out of his skin with love and pride, and there on the hospital bed was Abby, looking tired but thrilled. And in her arms was a small bundle that looked like a loaf of bread.

Except Carter scooped it up with tender care and it wiggled a little, and a wavering little cry came out.

And Jackson realized that wasn't a loaf of bread; it was a baby. "It's the smallest thing I've ever seen," he muttered as Carter deposited Ava Olivia into Becca's outstretched arms.

"She's perfect," Becca cooed as Sofia jumped up and down, chanting "I wanna see, I wanna see."

Becca turned the baby to the side, and Sofia squealed at the sight of the tiny red face.

"How are you doing?" Becca asked Abby, in a voice full of understanding and shared experience.

"Good now." Abby's laugh was faint. "I'm going to need to sleep soon. But I'm still full of adrenaline."

"I remember." Becca's smile was mysterious. Even though he knew so much about the woman next to him, from how she laughed at dumb movies to how she cried out when she came apart, he didn't know this side of her, the part that was forged in the same walls, the experience that had transformed her into a mother.

Carter was over by the hospital bed holding Abby's hand, gazing down at her as if she were a superhero who'd just diverted an Earth-ending asteroid from its fatal collision course.

Sofia and Becca moved to the plastic loveseat and were cooing over the baby.

"Do you want to hold her?" Abby asked.

"Who, me?" Jackson glanced at the impossibly small newborn and down at his big tan hands. What if he dropped it? Or it started crying? The slow realization was sinking in that he might know a thousand ways to make Becca happy, but he didn't know a damn thing about babies. And ultimately, he didn't think he would ever be able to do the first one without getting the second one figured out.

"Yeah you." Carter guffawed. "She won't bite. Not for six months, at least."

"Heh heh." He did his best not to cringe. The laugh sounded forced. "I'll let the new auntie soak it up."

"Are you sure?" Becca didn't break her gaze from her niece's face. "I'll share. I guess."

"Actually, I'm going to just head out and find a vending machine." He jerked a thumb at the door. "I need a soda. Back in a minute."

The hallway smelled like chemical disinfectant, but he could still breathe easier. He walked around the corner and then leaned against the wall, closed his eyes, and felt his heart pounding through his frame and into the drywall.

The fear hit him like a sledgehammer. What if he messed everything up? What if he let Becca and Sofia down? What if his own kid regarded him as a disappointment or, worse, a joke.

He had to figure out a way to get it together. A drinking fountain was on the wall diagonal to him. He walked over and took a long, slow drink of the lukewarm metallic-tasting water. Standing up, he glanced at the bulletin board above the sink and froze.

The flyer featured a photograph of a couple smiling together over the head of a small baby. It read:

Pre-Natal Classes
Geared to first-time parents

He tore off the number and email on the bottom
and folded it with care before pressing it into his
wallet.

* * *

"What's the baby doing?" Sofia whispered.

Ava Olivia was trying to shove her whole fist into
her mouth, her tiny brow furrowing in frustration as
she began to frantically shake her head.

"Oh, I think she's hungry." Becca stood up and
walked over to Abby, handing the baby over. "Can I
get you a pillow? How is breastfeeding going?"

Abby shrugged. "I've only tried once, and it
was a little confusing. She didn't seem to want it,
and yet she keeps acting like this, so I think she
is hungry."

"Do you want me to get a nurse?" Becca asked. "I
remember I had one with Sofia who was an absolute
lifesaver. She gave me all sorts of tricks and tips."

"That would be really great. I thought I knew
everything about kids, but turns out there's a whole
bunch I don't know."

"I'll come with you," Carter said. "I want to check
on Jackson. He looked strange when he left."

"You mean the whole thing where he took one
look at the baby and bolted?" Becca forced a laugh,
but it was hollow. She'd been trying to ignore that

fact, focusing instead on how good Ava's head smelled. There was nothing quite as wonderful as the smell of a newborn. "I'm sure he's fine, but if you don't mind, I bet he'd listen to you."

"Can I stay with Aunt Abby and the baby?" Sofia asked.

Becca glanced to Abby for confirmation.

"Of course, Peanut. You are going to be the best cousin in the whole wide world, aren't you?"

"Yeah." Sofia gave a toothy grin.

"Back in a second." Becca pushed out the door. "Hey, hang on a sec," she said to Carter once they got outside. "Can I just take a second to tell you how proud I am of you?"

Carter blinked. "You mean Abby?"

"Well, her too. She's obviously a rock star. But I mean you right now. Think about where we started. Think about everything we have survived together. And look at where you are now. You are a father. You've made it, you've got everything you ever wanted, and it's because you had the courage to chase your own happiness. You didn't let *him* win."

She didn't have to speak his name for her brother to know.

Their dad.

Robert Hayes.

The man who had been built like a brick wall from all his work on construction sites, who'd carried Carter and Becca under his arms as little kids as if they weighed less than a sack of potatoes.

The man who fell apart when their mom died, and who turned inward, mean and selfish, destroying himself in his grief, and wanting to make the world as miserable as he felt.

But the way to cope with a broken heart is not breaking the surviving children.

Becca had tried her best to be perfect, as if maybe getting the best grade or going to state with the high school debate team or getting accepted into a good college would be enough to make her father realize that she mattered, that she deserved his love.

Except no matter how hard she tried to twist herself into a pretzel, nothing was good enough. Eventually she learned to only rely on herself. She put her heart on an island, built a fortress around it, and made sure it was surrounded by a moat stocked with alligators.

Carter had to walk his own path. He didn't have a role model on how to be a good guy; he somehow was able to just walk away from the toxic narrative of his youth and embrace a path where he never raised his voice if he could talk logically, and he always made sure to center others' needs while never abandoning his own boundaries. She was so freaking proud of him.

He deserved every last little bit of happiness the universe could give him and then some.

"Sis...are you crying?" He looked at her with concern.

"What, no? Of course not." Her voice broke as she waved her hands in front of her face. "Sorry. I

just want you to know how much I love you and
how happy I am for you."

"Thank you" was all he said. It was all he had to
say. "And I'm happy for you. I think what you've
got with Jackson is good. I hope it works out."

"I don't even know what I have with him," she said
ruefully. "But I guess I've got to figure that out."

"Speaking of which…" Carter waved.

Becca turned around and saw Jackson striding
toward them, his face serious, determined almost.

"Everything good?" she asked.

"Totally." He nodded, absently patting his front
pocket. "You weren't putting out a rescue party
were you?"

"No. Abby needs to talk to a nurse to see if
there is a lactation consultant who can come visit
tomorrow."

Jackson nodded slowly. "I only understand about
half of what you said, but it sounds important."

"Hey, man, I need to go get Abby's toiletry case
out of the car. I forgot it when we were rushing
in, and she wants to take a shower soon. Walk
with me?"

"Cool." If Jackson looked confused that Carter
was seeking him out for some one-on-one time, he
didn't let on.

Becca flashed Jackson a quick thumbs-up before
making her way to the nursing desk. She'd had an
okay time feeding Sofia for the first few months; for
her it was easier than for some and harder than for
others. But when she started working again, it was

too hard to keep pumping, and she was so tired. When she shifted to formula, she felt guilty at first but also happy to have her body back to herself.

Every mother needed a choice that was right for them, and the most helpful thing she could do for her friend was to get her some assistance.

When she got back from the nurses station, Jackson and Carter were back. The restless nervous energy Jackson had exhibited earlier was gone, replaced with a pensive thoughtfulness. She glanced at her brother, wondering what he had said, but Carter had on his poker face. There were no clues to be deciphered from his features.

When the lactation consultant knocked on the door, ready to come help Abby, Becca took that opportunity to excuse herself, Sofia, and Jackson and let the new family have privacy.

Out in the parking lot, after getting Sofia into her booster seat, Becca shut the door and turned to Jackson. "I'm going to tell Sofia about Bolt."

"For real?" He stumbled a bit but caught himself. "When?"

"Today." Becca took an elastic off her wrist and caught her shoulder-length hair into a neat ponytail. "This seems like a good time, after meeting her cousin. The idea of a baby will hopefully feel a little more familiar and relatable."

"Do you want me to be there for the conversation?"

"I've been going back and forth, and I think I should do it alone. I don't want to overwhelm her with information—just give her the facts that a baby is coming and stuff like that."

"You aren't going to tell her I'm the dad?"

"I won't lie if she asks, but I'd rather just get the news out of the way first and wait and see if she asks more."

He gave her a look.

"What?"

"I think she is going to ask right off the bat."

And it turned out he was right.

After they got home, Becca gave Sofia a Popsicle and asked to talk to her out on the back stoop.

As Sofia slurped her treat, Becca cautiously explained that she had something very special to share.

"There is a baby growing inside me." Becca rubbed her belly, which had only the hint of a bulge.

"What? Really?" Sofia lowered the Popsicle with a stunned expression. "For real, or are you making a joke?"

"No joke, honey." Becca leaned forward and stroked her soft hair. "How does that news feel? Happy? Scary? Strange? Not sure?"

"What daddy put it there?"

Becca blinked. "What do you mean?"

"At Sunshine Corner, my friend Ryan said daddies put the babies in the mommies. Who is the daddy?"

Well . . . shoot. Jackson did try to warn her. Looks like she was going to serve herself a great big scoop of humble pie.

She cleared her throat, doing quick mental gymnastics. In the end, she realized the only way out of this conversation now was through. She'd have to tell the truth and bear all the questions.

"It's Jackson, honey."

"*Our* Jackson?" Sofia cocked her head, face expectant, oblivious to how her word choice hit her mom with the force of a sledgehammer.

Our Jackson.

"That's right. *Our* Jackson is the daddy of this baby."

"Okay!" Sofia went back to licking her Popsicle.

Becca waited and waited...until finally the silence got to be too much.

"Do you have any questions?"

"Can I have screen time? There is this one show where this kitty wants to be a mermaid, and then this mean witch comes and..."

Becca was unable to focus on the cartoon's convoluted plot. Sofia didn't seem traumatized or even remotely curious. And nothing in her expression hinted to the fact that she was burying confusion or hurt. It was as if the news was pleasantly received, and she had simply moved on to the next thing.

After Sofia was happily engrossed in her show, Becca walked to the kitchen sink, grabbed a glass off the drying rack, and filled it halfway, taking a long swallow.

"Well, heck...What a day." She slumped against the counter, thoughts jumbling together as a slow smile spread across her face. Today, Carter became a father, and Sofia learned she was going to be a big sister. The sky didn't fall. If anything, it felt more expansive, as if the world held so much possibility and all she needed to do was to muster up the courage to claim it.

Chapter Fifteen

Jackson sat in his truck on the dark street looking into Becca's house. Her kitchen light was on, and he could see her outline. Her studied her back as she stood facing away from the window. Her shoulders were narrow, too slight to carry the burdens that she did alone. He could feel a vague ache in his arms, the wish to take some of the weight from her, shoulder more of the load. The conversation he'd had earlier in the hospital with Carter played through his mind for the hundredth time.

His buddy had clapped him on the shoulder the minute they were alone together.

"You doing okay there, man?" Carter had asked. "You looked like you were freaking out back there."

Jackson had given a sheepish shrug. "Aren't I

supposed to be checking on you? You're the one who had the kid. But you look like you were born into it. And I…I guess I'm just worried that I won't be able to do the same."

"You kidding me?" Carter's chuckle had been low but amused. "I've been freaking out ever since Abby told me she was going to have our baby. Today, when I held Ava Olivia for the first time, all I could think was that I was shaking so hard I might drop her."

"For real?" Jackson hadn't been able to believe it.

"For real." Carter's nod had been genuine. "But I had to step up. And you're going to do the same. You might not know what you're doing, but you're going to figure it out fast, because we're the same…Deep down, the only thing that matters is family."

Those last nine words had been playing on a loop for Jackson. Somehow, he and Becca and Sofia and the baby were going to be a family. And the idea made him willing to walk through fire to deserve it.

His phone buzzed. He glanced down. It was his dad.

No doubt Alan wanted to talk about his future in landscaping management.

He'd need to have that conversation soon…but not tonight.

Declining the call, he flicked to the website that Carter had told him about. It compared the size of the growing baby to a seed, fruit, or vegetable each week, serving as a practical benchmark for intangible growth. Today, the baby was the length of a green bean. He thought of the small size, a sense of protection rising in his chest. On the dashboard was a small notebook he'd purchased a few days ago to keep track of orders for the business, but now he had a better idea. This was going to be his baby book. He'd record observations about Becca and the baby in it, keep track of growth, and jot any ideas or concerns he had. He wrote in the date and drew a small sketch of a string bean with a little happy face.

Then he flipped the notebook closed, stuck it in the center console, and climbed out of the truck. It was a Saturday night, but he had no desire to be anywhere other than right here. He opened the gate, and Becca turned at the sound, looking out the window with a wide smile on her face.

He bounded up the front steps and grabbed the door handle before pausing.

"Shoot," he muttered. He'd been about to just open the door and walk in, but he'd never done that before. He'd always knocked to announce his presence, even if Becca was expecting him. This was her space, and he'd always wanted her to know he respected it and waited for permission to enter. So, what had changed...?

The door opened and Sofia stood there, one earbud in, the other on the floor, dangling from a wire. The tablet she was holding at her side was playing a cartoon.

"Hi." She beckoned him forward. "And thanks!"

"What for?" He removed his sneakers before entering. While Becca hadn't grown up in Hawaii, she'd been raised to never wear shoes in the house, and she enforced that rule with all guests.

"I've always wanted to be a big sister."

His body tensed. "Sorry, what?"

"You put the baby in my mommy's body."

And with that, she wandered back to the couch.

He sensed movement and glanced right; Becca stood in the doorway to the kitchen.

He raised his brows.

She shrugged and mouthed *I know*.

He walked into the kitchen, chin tucked, hand fisting the hair on the back of his head. "I take it that you told her earlier?"

"Yes, but not in the way that she took it." Becca paced in the kitchen. "I'm all for facts, but can you imagine her at Sunshine Corner telling the parents at pickup that you put Bolt in my body?"

He burst out laughing. "It will be on the front page of the newspaper by midweek. I hope you're ready for the yard to be filled with reporters. Paparazzi in the driveway."

He was exaggerating, of course, but like all small towns, Heart's Hope Bay was fueled by gossip. There hadn't been any scandals lately, so this would likely set tongues to wagging.

"Should I be worried that she's taking it so well?" Becca crossed her arms. "Tell it to me straight, because I'm really not sure."

"To me, it's a sign you're a great parent. She's

confident and secure, so the idea of a baby isn't a threat or competition. Instead, it is..." He trailed off, the rest of the sentence feeling suddenly corny.

But he should have known that Becca would never let it go. "What?"

He sighed. "Instead, it is just more love."

A strange look passed over her face, one he'd never seen, but it was gone before he could decipher it, and replaced by a cheerful, upbeat smile. His Becca, when she wanted to put on a brave front.

Wait a second. *His* Becca? As much as he wanted to hit rewind on the thought, he couldn't; it was in his brain now. And why couldn't it be there? What if he, finally, for once, just admitted that he was crazy for this woman, and that he was beginning to realize that he'd always been, even when they were teenagers. The issue wasn't the wanting; it was having the balls to see if someone like her would take a chance on a guy like him. She had everything going for her, from looks to brains to a great personality. He knew women found him attractive, and he didn't lack in self-confidence, but with her...he just always knew that he'd need to play his cards exactly right, and he wasn't quite sure if this was a good time to hold or go all in.

"I've got to put Sofia to bed. Do you mind hanging out and waiting?"

"No, no. Of course not. You go, I'll just...uh..." He eyed a fashion magazine by the mail pile. "I'll read this. 'Must-Have Sandals for Summer.' I'll definitely learn a thing or two."

"You'd look smashing in espadrilles."

"Spa—huh?" he asked as Becca yelled, "Sofia, baby, time for bed. Go brush your teeth, and I'll tuck you in."

"No! Both!" Sofia hollered back.

"Don't argue! It's bedtime."

"I know. I'm tired. But I want both."

"What do you mean, *both*?"

"Both you and Jackson to tuck me in."

Becca gave Jackson a quick glance. "You don't have to if you don't want to This is so not an obligation. I can tell her—"

"You kidding? That kid is never an obligation." And he meant every word. Sofia cracked him up. She was feisty but sweet, and he always enjoyed hanging around her. He rubbed his hands together as he walked back to the living room. "You want me to tell you a story about Banjo?"

"Banjo? Who's that?"

He opened his mouth in a perfect *O*. "Sofia Hayes, are you trying to tell me that you don't know who Banjo Lowe is? How is that even possible?"

She giggled and picked up the stuffed frog beside her. "I don't, though. Who is it?"

"Only the greatest dog that ever lived this side of the Mississippi. He lived in my house when I was your age. He was a rough collie, which means he had lots of long shaggy brown and white hair, and a long, serious nose."

"Tell me about him."

"I can't wait," he said, "but first you need to listen to your mother and brush your teeth."

"Ugh. Fine." She stalked off, giving a very uncanny impersonation of the kind of teenage attitude she might deliver one day.

"You sure you haven't parented before? Because I have to say, you might be a natural."

Natural. You might be a natural. The words beat inside him like a slow, persistent pulse. And just like that he had the courage. Tonight he was going to do it. Put it all on the line and lay it out for Becca—give her the ball and let her decide what to do in the court.

* * *

Sofia loved the Banjo stories. She propped herself up on one elbow, her nose adorably scrunched in concentration, and ate up the stories. Like the time Banjo ate his homework—although technically it was sort of Jackson's fault because he'd been doing math work while eating bacon. The smell had gotten absorbed into the paper, and the rest, as they say, was history.

Becca sat watching them from the rocking chair in the corner, the one that used to be her mother's. It was the single item she took from her childhood house, sneaking in one night when her dad was passed out at the kitchen table, empty beer cans piled at his feet like spent bullet casings. Just another night, another act of violence against himself.

She'd removed the chair while pregnant with Sofia, wanting—needing—to be close to her mom's memory, and her dad would never have willingly parted with it. He clung to every memory of his wife, every last thing she owned, hoarding it like a dragon with precious gold.

He never noticed the missing chair—or if he did, he never came looking for it.

This was her safe place. Where, as a new mom, she'd rocked her baby, singing "Pua Liliehua" just like her mother had, the words meaning "love is bound fast, with an eight strand lei, there is nothing to separate you from me…forever." It was a song that made her feel close to her mom and her beloved islands. She'd taken more trips with her mom as a little kid than Carter, as he'd often stayed back in Oregon for summer sports camps. And so she had soaked up more of the culture from the luau to eating lilikoi straight from the vine, and spending days at a time wearing nothing but her bathing suit and plastic slippers.

And now her mother's rocker was a vantage point from which to watch Jackson, his frame absurdly large next to Sofia's little single bed. He was built like a redwood tree, all length and power. She was built more like a little shrub. And judging by Sofia's growth to date, her daughter was similar. Becca placed a hand over her belly. Who was this mysterious being inside her? Would they be tall like their father?

Jackson had finished the story, and Sofia's

breathing was beginning to slow, her eyes slowly blinking in the changing colors of her rainbow night-light.

Becca flashed him two thumbs-up, and Jackson swept out his arm with a flourish and dipped his head, clearly pleased at the great success of his effort.

She pointed toward the door and pressed one finger to her lips.

Sofia's eyes had closed, and when she was out, she stayed out, just like a light bulb.

Once they'd tiptoed back to the living room, Jackson flopped onto the couch. "Man, it was easier sneaking out of my house in high school to go to one of Barry Lohman's parties out on his farm."

"Now there's a name I haven't heard in a while." Becca sat beside him, keenly aware that only a few scant inches of space remained between their legs. "Those were crazy parties."

"The bonfires." They glanced at each other as they said the same thing.

She burst out laughing. "Now when I recall those memories, I'm genuinely shaken as a parent. Like... those fires were gigantic."

"Right? I'm pretty sure you could have seen them from up in space."

He leaned back and ran a hand through his hair. His smell drifted toward her, that delicious scent of salt and sunshine.

He gave her a side eye. Their gazes locked and held.

Busted.

He slowly shifted so he faced her straight on. "Are you checking me out?" It was a simple question, but behind it was so much more.

She wanted to say no. The word was on the tip of her tongue. But she couldn't lie to him.

"And what if I was?" she said slowly. "It's a free country, and you're in my house."

"Is that a fact?"

The silence lingered. It was clear he was waiting to see where she'd take things. And the problem was, she didn't know what she wanted to do. Because if she started reaching out to him, how would she ever be able to stop?

His eyes hooded as his irises seemed to darken. He brought a hand up to his face, absently rubbing his long pointer finger against his full bottom lip.

She'd tasted that lip but not enough that the flavor was imprinted on her senses. But something in the way he'd ever so slightly leaned toward her, as if she were a magnet, made her wonder if she'd be getting another opportunity for research.

"Would you...hold me...for a little bit?" She ducked her head, pushing hair behind both of her ears. The request was simple, but it still made her feel shy. This was Jackson. Her friend. But he was also becoming this new Jackson, and that person sometimes made her feel different things.

"Bring it in." He opened his arms so wide that the sleeves on his cotton T-shirt appeared to be crying uncle as the thin fabric stretched over his biceps.

She crossed the space and nestled her head on

his hard chest, not quite believing how good this moment felt, or how natural it seemed to cuddle up on the couch, lost in his embrace.

He gently rested his chin on the top of her head.

"Can I tell you a secret?" he asked, running a hand up and down her spinal column.

"My lips are sealed."

"I like this." He pressed his lips to the top of her head.

Tingles moved up and down her body as if she was being burned by tiny sparklers. "What do you like about it?"

"Being with you," he said without missing a beat. "It's hard to ever be in a bad mood around you."

"You are being silly." She slapped his leg. "I was being serious."

He tilted her chin up so she was forced to face him dead on, absorbing the full power of his unbroken, seemingly unblinking stare. "I am too."

She licked her lips and noticed how he homed in on the action, and that his pupils had dilated. She'd read enough romance books in the last five years to know exactly what it meant when a man's pupils dilated. It felt good, to have this power, to be in the arms of this beautiful, physically powerful man who wanted her, and to be open to the fact she wanted him back.

"I like you," she said quickly before she lost her nerve.

"I've always liked you." He watched her uncertainly.

"Ugh, do you really want to make me do this?" Her cheeks heated, but she was on a committed course now. Sink or swim, and she wasn't drowning today.

His lip twitched in amusement. "I don't mind hearing it."

"You've always been special to me as a friend. But now you're becoming special in this whole other way."

"Are you saying you have feelings for me?"

She buried her face in her hands. "Shut up, or I'm going to make you a friendship bracelet."

"Becca?" He gently removed her hands and held them tight. "I know this is strange, because we've been friends for so long. But look, I'm into you. Like I said, I've always been into you. I tried not to focus on it, but it's always been there, this spark."

Her shoulders rose and fell as she took a deep inhalation. "I think I've been nervous to acknowledge it. Your friendship means the world to me, and I don't want to risk anything messing that up, you know?

"Why do you think I've kept my mouth shut for so long? But now that it's out on the table..." A flame kindled in his eyes and his gaze began to smolder. "Can I kiss you?"

She blinked, her mouth parting slightly as the tip of her tongue touched the center of her top lip for just a fraction of a second. Even though they were on solid ground, it was as if the Pacific Ocean had risen and was lifting her house off its foundation, gently rocking her off balance. "I'd be open to that."

With a swallowed groan, he moved in. That sexy deep, gravelly chuckle was barely audible. Ooh boy, she was in trouble now.

"Only kissing, right?" He swept her hair back off her neck before leaning in to nuzzle the edge of her jaw.

The pressure of his lips against her skin threatened to sap her strength. Her thighs quivered, but she squeezed the muscles tight, locking them into place. "Not just kissing." Her words were little more than breath.

His breathing grew increasingly ragged. "A little more? Or a lot more?"

She reached out and cupped his cheek, feeling the tension locked in his jaw, the same pressure welling in her core. "Tonight, I want everything. Are you okay with that? Because if not, then—"

"I'm great with it." Hyperawareness flooded her body as he slid one hand to her lower back, the other beneath her thighs. And then he was scooping her up off the couch, cradling her in those powerful arms, crushing her to his chest, and striding to her bedroom. He carried her to the edge of her bed and set her down, bending down to taste her lips as if he'd never grow tired of her taste. She went to lean back, holding her weight up with her palms, but then stopped herself. She'd been holding herself up for so long, she didn't know what it was like to rely on another person's strength. Reaching up, she looped her arms around his broad shoulders, feeling his hard muscles bunch and shift from the contact.

The deep shudder that jolted through his body released some hesitancy within her. She could undo this big, beautiful man with just a few touches. What if she took more? During their one magical night together, she hadn't boldly explored his body, the physique she'd watched shift from a handsome boy to a whole man. But tonight, they had time, and she could take the scenic route.

Slowly, she dropped her fingers down to tease up the bottom of his soft, well-worn T-shift. With a low groan in the back of his throat he reached behind him and fisted off his shirt in one clean motion that was so incredibly hot.

And then he was there, before her, all bronzed skin, hard pecs, and trim waist disappearing into faded denim.

She wasn't sure exactly where they were going, but it was time to have the courage to explore all possibilities.

Chapter Sixteen

It felt as if all the lovemaking was tattooed over Becca's body. The night she and Jackson had conceived the baby, they'd only done it once. But now, maybe it was the pregnancy hormones, or maybe it was all the longing, but she couldn't get enough. It was like she was turning into some sort of a sex fiend, and he kept joking that she was draining his life essence.

Thankfully none of the other parents at preschool drop-off seemed to suspect that beneath her cute but sensible mom jeans and fitted T-shirt she'd been ravaged last night and did her own fair share of plundering. She subtly stretched out her hips, rocking from one side to the other, feeling the sweet soreness at her center, a secret souvenir that was just for her.

Becca was just preparing to leave from drop-off when Abby came in, her hair in a messy bun and her T-shirt on not only backward but also inside out.

"Hey, lady," Becca said slowly. "You doing okay?" They'd only been home from the hospital a week.

"Yeah, I'm fine. Great. Better than great! Just wonderful. Hashtag *blessed*." Abby flashed a silly peace sign, but her attempt at a smile looked like a hostage's proof of life photograph.

"What's going on?" Becca still remembered the first few days home from the hospital as a new mom. The idea that they let her just walk out of there with Sofia and didn't even provide an instruction manual was pretty darn wild.

"It's nothing." Abby waved a hand. "Ava's just had a hard time settling down. She's sleeping right now, so I wanted to pop down and see how everything was going."

Abby lived above Sunshine Corner in a small but well-appointed apartment.

"Don't worry." She held out a monitor. "I've got this in case—"

A high newborn cry emanated from the speaker.

"I guess duty calls." Abby's upbeat tone was at odds with the unshed tears thickening her voice.

"Can I come up?" Becca said quickly. "I don't have any early morning meetings today, and I'd love to see my baby niece for a few minutes."

Abby looked doubtful. "It's a mess. Carter says not to worry about it, but how can I not?"

"Mess, shmess! That's just how new parents roll."

"Well, I'm rolling so hard I could be a…a… fancy car. Just don't ask me to name a make or model, because I swear to God, I'm not even sure of the day of the week or when I last took a shower."

"Yep, that's it. What you need is to not come down and check on how things are going with the school. Let's go upstairs. You get in the shower. I'll rock the baby."

"Is everything okay?" Hilde approached wearing an apron covered with daffodils.

The sound of baby Ava crying came through the monitor even with the turned-down volume.

"I'll get her." Hilde moved to take off her apron.

"No! I mean it's okay," Abby said quickly. "No offense, but you're just such an incredible baby whisperer. Honestly, I need to practice being a mom." She shook her head as tears filled her big eyes, making them shine. "I just figured since I knew how to run a preschool, I could handle a baby who is a week old. But it's like my body is stuck in slow motion, and the baby can't wait. But I need to figure this out. Me."

"I see." Hilde's brows drew together even as she inclined her head, nodding in agreement. "And I support you. Go on then, and if you change your mind, I'll be over in the maker space helping the children with their play dough."

Becca followed Abby back up into her apartment.

"Is Carter here?" She glanced around. The space was open and bright. There were no dishes in the sink. No piles of laundry. No outward signs in the home that Abby was struggling.

"He had to drive up to Portland for a meeting." Abby headed to the bedroom to scoop up little Ava. "He's supposed to be taking paternity leave, but there is this one client that he can't afford to put off. I support it. In fact, I told him to go, so he isn't the bad guy here."

She collapsed on the couch and hiked up her shirt. "But look at this." She reached into her bra and pulled out a cabbage leaf. "I have cruciferous vegetables in my bra."

"Uh..." Becca scratched her cheek. "Is that for a snack?"

"No!" Abby hiccupped. "I don't even like cabbage. I'm having horrible breast engorgement, and Hilde said it would help. I think it's doing something, but also it's making it hard for Ava to get a good latch. Do you mind handing me that?" She jutted her chin in the direction of a *U*-shaped breast-feeding pillow near the reclining chair.

"Of course." Becca snatched it up and brought it over to her friend, who was adjusting the baby, trying to find a good angle. "Did the lactation support help in the hospital?"

"Mm-hmm," Abby murmured, wiping back a few more escaped tears. "I mean, it was still hard, but with the nurse's help, I felt like I could do it. But once I got home? I'm afraid she isn't able to eat enough. And when she can't eat, I get more swollen. And then it gets harder for her to try. And beyond that, she really does hate to be swaddled, but she gets fussy if I hold her for too long, but then she gets lonely if she's in the crib." She dropped her head so that her red hair hid her face like a glossy curtain. "What if I'm just a bad mom?"

"Honey." Becca's heart ached as she walked around to the back of the couch and began to rub her friend's tense shoulders. "I know this is a huge adjustment. And even though you felt so prepared, your body just went through an epic ordeal, not to mention your hormones are basically at a Six Flags riding on roller coasters. You aren't a bad mom. Ava loves you. It's just that it's a hard business to be born. For nine months she was quiet and snug inside you, and all her needs were being met without any effort. Now, she's out here in the world. The temperature changes. She has to eat. Pee. Poop. Adjust to sunlight. It's a lot. But you're both going to get there."

"Do you promise?" Abby's expression looked hopeful even as her chin quivered.

"Cross my heart. I have no doubt you're doing your best, and your best is all you need to do. You have cabbage on your boobs. How can you even begin to think you are a bad mom?"

That earned her a snort laugh.

"I love Hilde so much, but since coming home

it's been a little hard. She's the baby whisperer of Heart's Hope Bay, you know? And I feel as if she knows all the right things to do at the right time, and there's a part of me that might be jealous, which is so dumb. And part of me worries that if I just stand back and let her do it, then I'll never learn."

"Have you spoken to Hilde about your worries?"

"You sound just like your brother." Abby sighed. "And no, I haven't. At least not candidly, like I just did to you."

"I don't know Hilde like you do, of course, but I think she is one of the best listeners I've ever met. You aren't saying anything that is hurtful or mean. This is all normal. And everyone who knows you adores you and wants to support you."

"Thank you." Abby sucked in a breath. "Oh! She just latched. Ava, good baby. Yes, good." She sighed with relief. "Thank goodness, it was beginning to really hurt."

"I think that's my cue to leave, but before I do, let me fix you up a quick snack and bring over a drink of water. You don't need to do anything else today except what you're doing now."

After she cut up some fruit and put it in a ceramic bowl and popped a lemon slice in a glass of filtered water, Becca excused herself.

Abby didn't seem as if she was on the brink now, but she was clearly struggling. Becca hadn't experienced postpartum depression with Sofia. Could Abby be in an early stage? She frowned. The best thing she could do is call her brother later and get his take on the situation. He'd move heaven and earth for that woman.

As she stepped outside, she put on sunglasses to ward off the bright sun.

Would Jackson do the same if she struggled this time around?

Chapter Seventeen

Jackson pulled up to the large vacation rental house out on the point above Heart's Hope Bay, parking next to the other trucks from Lowe's Landscaping. It had 180-degree views of the coastline, and while bigger than any other home in town, it wasn't flashy. Instead, it had been built low, using neutral colors and glass, making it seem as if it had sprung up along with the salt-hewn stone and scrub brush. He always enjoyed working on this site.

He checked his watch before jumping out. Crud. He was fifteen minutes behind. He'd slept in, a dream of Becca keeping him happily unconscious until he'd bolted awake, realizing that the alarm had been beeping.

But when he walked around the house, the crew

was already at work. He frowned. It wasn't that he didn't want people taking the initiative, but they didn't have the work order. How could they have started when they didn't even know the tasks?

"Reggie?" he called, approaching a worker who was standing to the side of the property, looking over a piece of paper. "What's going on?"

"Huh?" Reggie looked up, blinking at him blankly. "What are you doing here?"

Now it was Jackson's turn to blink. "Dude, what? I work here."

"But your dad said that I was the crew leader now. This morning, when he promoted me." Reggie held up the paper in his hands, which Jackson noticed was the work order. "Didn't he tell you?"

"No. No, he didn't." If a meteor cut through the atmosphere and hit him on the head, Jackson wouldn't have been more surprised. Was his dad firing him? What the hell was going on?

"I was planning on it." Alan's baritone cut through the din in Jackson's brain. "But when you were late, I had to get the crew started, so I let them know about the changes."

The rest of the crew kept working, but Jackson wasn't dumb. They all had their ears craned like satellites hoping to pick up the smallest bit of gossip.

Alan seemed to realize it too. "Walk with me," he said, taking off toward the point, far enough away that no one could eavesdrop.

"Dad, you serious?" Jackson glanced around as

if the answers he sought were on the lawn or in the sky. "Reggie is crew leader now? I'm out? You...you fired me?"

Alan's sigh was long. "I'm not firing you. I'm hiring you."

Jackson swiveled around. "What are you talking about?"

"I'm putting you in charge. I waited for you to get back to me after my last call. You didn't. So, if you aren't willing to make a decision, guess I'll be doing it for you."

"You can't do that!"

"No, what *you* can't do is go get a woman pregnant and not have a plan." Two blotches of color spread across Alan's cheeks. "I don't know what you're thinking, son, but you're clearly not thinking with the head that I need you to be using."

"That's a low blow."

"I like Becca. I like her daughter. And I will support any grandchild of mine. But what I will not—no, what I *cannot* do is stand to the side watching you bop along like you don't have a care in the world. Actions have consequences. And you need a stable livelihood."

"Do you think I don't know that? Do you think I wouldn't want to provide for my child?"

"Honestly, I don't know what you think." Alan's voice went up a fraction, his throat muscles straining as his hold on his temper weakened. "What I do know is that I hear you say 'don't worry, Dad' and then I see you out on the goddamn surfboard day in and day out, and guess what? That makes me worry."

"Well, I've been thinking through my options, and you know what? I think there is a real opportunity to explore with surfing. Maybe I can figure out a way to make it work as a business...doing rentals, surf school, and I don't know...retail." Jackson stumbled on his words and hated that he didn't sound as confident as he needed to be to convince the old man. He'd been keeping these thoughts close to his chest and wasn't sure he was ready to have them out there, especially with his dad. They still felt so private. They were his dream, fragile and still as easily popped as a soap bubble.

"Surfing?" His dad rolled his eyes. "Don't speak nonsense, son. If you aren't going to make the right call here, then I'm going to do it for you. And that's you stepping up to take over our operations. Here's how this is gonna go. You follow me back to the office. We're starting management training 101 in thirty minutes sharp. And don't look at me like that." He walked past, patting Jackson's shoulder. "Someday you're going to thank me for it."

After seven hours with his butt in a chair, Jackson wanted to say a lot of things to his dad, and none of it was grateful. Outside, the sun was shining, but here he was in a cramped office with bad lighting, hunched in front of a computer going through spreadsheets that were making him cross-eyed. There was the pesticide charter he was ordered to read and an online folder full of workers' comp and employer liability law.

When five o'clock rolled around he was up like a shot.

"How did it go?" Alan peered over the top of his wire-rimmed glasses as Jackson stormed out of the back office.

"I looked over everything you asked me to review," Jackson said tightly.

"Good. Good. I'll quiz you on some of the specifics tomorrow. I expect to see you here at seven thirty sharp. Not seven forty-five, not seven fifty."

"I was late one time." Jackson spoke through gritted teeth.

"Your name is on the side of the trucks. If you don't take yourself seriously, how can you expect your employees to do the same? I have always expected nothing less than absolute excellence for myself. And as a result, people know not to cut corners, not to shirk."

"I get it. I get it. You're amazing."

"Knock it off. You aren't a child. I'm not tooting my own horn for entertainment. I'm telling you that I don't expect anything from those around me that I don't expect from myself. It made me tough, but I'm fair."

"Yes sir." Jackson wasn't sure he fully believed his father, but he knew Alan believed the truth of his words. "I'll be here tomorrow."

"Have a good night. And think about it: If you're going to be a father, what can you be bringing to the table to be the best man you can be for Becca and this child? If this isn't the way, tell me what is, because I'm all ears."

When Jackson got into the truck he flexed his hand into a fist, tempted to take out his aggression on the steering wheel, but that felt like proving his father right.

"Damn it." He growled the words and fisted his hair into an angry tuft.

The trouble was, as much as he wanted to make his dad out to be a villain, he knew that much of what he was saying came from a place of common sense. But Jackson was coming from that same place too, and Alan just refused to see it. Sometimes it felt like everyone did. It was as if all they could see was his laid-back, fun-loving personality, and they assumed that meant he was allergic to responsibility.

Yet here was Becca giving him a chance. He couldn't afford to screw this up.

But wasn't there a way to step up, and be the man he needed to be, without walking out on himself?

Chapter Eighteen

Becca leaned back on her elbows, letting the July sun kiss her cheeks. She'd put on a hat soon enough, but for a few precious minutes she wanted to bask in the warm glow. The beach was busier than usual on account of the holiday crowds, people coming from inland to celebrate the Fourth with some sand between their toes. She understood. Digging her own feet into the sand, she closed her eyes and just breathed.

What a treat it was to pause for a moment and do...absolutely nothing.

While work was never not busy, she'd been able to knock off all the pressing items on her to-do list. The house was in decent shape. Sofia was playing nearby with Rosie under the watchful eye of

Savannah. And—if she opened one eye and squinted out into the water—there was Jackson, his bleached shaggy hair as visible as his wide shoulders were admirable.

"Need a drool bucket?" Gia whispered from the towel beside her.

"Hmmm?" Becca feigned innocence even as her cheeks heated. *Dang!* She was so busted.

"Girl, you've been sitting there for a minute biting your lower lip. And I know you aren't watching the seagulls."

"Shhhhhh." Becca shushed her.

"Everyone knows about you two." Gia lowered her sunglasses and wiggled her brows. "I heard Mrs. Briar at the grocery store say that she heard from her sister who heard from one of your neighbors that Jackson's been spotted leaving your house in the morning not once, not twice, but *three* times."

"I see." Becca's neighbors were very sweet, very retired, and, apparently, very chatty.

"I'm just saying, I love Marco to bits, but I get why you wouldn't kick Jackson Lowe outta bed for eating crackers."

"Shusssssssh," Becca hissed through a wide smile. "He's coming over. Not a word if you want to live."

"I'll go check on Marco." Gia pushed herself up and walked over to where her husband was trying to stop their baby from putting a shovel full of sand into his tiny mouth.

"Hey!" Jackson tossed back his head, and flecks of water flew up, catching the light like a halo. "You wanna come out for a bit? Water's warm enough. You don't need a wet suit."

"Says who?" She giggled. "How many times have I ever gone swimming with you? Hawaii water is lovely. Oregon water is meant to teach character."

"Come on." His smile grew in intensity. There came the hint of a dimple by his left lip.

Ugh! She was powerless to resist a direct charm offensive.

She glanced back at Noah and Savannah, who waved her off.

"We're fine." Savannah flashed a thumbs-up. "The girls are doing great."

They were engrossed in digging a hole and didn't even look over.

Down the beach she could see Carter and Abby making their way over. Carter was carrying a cooler and an umbrella, a backpack strapped to his large frame, while Abby had the baby in a chest carrier.

"Tell Carter and Abs that I won't be long." She stood up and put her hands on her hips. "You know, I'm not sure about this."

He winked. "I consider it a personal challenge to give you pleasure out there."

Noah choked behind them, and Jackson called out, "Not like *that*. Get your mind outta the gutter, bro!"

Becca couldn't turn around. If she looked at her friends she'd keel over in embarrassment. Still, it was pretty funny how Jackson had walked into that with no sense of irony. For being such a big manly guy, he had an innocence about him that always surprised her.

When they got to the water's edge, she stopped. "Do you think it's okay? With the baby?"

He nodded. "I'm not going to put you on a board. I thought we could just swim past the breakers. Cool off. Have fun."

"You think you can make a cold-water ocean lover out of me, don't you?"

"I'd be a liar if I said that I didn't want to try." He broke into a wide smile and held out his hand. "We go in on the count of three?"

She took his hand and smoothed her other one over her black one-piece, and the slight swell in her belly. It wasn't enough yet to be an obvious bump, more like she ate a large burrito.

"The baby will be fine. Remember, I'll be having him or her on a board by the time they can walk."

"No!" Becca shivered. "That's terrifying."

"Then you'll want to be out there with us, supervising." He ran forward, pulling her. "Let's go."

The only way to adjust to the temperature was to dive right in. Becca plugged her nose and ducked beneath a wave, jumping up behind it, gasping as the shock of cold blasted her skin.

"Oh!" she cried out, arms flailing.

"Good, right?" Jackson flipped onto his back and began to swim away.

"Come back!"

"Catch me."

As much as the water had threatened to take her

breath, she was adjusting now, and she admitted to herself she felt more alive, the sluggish beach sleepiness doused, replaced by skin that felt electric, every nerve ending on fire.

"I like this." He knocked his foot against hers underwater. "I needed to get out here so bad, and I'm glad you're with me."

"Has it gotten any better?" He'd told her how his dad had railroaded him into a desk job running the landscaping company. While she understood that he chafed at the idea of being indoors, she'd felt some relief that he was committing to something stable moving forward, an opportunity to level up into a more secure job.

Jackson's smile didn't dim even as clouds seemed to pass behind his eyes. "Aw, let's not talk about that stuff today. It's too nice out. Besides, I was serious earlier. I want to teach the baby how to surf at some point. I can't imagine having a kid who doesn't know how. But that being said, I wanna teach you and Sofia too."

"I've lived by the ocean my entire life and never been on a board a single time."

"Then let's fix that." Jackson splashed some water playfully in her direction. "You trust me, Fun Size?"

Underneath that teasing tone lurked a more serious question. "I do."

And that was the truth.

They might not see eye to eye on everything, and she might be happier inside watching a movie than floundering in the waves, but they could try to meet each other in the middle.

Maybe that's where they were now too—between their past and the future, with possibilities spread out before them as wide and boundless as the horizon.

The prospect of having everything she'd ever wanted lifted her up, just as the ocean rolled with the incoming set. But then the wave pounded down, flipping her off her feet, sending her spinning like a sock in a washing machine until Jackson's big hands grabbed under her arms and pulled her back up to standing.

"You okay?" He smoothed back her hair, checking her over. "I thought you were going to duck under."

"I stopped paying attention for a second." Becca gasped. She was fine, just a little stunned. Unease lapped at her with a quiet persistence. The horizon might be wide, but if she focused too much on the idea of big dreams, she risked getting pounded in the head by reality.

"Do you want to go back in?"

"Would you mind?" Her teeth were beginning to chatter.

"Let's go."

It didn't take long before they were back by their friends, and Becca was wrapped in a cozy Turkish cotton towel, a can of lime seltzer water pressed into her hand. Jackson was behind her, a human wall for her to lean on. It was a little weird to be touching him around their friends and Carter. It wasn't like they were engaging in any sort of PDA, but even doing this made it clear they were more than just buddies.

"I can't believe you were out in the water," Savannah repeated for the third time.

"Why is it so shocking?" Becca took a sip of seltzer, pulling the towel tighter around her shoulders.

"Uh...because you've always said that unless you are in Hawaii, you are never touching the water," Carter quipped.

"Well, I even got her to promise to let me teach her how to surf after the baby comes," Jackson drawled, pride evident in his voice. "Sofia too."

"Me!" Sofia glanced over from the hole she was still digging...where was that child planning on going?

"Would you like that, baby?" Becca called out.

"What about sharks?" Sofia frowned.

"Sharks live in the ocean, but they aren't interested in you. They like big seals."

Sofia giggled. "Okay. I'll do it."

"It's so strange that there isn't a surf school in Heart's Hope anymore," Gia said. "That one company seemed like it did a good business. Didn't you work there, Jackson?"

"Sure did. Long time ago now." He sounded wistful.

"Hey, who wants to throw a ball around?" Marco lifted up a football.

All the guys except for Jackson clambered up.

Becca elbowed him. "You should go."

"But I'm your back support."

"I think I can manage."

"Sure," he said incredulously.

She shoved him harder this time. "Go."

"Okay, okay." He jumped up on his feet and jogged down the beach to catch the other guys.

"He is so smitten," Savannah said. "I've never seen my brother be such a total goober. I'm glad it's you."

"Why?" Becca was surprised. It was so strange to have these conversations in such matter-of-fact ways. Savannah hadn't missed a beat in transitioning Becca from her good friend to her brother's baby mama to possibly something more.

"He's unruly, and he's had his troublemaker days, but he's a good guy. And the youngest boy. I think sometimes people forget that even though he's so big, he's sensitive too."

"Yeah. I see that." Becca nodded slowly, her heart aching for the truth in his sister's words. "I don't know if he's loving working for your dad."

"I haven't heard much, but I wouldn't be surprised. Lowe's Landscaping is my dad's dream. It's not Jackson's."

Becca shrugged. "But it's an established business. It does well, and he's worked there since he was a kid."

"I know." Savannah blew back an errant lock of hair. "I guess sometimes I wish Jackson was just given the space and confidence to chase his big dreams. I think he'd surprise everyone. He just needs the right support."

Becca heard the silent question in her friend's statement, the one that asked, *Are you that support? Could you do that for him?*

"Ow!" Abby yelped from her beach chair. "Sorry! I'm fine. I think I am getting a clogged duct. My right boob is getting sore, and I don't feel like enough milk is coming out. Have you ever dealt with that?"

Gia shook her head. "I had the opposite issue. My milk came out like Niagara Falls. It still can shoot across the room during a letdown."

Abby laughed, even as strain etched her features. She was pale by nature, but her skin had more of an ashy hue now, not helped by the dark circles under her eyes.

"Is my brother helping you around the house?" Becca asked, grateful for the distraction from her conversation with Savannah. She needed more time to process the question.

"Yes. He cleans all the time for me. But with the baby...I don't know. I feel like I need to establish this bond."

"He's the dad too," Gia said gently.

"I know. And I know he loves her. Hilde wants to help all the time as well. She's always asking if I want to take a nap."

"That answer should be yes," Savannah said. "You are allowed to rest."

"I know, I know. But it's hard to sit still when I think of all the things the baby needs."

"You're a human being, not a human doing," Gia said.

Abby furrowed her brow, mulling it over. "That's pretty smart."

"Thanks! I saw a tourist drinking out of an insulated mug that said that at the grocery store last night." Gia laughed. "But it's wild how much a baby changes plans, isn't it?"

"I'll say." Savannah gave a cute pout. "Remember how we were going to go to Italy, Becs?"

"Florence. Tuscany. Eat all the carbs. Drink all the wine." Becca sighed. "How could I forget? But you can still go. Take Noah."

"You wouldn't be mad?" Savannah asked cautiously.

"Of course not. I want you to go have the time of your life. And besides, what's better than a romantic vacation? We'll watch Rosie! She loves hanging with Sofia."

The girls cheered.

"Well, I'll look at tickets." Savannah flipped her hair into a messy bun and held it in place with a scrunchie. "But if I do that, then you need to do a getaway too. A babymoon with my brother."

"Yes!" Gia pumped a fist. "I took a babymoon up to the San Juan Islands. It was so romantic. We had a little cottage where we could see orcas from the dock."

"I...could..." Becca mulled the idea over. A few days alone with Jackson, without responsibilities, without...clothes? "That could be fun."

"You have a devilish look in your eye." Savannah wagged her finger. "Don't take advantage of my brother, missy."

They all laughed.

And as the day faded into twilight, coolers were opened and potluck treats were dispersed. Sofia was on Jackson's lap, resting her head on his chest by the time the fireworks came out. He opened his free arm to bring Becca in, and she snuggled against him, grateful for the body heat in the cooling evening air.

And as Jackson looked up, watching the lights crash and crackle and explode, she felt the same eruption in her heart.

He glanced over, and then down at her daughter. "Sofia," he murmured.

"Huh?"

"Your mom is pretty gorgeous, isn't she?"

Sofia gave her mom a curious glance before shrugging. "I don't know. She's just my mom, I guess."

"I know so." He leaned in, brushing his lips over hers with a soft kiss.

"Mom, you just got Jackson's love cooties!" Sofia squealed.

Becca glanced up at Jackson before turning back to her daughter. "Do you want him to stop?"

"No!" Sofia clapped her hands. "Do it again. Do it again."

And that's just what Jackson did.

Chapter Nineteen

Becca looked out into Savannah and Noah's back-yard, where Rosie and Sofia were running around with fairy wings and rainbow ribbon streamers. "Should I call her back for one more hug?"

Savannah grabbed her shoulders and steered her back toward the front door. "Think of it like a child's first day at Sunshine Corner," she said kindly, but firmly. "Don't drag out the leaving. The kids adapt quickly. Noah and I are going to give Sofia a great time. Rosie has been planning all the activities and snacks and movies and dance party mixes. She'll be safe. She'll be happy. And all you need to do is focus on having the best babymoon in the world."

"Can you give me a tiny hint where we're going?"

Becca pleaded as she reluctantly let herself get led away from her daughter. She'd rarely ever left Sofia for a night, and she had certainly never gone out of town without her. While this was for the best, and she needed it, the invisible umbilical cord that tied her to her little girl already seemed to ache.

"I absolutely cannot." Savannah's tone brokered no hint of weakening. "Jackson left all the contact details with me in the very unlikely event that we need to reach out for anything, but he wants to surprise you! So let him."

"I just don't know if I'm big on surprises," Becca mumbled. "I didn't even really know what to pack."

"Then think of this as a stretch moment. Go out of your comfort zone a little and see what else is out there. I want you to focus on the moment. Promise me that." She scrunched up her nose. "And promise me that you'll give me not a single solitary clue that you hooked up with my brother, because while I love you two, separately and together...you know..."

"I do." Becca giggled, her blush deepening. "And trust me, I get it. I love that Abby is with Carter. I'm so happy they are together. But I mentally pretend that they sleep in separate beds and that Ava Olivia was conceived through the pure power of positive thought."

"Amen to that." Savannah held up a hand, and Becca slapped it in agreement before walking to the front yard, where Jackson and Noah were casually shooting hoops. "I do love small-town life, but maybe we are beginning to inbreed just a little."

"Who is inbreeding?" Noah called out.

"Never you mind," Savannah sang back sweetly. "It's not something *we* have to worry about."

Becca nudged her in the ribs as Jackson jogged down to open up his truck's passenger door. "Your chariot awaits."

"Have a great time," Noah called, slinging his arm around Savannah.

Becca grinned at the sight. They made such a cute couple, and it truly warmed her heart to know that Sofia would be with them, safe and happy.

"Don't do anything we would do," Savannah teased as Jackson got the truck roaring to life, and then they were pulling away.

Becca waited five minutes. It felt like five hours, but she was trying her best. "You really won't tell me where we're going."

"I like surprises." He side-eyed her. "But I can see that you're having a hard time."

"I'm not great without parameters. Maybe that makes me super boring, but I like to know my homework assignments. I want to know the plans. I get anxious when I don't know what's expected of me."

"All you need to do is have fun."

"But is fun bungee jumping, or a winery, or going deep-sea fishing?"

"Seeing that you're pregnant and get seasick on boats, none of the above."

She stuck out her bottom lip, and he groaned.

"Fine. A hint. One. And look, you're going to figure it out soon enough with the road signs. We are going to the mountains."

"Iiiiiinteresting." Becca tapped a thoughtful finger on her lower lip. "In Oregon?"

"Someone is fishing for more than one hint," he teased. "But yeah. We're staying in the state."

"Do I have to climb one of these mountains?"

He shot her a sideways glance. "Do you *want* to climb a mountain?"

"Not really." Her grin was bright. "But I wouldn't mind looking at some."

Jackson's chuckle rumbled low like summer thunder. "Let's just say I figured as much. You'll get your view."

"Okay." She poked his bicep. "Thanks for spoiling at least a tiny bit of the surprise."

"Oh, I plan to spoil you this entire trip." His wink was less innocent than his grin, and she found herself needing to press her legs tight together.

The time passed quickly. They played the license plate game and listened to a couple of podcasts. Eventually, Becca was able to guess the location.

"It's Sisters, isn't it?"

Jackson flashed her a thumbs-up. "How'd you guess?"

"Well, there aren't that many mountain towns left this way, and I remember you used to come up here sometimes when you were younger."

"Yeah, with my dad. He'd take me and my brothers fishing." His voice faded away and he appeared lost in thought, a slight frown stamped on his features.

"That's right. And hey." Becca reached out and touched his leg, giving the hard muscle a soft squeeze. "How are things with your dad? Are you working your stuff out?"

"If by working out you mean I'm doing what he says, then yeah, it's going great." Bitterness clung to every word. What thirty-one-year-old guy wanted his dad treating him like a kid?

"You're still not liking the idea of taking over the company?"

"Nope." He popped the *p* sound for added emphasis. "It's boring. And I feel like I'm going to prison every morning."

What Becca wanted to say was *Except instead of being locked in a cell, you're running a small business that employs a bunch of locals and provides a decent income.*

But this was meant to be a fun getaway, and thoughts like that weren't fun, nor would Jackson welcome them.

And yet…this kind of black-and-white thinking was playing right into her fears that he wouldn't be ready to take on the coming responsibilities of fatherhood. It wasn't that she expected Jackson to sign over every paycheck. She wasn't a gold digger, and besides, she liked her job at the bank and planned to keep working after her maternity leave was over. But she did need him to show some stability. She knew firsthand what it was like to have a father who couldn't commit to regular work and all the uncertainty and insecurity that played into it.

Being a child of an alcoholic left scars that weren't visible on the surface but ran along her bones. While that wasn't the path Jackson was on, it didn't change the fact that for her to feel safe, she needed someone dependable.

"Well, there must be some parts of the job you like," she ventured. Maybe getting him to see that the glass was half full rather than half empty was a better strategy.

"I'm not saying I don't want to work hard. But I'm not sure that I want to live to work either. My dad was able to provide for five kids with this landscaping business. I get it. I understand the parts that are practical. It's just...I guess I want to look forward to going to work. And more than that, it's a lot of hours. Growing up, my mom was with us way more. Dad left before I woke up in the morning to go to school. He was often home by dinner, but then he was vegging out on the couch after to watch whatever sports game was on that night. And that's not me. I guess I want to do something different. Something fun."

"Fun? But life isn't always fun. Sometimes it's hard work." Becca's thoughts went to all the times she'd experienced as a parent that weren't fun. The time that Sofia once woke up in the middle of the night, climbed into Becca's bed, and vomited right on her face. Or when she got lice. Or pinworms. Or didn't want to eat any green vegetables.

"But you like working at the bank, right?' Jackson didn't seem to have a clue about the tension building inside her.

"Yes. But it's not the same as going and getting a pedicure or eating chocolate ice cream." She hoped her tone wasn't too snippy.

"Of course. I get that." He ran a hand through his hair. "Shoot, maybe I'm explaining this all wrong. I think I just want to look forward to my day. It doesn't mean that I don't want to work hard, or that I need to have every moment be full of pleasure. It's more that I want to feel as if it's where I'm meant to be." He glanced over, his blue eyes pleading for her to understand him.

And she wanted to. She did. But a part of her wished he'd just suck it up and be grateful for the opportunity being gifted to him.

Her dad never handed over a lucrative business. Instead, he'd call too late and rant at her about needing some money to keep the power on.

"I promise I'm not going to do anything that is going to put me in a position where I can't be a good dad. And I mean that in terms of time, too, not just money, okay?"

She forced a smile. He was saying the right words, and they helped, but still, it was hard to trust them. Not just because he was happy-go-lucky Jackson, but because of the way she and Carter had to learn to trust only in themselves and each other. What would happen if she went all in on Jackson, let down all her lingering guard, and opened up her heart? Would he remain by her side even during the moments when life wasn't all blue skies and good surf?

He could hurt her. Or disappoint her.

And she'd been hurt and disappointed enough for a lifetime.

"We're here!" He turned into the parking lot of a mountain lodge, the view of the Three Sisters spread out around them, and the sight was magical.

"We have a cabin booked with mountain views. You have a massage tomorrow. And they'll be bringing breakfast in bed. Did I do good?"

The fact that he looked as trustworthy as a golden retriever pulled at her heart.

This was Jackson. He was a good guy. He deserved a chance.

And she'd give him one.

But she was still going to keep some protections up around her heart...just in case.

* * *

"Rise and shine, Princess." Jackson opened up the blackout curtains, and Becca rubbed her eyes, disoriented as she went from a snug dark cave to a bright bedroom with floor-to-ceiling windows looking over North Sister's peak.

"What time is it?" she mumbled, collapsing back

into the king-sized goose down pillow. After they'd gotten in at sunset last night, they had taken a walk down to a creek that flowed adjacent to the lodge. When they got back to their rooms, a table for two had been set up, complete with white linen and candles, pasta, fresh greens, and garlic bread still warm from the oven. It was as if magical elves had been at work, but she knew that Jackson had organized it with the owners. She had been touched by his thoughtfulness.

Although she'd repaid him by almost falling asleep before dessert, and only just managing to slip into her nightshirt, wash her face, and brush her teeth before pregnancy sleep knocked her out.

"It's ten o'clock." He handed her a coffee.

"Shut up! You're just teasing me."

He pointed at the wall clock, which backed up his words.

She blinked. "Oh my gosh. I haven't slept this late since…high school."

"Fun Size." Jackson sat down beside her, his weight dipping the mattress, causing her to tilt toward him. "I remember you in high school. And you were still an early bird determined to get worms before anyone else."

"I'm sorry. You took me all the way out here, and look at me. I'm just snoozing the day away."

"Snoring is more like it." His tone was teasing.

"I don't snore." She rolled her eyes.

"Says you."

She glanced back in alarm. "Do I really?"

"It sounded a bit like my dad's tractor at one point, but it was cute."

She set the coffee on the nightstand and covered her head with a blanket. "Don't look at me. I'm so embarrassed."

He tugged the blanket back and crawled in beside her, his jeans rough against the skin of her bare leg in all the right ways.

"I like you," he said simply. "I like you all the ways. Even if you're so tired from all the hard work of growing Bolt that you end up snoring. I'll take you any and all ways, Rebecca Hayes, so you don't ever have to be embarrassed around me."

And just like that the walls she had attempted to keep high around her heart came down a little, letting in the same warm sunlight that filled the room. She felt bright, alive...hopeful even.

"Hey, I wanted to tell you something," he said, suddenly serious.

"O-kay." She glanced at him, but he didn't seem like he had bad news up his sleeve. Instead, he seemed a little nervous. "What's up?"

"This might seem presumptuous, but I did something." He pulled a folded piece of paper from his back pocket. "Take a look and tell me what you think."

Tentatively, she opened it up, freezing as she read the words. "A birth class?"

"I signed us up. I hope you don't mind." He spoke quickly, as if he needed to convince her. "I know you've had a baby before. And that you're the one who'll be doing all the work. But, uh, this is new for me, and I thought it might be good if I learned some ways to, uh, you know...help."

She glanced up at him, and the vulnerability on his face nearly took her breath away. It was as if his kindness was a catapult, and this time, her walls didn't just drop; he'd smashed a hole right through. But for the moment, she didn't mind being defenseless.

"You signed us up for some birth classes so you could learn ways to support me in labor?"

He nodded. "And after. I mean I've read some of the books too. But I spoke to the instructor, and she said they'd also show us how to put on diapers and do swaddling. Plus they give advice on the best carriers so we can take turns wearing the baby."

Becca reached out and put a hand on his cheek, holding his gaze on hers. "Jackson, you are full of surprises."

"Does this mean you'd like to do it with me?"

"Oh, trust me." She wiggled her brows, suddenly much less sleepy. "I'd like to do a lot with you."

His shy grin deepened. "So that means I did good?"

She reached out, popping open the brass button on his jeans. "Oh yeah, you've done real good. Trust me, there is nothing as sexy as a man who wants to learn to put on diapers."

He pushed up her nightgown, and she gasped as his big hands moved to her bare waist. "Well, then you are in for a treat. Because I haven't even gotten into my thoughts on disposable versus reusable."

She giggled and arched against him.

"You wanna call me Daddy?" A low chuckle rumbled from his broad chest.

She laughed. "Shut up and kiss me senseless."

And that's just what he did.

Chapter Twenty

Get 'em! On your left—no, no, your other left! Damn! He got me. Come on, guys, you gotta cover me." Noah perched at the edge of the couch, his thumbs working the video game controller.

Caleb's voice came through the headset. "I'm trying, dude. I'm taking fire over here."

"I'm going." Spencer's avatar began running toward the active fighting.

Jackson had his brothers and buddy over to play No-Man's Land, one of their favorite video games, simulating World War II battles.

Empty pizza boxes were strewn on the floor, while beer and soda bottles covered the coffee table. This morning, after he got back from the babymoon with Becca, his brothers had informed him that they were going to crash his cottage for a day of marathon gaming. Given that it had been raining steadily today, and the wind conditions made the surfing crap, this seemed a perfect indoor activity.

"Did you just shoot me?" Aaron turned to Spencer, aghast.

"Oh, sorry, bro, bad luck. You were collateral damage."

"Wait, shit. Guys incoming!" A blast sent the screen into a wall of fire.

"Did we just get bombed?" Jackson glanced at Noah, who was currently sprawled dramatically against the couch, his mouth locked in a frozen *noooooooooo*.

"Dude, I told you guys we should have worked on building up our fortifications, but you all just had to go gun happy." Caleb's disembodied voice was annoyed but amused.

"There is only one thing that will fix the situation." Aaron pushed up off the floor and headed to the kitchen. "Who wants a beer?"

Their hands all went up.

"Me," Caleb called from the headset.

"Why haven't we done this more?" Aaron asked after settling back in and cracking off a bottle cap. "Oh, I know. Everyone's breeding. Puts a cramp on things."

"Way to go," Spencer said. "Cheers to Jackson and Caleb for blowing up the band, er, our regular gaming. Say hello to walks to the playground and Little League."

"Ew." Aaron shuddered.

"Uh, hello?" Noah looked around with a frown. "I'm right here. Dad. Friend. Someone who still hangs out? Fatherhood doesn't end your life."

"We're just giving you all some crap," Aaron said. "But Rosie's getting bigger. She's like a full kid at this point. And a cool kid to boot. But when she was a baby? I feel like we went a cool year where we didn't see you."

"Or if we did, you looked like you were an extra on *The Walking Dead*," Spencer quipped.

"You all should be life coaches," Caleb said wryly. "On that note, I'm going to sign off and bid a fond farewell to my free time. And make my beautiful wife some dinner, because I gotta say, she's a lot more fun to look at than you four."

"Bye, bro!" Aaron shouted as Caleb vanished from the corner of the screen.

"I don't think the baby is going to change me that much." Jackson tensed as the three guys in the room pivoted in his direction with facial expressions ranging from bemused to sympathetic. "We're going to take a birth class, you know. And I'm learning how to put on a diaper, and how to wrap the baby up nice and tight like origami."

"Give him the real talk," Spencer said to Noah. "There's more to it than he's saying, right?"

"That's right. Remind our little bro that it's more fun making the baby," Aaron quipped. "Just kidding, though. Rosie's great."

"Here's the deal," Noah said, propping one foot

up on his knee, frowning at the television. "Will it change your life? I mean...yeah, more than I can tell you. It's something that you've got to experience to understand. But here's the thing these two chuckleheads don't know." He jerked a thumb at Spencer and Noah. "It's the hardest but best work you're ever going to do in your life. I'm going to be real, the hard part is really hard. You lose sleep. You lose free time. You lose brain cells watching the ninth mindless princess cartoon. You lose your temper, and sometimes you won't be proud of it. And you and Becca? You're going to see yourselves at your best, but also your worst. Parenting is one hell of a wild ride.

"Here's the way I see it. Imagine your day is put into three columns. In column one, you gotta invest time in your career, because you gotta provide for your loved ones. In column two, you need to invest time in family, because you need to be there for all those dinners, and bath times, and bedtime stories. They are important. And then the last column? Well, that's your fun and free time. And that gets whatever is left over. And during some seasons, there's just not a lot. And that's how it goes."

A low rumble of thunder shook the windows as if to emphasize his friend's point. Rain lashed the windows in earnest.

"It's all good." Jackson swallowed hard. "I got this." But while the other guys all nodded and returned to loading a new game, he couldn't shake the chill that settled over him. First, his dad had come for his freedom, trying to give him golden handcuffs to the family business. And then, man, having a child was going to be a full-time job. He knew that, and he was up to the responsibility, but it still felt a little overwhelming to think about not being able to just waste the day with the guys every once in a while. Things were changing fast, and every so often he caught a twinge of whiplash. For years he'd invested all his time in the third column, the one that was going to shrink fast.

Suddenly, he was all too aware of the mental walls pressed in around him, thick and opaque. And for the first time since Becca had shared the news with him, serious concerns bubbled up. Was he going to lose his identity? Would fatherhood force itself in and push all the other parts of himself to the edges? He took a deep breath and released it slowly. Nah. This worry was probably just coming from a place of the unknown. Fears were a normal part of life, and the measure of a man was how he faced them down—and for Jackson, he'd hoped it was with integrity and the confidence that he would get his priorities centered.

* * *

Becca hit Send on an email and stretched. She'd been using a standing desk to work for over a year and normally enjoyed not being stuck in a chair. But today? Her swollen feet were killing her. Reaching underneath, she found the little button that lowered it, and then she collapsed into the leather chair. Her calendar pinged with a reminder to reach out to a customer who was looking to refinance their house. She was getting ready to pick up her phone when it rang with an unlisted number.

"Rebecca Hayes, financial services, Heart's Hope Community Credit Union."

There was a pause.

She had opened her mouth to repeat herself when she heard a click and then a rough male voice that set her teeth on edge.

"Hey, Boogaloo. It's your old man."

"Hey." Her body went rigid. "You're calling on my work phone? What's up?" It was one of two things: He was in jail, or he needed money.

"Listen, I got pulled over last night. Cops said I had too much to drink, but it was just a couple of beers. Then I had a warrant, which didn't even make sense, and long story short...I need you to come post bail."

"I see." Okay, he was in jail *and* needed money. Cool.

"You're my one phone call, so you coming?"

She glanced at her packed, color-coded calendar. None of that mattered now. As always, when her dad went into chaotic mode, he played the tune, and she'd have to dance along.

Twenty minutes later, she walked into the Heart's Hope Bay police station.

She'd only ever been here to deal with her dad.

The woman behind the front counter didn't even look up. "What are you here for?"

"I need to bail out my dad. Robert Hayes."

After a few minutes, they brought her father out. She hadn't seen him in a few months. She used to check in on him more regularly, but he'd gotten leaner and meaner, so she'd been keeping her distance, always offering to pay for him to get treatment, anything to stop this slow decline. He looked horrible, gaunt and unwashed, his eyes small and mean. He sized her up in her maternity skirt and smirked. "I never got an invite to no wedding."

"I'm not married," she said quietly. She put her hand over her five-month bump as if to protect Bolt from his mockery.

"So, you just give the milk away like a stupid cow, is that it?"

"I'm going back to work; you can walk home." She turned and beelined for the door. For a hot minute she was frustrated that Carter didn't have to be the one to deal with this, but he'd borne the bigger brunt when they were kids. She could do it. She wouldn't let her dad get her down.

"You can talk all fancy and dress like you are somebody, but you aren't. You know that, right?" When he smiled, there was a gap where his left front tooth should be. "You're trash, just like me."

"I'm not. And you don't have to be. If you'd agree to go to rehab, I'd cover the cost. I've told you that before, and the offer stands." And she meant it. While the man in front of her felt for all intents and purposes like a stranger, he was her dad. And for the memory of her mom, she'd help if he was willing to accept it.

"You just keep talking like you know something. I'd rather walk home. Better to be alone than with a daughter who can't stop getting knocked up."

He staggered off in his stained jeans and threadbare flannel. It hurt to watch him go, but he was fighting a battle that didn't involve her. Still, she felt a hundred years old now.

And while she knew his comments were all things she should let wash off her back as she paddled away like a damn graceful swan, a few barbs stuck.

But while he might be able to get a few sucker punches in, he couldn't knock her down. She was too strong for that, and even stronger now with Jackson beside her.

Chapter Twenty-One

Becca was a little late getting Sofia to Sunshine Corner. Heartburn had been making its presence known, as had the increasing need to pee with a great frequency. But the tradeoff was that she'd started to feel the baby. At first, it had felt like the lightest sensations, a sense of a tiny butterfly beating its wings in her abdomen or a small cluster of bubbles popping. A few days after that, she'd been able to focus in on the feeling when she was lying down, especially if she'd recently eaten and it felt as if there was a disco going on inside her uterus.

"Hi there." Becca paused near the kitchen area, where Abby's grandmother was kneading dough for a bread project the over-three kids were going to be working on later today. Groovy New Age music played from a speaker nearby.

"Oh! Rebecca! Nice to see you." Hilde's silver hair was pulled back in her usual neat bun. Today she had on a wine-red velvet skirt with little silver bells at the edges that tinkled when she moved.

Heart's Hope Bay's famous baby whisperer always carried herself in a positive and cheerful manner, her gaze clear and far-reaching.

But as she smiled now, Becca noticed that the older woman seemed deflated somehow, more gray, more clouded. And Becca immediately suspected the reason.

"Is it Abby?" she asked quietly.

Hilde gave a single nod, then stepped out to look up and down the hallway before pulling the kitchen door closed. "I would have never predicted this." Her voice was thick with emotion. "That poor girl is struggling and doesn't want me to see. She pretends as if everything is fine, even though I see her unraveling, and I'm afraid if I point it out, it will do more harm than good."

"Is it breastfeeding?" Becca knew her friend had been struggling with that area of new motherhood as well as possible postpartum depression.

"Among other things. I think Abby felt that since she ran Sunshine Corner, she'd sail through motherhood. But it's a different job when you do it twenty-four seven."

"Absolutely." Becca's heart hurt for her friend, the one so many of them had looked up to for being so amazing with kids, who now needed her own helping hand.

"Is she home? I think I saw her car parked out front."

"She is." Hilde's lower lip trembled. "I want to be of use. But she seems to feel as if she's letting herself down if she admits that she can't do everything by herself."

"And no new mom can." Becca was adamant on this fact. "It takes a village."

"Right now, Abby has made herself an island. And she doesn't want me to build a bridge." Hilde reached out and took Becca's hand. "Ava is fine. She has had a touch of colic and is taking time getting used to nursing, but these aren't uncommon problems for a baby. Abby is just being so hard on herself. She didn't realize that she'd feel so out of her element."

"I understand." Becca gave the older woman a soft squeeze. "I'll go up and check on her now."

Hilde hugged her. "Thank you, Rebecca."

Carter answered the door after a few knocks. He was in a pair of flannel pajama pants, and his hair was a bit mussed in the back. Ava was sleeping on his shoulder.

Hi, she mouthed.

Carter stepped out onto the landing. "What's up?" He looked friendly enough, just tired.

"Hilde asked me to come up and check on Abby." Becca put her hand on his arm. "Is she okay?"

He raised one hand and tilted it back and forth

in a "so-so" gesture. "I'm glad you're here. She is in bed right now watching a show. I asked her to take a break because she had a hard time sleeping last night. I know Hilde would love to be up here helping, but Abby feels as if accepting help from her grandmother means she is somehow failing."

"It might not seem rational, but postpartum feelings are no joke. I'll check in. Is that okay?"

"Of course. I'm glad you're here."

Becca sniffed the air. "And what smells so delicious in there?"

He grinned. "I'm grilling chicken with Mom's recipe for huli-huli sauce. I'm making lunch for Abby. It's her favorite. Every little bit helps, right?"

"Right." She stared at her big brother. He'd always been a rock, first for her, and then his partner. But right now, he appeared like a mountain. A tower of strength even as he held his tiny baby daughter with such care and delicacy.

"You have grown up so well. I know you had no role models, and Dad didn't teach you how to do more than microwave a burrito, but you did it yourself. Abby is so lucky to have you."

"Thanks, sis. But remember, you're lucky to have Jackson too."

She glanced over at her brother. "You really think so?" It's not that she wasn't getting used to the idea of leaning on Jackson, but she trusted her overprotective brother, and if he was being positive, that meant a lot to her.

"Sure, he likes to joke around and have fun, but

sometimes I worry you take stuff too seriously. You grew up fast. Quicker than you should have."

"You were the one who would try to balance Dad's checkbook so we could pay rent each month."

"And you were the one who worried. And made plans. And I've seen the old man, what, one time in the last decade? You've had to handle him whenever he needs handling. I know I've put that pressure on you. And I'm sorry. But I've never seen you laugh like you do when you're around Jackson, and that's a fact. When I see it, it makes me hope you'll get a chance to have what I do. An opportunity to make a new family, to move forward and not look back."

Becca nodded slowly. "He does make me laugh."

But is that enough?

If she ever cracked, would Jackson be there to pick up the pieces, even if it wasn't fun and games? Signs were starting to point to yes, but she needed to be cautious. It wasn't in her nature to jump into anything with two feet and no plan.

She was still mulling the question when she tiptoed into the master bedroom. Abby looked small on the bed, her red hair spread out like a fan.

"Hey, you," Becca said, taking a seat on the edge of the bed. "I hear you're not sleeping great."

Abby's smile was pained. "Apparently I'm not doing anything great at the moment. I was looking at Gia's social media. And before you say anything, don't judge. I know it's unhealthy. But look...she has always been a boss babe, but she was so nervous and skittish about everything baby. Now she's supermom. And here I am, childcare is my literal profession, and I'm acting as if I've never seen a baby in my life. What the heck. Do I lack a mommy gene or something?" The tears gathering in the corner of her eyes belied her joking tone.

"You know what? Being afraid isn't a bad thing. Fear can mean that you care so very much. It's just your hormones are unbalanced right now, so it's throwing you off. You do not lack anything. You got this, and you are everything that little baby needs. I promise you."

"But..." Abby trailed off, and Becca didn't push. She wanted her friend to take all the time she needed to share the burden that was sitting on her heart. At last her shoulders collapsed inward. "What if I don't?"

"Well, I also know it's very normal and healthy to ask for help when you need it. And honestly, I understand how you feel. When I had Sofia, and her dad left a few weeks after her birth to go back to England, it was hard. But what was even harder was the idea of asking anyone for help. I felt like I was a nuisance. But it was more than that. I felt that if I asked for help, it would show my big deep dark fear, which was that I really didn't know what I was doing. And here is the biggest secret of all." Becca leaned in close. "I didn't. I didn't have a clue."

"Really? But you always seemed like you're so together."

"Some of it is the fact that at this point, I'm confident in knowing that I don't know everything.

But I know that good support makes all the difference. Sunshine Corner has saved my sanity more times than I can ever count. I'm so grateful for the space. And if I can pay you back even a fraction of what you've given to me, I'd love the opportunity. Please. Taking some more time to rest is a good idea. Hilde loves you. She loves Carter. And she loves Ava. She is family. And so am I. And family is always here for each other, in good times and hard times. Just take this one moment at a time."

And as she hugged her friend, she realized she should take her own advice. There wasn't a need to define her and Jackson's long-term future right now.

One day at a time.

Chapter Twenty-Two

Just so we are crystal clear, you don't want to know the baby's biological sex." Dr. Fridley had walked into the examination room for the twenty-week ultrasound with hair the same color as a yellow highlighter.

"We'd like it to be a surprise," Jackson responded firmly. He knew Becca was willing to humor him, but he could see that glint in her eye. The itch she had to plan for every outcome.

But still...she was doing all the work. It wasn't like he could control the narrative. What grounds did he have if she really wanted otherwise? "You good with that, Fun Size? Because I know I pushed for not knowing. If you want to find out..."

"How about this?" Dr. Fridley glanced between

them. "I'll write the sex on a piece of paper and put it in an envelope and give it to Becca. If you decide at any point you'd like to know...then you can make that decision. Sounds good?"

Jackson relaxed at the relief flooding Becca's face. "I really love that choice, thank you," she said. Turning to Jackson, she reached out her hand. "Even though I think I want to be surprised too...it feels better knowing I *could* know. Does that make sense, or am I being ridiculous?"

"Never ridiculous." Jackson would have kissed the furrow between her brows away if the doctor wasn't a few feet away.

"Okay, let's get to it then." Dr. Fridley squirted a clear gel over Becca's belly, which was beginning to swell.

God, he loved looking at that baby bump. There was some sort of primal sense of "mine" coupled with a feeling of gratitude and awe that threatened to send him to his knees.

"Today we're going to be doing the twenty-week screening scan. At this time, we can look in detail at the baby's bones, heart, brain, spine, abdomen, and even their kidneys. You ready to say hello?" She directed all her questions to Becca.

Jackson positioned himself on the other side where he could hold her hand but also have a clear view of the screen.

It didn't take long before the baby came into view.

"Whoa, it's so much bigger," he breathed.

"Yep." Dr. Fridley sounded amused, even as she

kept her focus on the screen. "Welcome to parent-hood. You'll be talking about how fast they grow for the next two decades."

"Do you have any children?" Jackson bit his cheek the minute the question was out of his mouth. "Sorry, I know that's not my business."

"Oh, it's okay," Dr. Fridley replied as she took some measurements. "I haven't physically carried a baby. But my wife and I did adopt twins a few years ago."

"Twins! That'll keep you busy," Jackson said at the same moment Becca piped up with "You don't see twins in there, do you?"

That earned another chuckle from the doctor. "One is enough for you?"

"Considering I already have a four-year-old, I think this seems like the perfect amount. The baby stage is hard as it is. Don't even have the first clue how you manage to run the newborn gauntlet with multiples."

"Tiredly," Dr. Fridley cracked. "And I just see one baby. No surprises hidden behind them. And the good news is that everything looks healthy from the heart to the kidneys. Appears like you're still the same as you've been this entire time...moving along with a perfectly healthy, boring pregnancy."

Jackson thought that apparently this must be Dr. Fridley's catch phrase, but he didn't mind. It was music to his ears.

"In this case, boring is the best news!" Becca's smile filled his heart.

"Would you like to see a 3-D image of your baby?" Dr. Fridley turned around to look at both of them. "I'll keep the focus on the face and none of the genitals."

"I'd love that." Becca clapped her hands. "I was going to ask but wasn't sure if it was okay."

"Of course it's okay!"

She glanced at him. "Do you want to see Bolt?"

Jackson frowned, a little lost. "What's a 3-D ultrasound?"

The question had barely left his lips when the image on the screen, which looked a lot like an alien, shifted into a bumpy-faced ball of pudding. But then the baby moved a little bit, and the features cleared.

"Oh my God! Jackson." Becca gasped, covering her mouth behind her hand.

He blinked and blinked again. The face he was looking at somehow was him. But it was also Becca. He recognized her nose and his chin. His forehead and her cheeks.

"It's...it's us." Jackson wasn't a crier by nature. He couldn't think of the last time he'd teared up. But here he was in the middle of this small room, seconds away from breaking down.

The surge of love that hit him was like stepping onto a freeway and turning to face a Mack truck.

They watched in hushed wonder as the baby scrunched up its nose, yawned, and then grimaced before rubbing its face.

"I didn't expect to see the baby like this," he kept repeating.

"Would you like me to print out a few pictures?" Dr. Fridley asked.

"Yes!" they chimed in unison.

"I'll go get those printed, and while I do that, you can clean yourself up." She handed Becca a small towel to remove the gel from her bump.

As soon as she left, the room went quiet.

"How do you feel?" Becca whispered.

"Like I could do anything." He knelt down beside her and covered her belly with his hands, feeling the heat from her skin seep into his palm. "I promise that I'll do everything in my power to give this baby a wonderful life."

Beneath him, as if in answer, came the tiniest nudge.

He raised his head, and Becca was staring back, eyes as wide as his felt.

"Was that Bolt?"

"Yeah." Becca's lower lip trembled from emotion. "You felt it."

"Do you mind if I talk to it?" Jackson's voice was quiet. He'd never felt like he did in this moment. It was as if he'd spun himself dizzy on swings at an amusement park, but he was also full of clarity and purpose.

"Be my guest." Becca patted the side of the bump. "Hey, Bolt, Daddy wants to talk to you."

Daddy.

He pressed his lips to the side of her belly. "Hey

there. It's me. I'm your, uh, okay, so hello there! I'm your dad. Nice to meet you."

Becca giggled. "It sounds like you are about to invite it to a working lunch meeting."

"Listen up, troublemaker." He tickled her, grinning as she swallowed back a yelp. "Cut me some slack, I'm figuring this out."

She threaded her fingers through his hair. "Me too." Her sigh was soft. "It felt real today. Like this baby is coming, ready or not."

"And we'll be ready," he whispered to her bump. "I promise you that." And then he moved up to Becca's face. "And I promise I'll always be at your side. Or on top of you."

"Or below." She whacked his chest. "You're bad."

And while that might be true, how could she ever know how badly he wanted to get this right.

Chapter Twenty-Three

Jackson and Becca walked into the classroom in the back of the hospital. Four other couples were already there, rolling out brightly colored yoga mats.

"Hello and welcome!" A kind-faced woman in her midfifties waved to them from a pile of pillows. "My name is Deb Klager, and I'm the nurse practitioner who runs the childbirth classes for Heart Hope's Bay Hospital. Please sign in and take a yoga mat and a pillow. We want you to be comfortable. I see you read the instructions for how to dress."

Becca pinched some of her yoga pants fabric. "Don't have to tell me twice to wear comfy clothing, especially lately."

A few more couples came in.

"Okay, everyone is here, so it's time to get

started," Deb said. "The first thing I want you to do is to make a line and imagine that the left side of the room is zero and the right side is a ten. Decide where you fall on the spectrum for this question. "How much do you know about having babies?"

Becca glanced at Jackson.

He kept a brave smile plastered to his face. "This is where we split up, I guess. Because I'm heading to zero, and you're at the top of the class, as usual."

As the group divided, Jackson couldn't help but notice that he was the only person down at the zero mark. The others all shared that they had babysat or had other kids before. Only Jackson was a zero. But all that served to do was light a fire. Because when he looked up the row and saw Becca near the top, she looked so pretty and confident with pink cheeks and a slight swell to her middle. The idea that their baby grew inside her didn't give him a hard-on; it gave him a heart-on. The sweet pain in his chest was sharp. He couldn't stay a zero, nor could he leave her or Bolt alone, especially when he'd learned today that Bolt was the size of a turnip as he made another entry in his notebook.

After the line-up, they did some prenatal yoga, and Deb taught the partners some massage tips to ease their partner's pressure during labor. Afterward, he was able to collect some pamphlets and books to bring home to study. School wasn't always his happy place, but now he had the motivation and internal fire. He couldn't afford to stay at the bottom of the class.

* * *

"And then he said, I'm gonna huff, and I'm gonna puff, and hang on to that short, curly tail because I'm going to blow your house down!" Jackson growled, lunging forward, arms open, hands twisted into claws as Sofia and Rosie shrieked with delight.

Becca turned her attention back to the oven, checking on the roasting chicken. It looked almost perfectly done, and the kitchen was infused with the scent of rosemary.

Savannah and Noah were away for a week in Italy, and in order to give Noah's mom a bit of a break, Becca volunteered to take Rosie, a reasonable trade seeing that they'd been so great with watching Sofia during her babymoon.

Tonight, Jackson had spent the better part of an hour giving the girls an entire performance. While it was Three Little Pigs at the moment, he'd also been through Jack and the Beanstalk, Rumpelstiltskin, and Rapunzel. The girls had barely budged, hook, line, and sinker in his thrall. No one had asked for a snack. No one had needed her for a single thing.

And Becca had to admit it was nice having the pressure off for a second. As a single mom with a dad barely in the picture, Sofia had grown up expecting and receiving her full attention. Most of the time it was fine. But sometimes she needed a moment. And she was having more and more of those occasions as she marched through the second trimester. She wasn't having a lot of physical symptoms—thank goodness. But emotionally she needed a little space. It was as if her heart was expanding to let more love inside, while her brain was shrinking.

She often found herself zoning out, just staring at a wall while her cup of herbal tea cooled on the table, forgotten beside her.

This was why even though Becca was reasonably positive that the three sweet old biddies who lived on her street hadn't missed the fact that Jackson was sleeping over more nights than not, she didn't have the mental or physical energy to ask for space. Nor did she want to.

It wasn't just the physical release he could bring to her in bed. It was the comfort and companionship. And the way he held her? It was as if her body had been designed to fit with his, and the sound of his steady breathing as he slept seemed to drive away any bad dreams.

They hadn't had any conversations about him moving in. It hadn't felt like the right time. It also felt like maybe it was too fast. Should they wait for the baby to be born? Wait to see what happened between them? She needed a plan, but right now she felt as if she'd somehow drifted off the map, past the signs that said HERE BE DRAGONS.

Relationships felt scary.

Especially since she'd had so few in her life.

But Jackson was someone she could count on for so many things, from always taking her side to making her feel supported and affirmed. It was a great feeling, stabilizing and strong, but what if she relied on it too much and they ended up not working out?

That pain might be too much.

"Mama?" Sofia stood in the door, scratching the side of her nose. "Rosie is bleeding again."

"Oh dear, let me see." She grabbed a box of tissues and strode briskly into her living room and down the hall to the bathroom.

But when she opened the door, she quickly realized she was superfluous. Jackson already had the little girl's head tilted back and a wad of toilet paper was clutched in his hand.

"Everything okay?" Savannah had mentioned that Rosie got frequent nosebleeds, and so far that tip was checking out. Rosie had had a nosebleed on her first day with them.

"She's doing great, aren't you, kiddo?" Jackson said. "Or at least I think you are. Let's hear from you."

"Yep, I'b dowing gwate." Rosie's high sweet voice was distorted because of the tissues. "Keep telling dat stowy, pwease."

He glanced at Becca. "We're just getting to the good part."

"Okay, well, I'll have dinner done in about ten minutes, so I'll see you then." She turned but looked back, unable to resist taking in the sight for a second time. Jackson was utterly focused on Rosie. He'd been getting up with the girls every morning before seven to ensure they got their cereal. He played outside in the jungle gym in the backyard. He'd also let them style his hair—all the way down to using unicorn sparkle clips and tiny pigtails. Two were in his hair even now. And the most amazing thing of all was that he appeared to actually enjoy spending time with the girls.

This is what she needed to see. Tangible proof that Jackson Lowe was ready to be a grown-up. She adored his boyish personality, but that carefree live-and-let-live attitude wasn't the sign of a man someone like her could settle down with long-term.

Fun and games were great. But at the end of the day, she had to think practically. And the fact that he was making an effort with his family's business and showing great attentiveness as a caregiver was honestly hotter than his ripped abs.

She shook her head, bewildered. Apparently that's what happens when you get pumped full of pregnancy hormones and stare down thirty. Priorities shift.

She got out her vacuum and went to work on a few crumbs in the kitchen, waiting for Jackson and the girls to come in.

Yes. It was better this way.

This was exactly what she needed.

Maybe if she repeated those thoughts over and over, they would become true, and she wouldn't have a lingering feeling that maybe she was putting too many strings on Jackson. Shouldn't love be unconditional?

But her mom had loved with an unconditional heart, and look how her dad turned out.

There were feelings. And there were facts.

And she wasn't alone in any of this. Whatever path she took was going to affect both Sofia and the baby. They needed to be the priority—no compromise.

Jackson came in with a girl tucked under each broad arm. She put the vacuum back on the charger, admiring the sight of those hard-won muscles, earned from years of hard paddling in an unpredictable ocean. It was amazing how he could move through the surf with such force and strength, and yet hold her with such care and be so gentle with the girls.

Heat surged up her thighs, and she had to swallow back a gasp. This was not the time to be feeling frisky.

And this was the real issue with Jackson. He had the looks and the personality to make smart girls stupid.

And she couldn't afford to be stupid.

Chapter Twenty-Four

> This is Week Twenty-Nine. Welcome to the
> start of the third trimester. Your baby is as
> big as an acorn squash.

Jackson propped his elbows on his desk in the
Lowe's Landscaping office and scrolled through the
email. He'd signed up for notifications from the new
parent class, and now every week he received an
update on the baby's size.

> Your baby has learned a new skill...
> smiling! And it's starting to put on the
> pounds, so expect to feel those cute lil'
> kicks and rolls to pack a bigger punch.

Physically, you might not be feeling your
most attractive. Varicose veins might be
putting in an appearance. While many
women don't like the look of them, they
aren't dangerous. That growing uterus is
putting a lot of pressure on things below.
You might even get hemorrhoids. Addi-
tionally, heartburn and indigestion might
be an issue. Try to avoid snacking after
seven p.m., and also avoid food triggers
like coffee, chocolate, and spices.

"Okay then." He pulled out the small notebook
he had started keeping in his back pocket and wrote
out another update on Bolt and Becca.

He hadn't noticed any veins popping anywhere,
but she had been complaining about diet-related
stomach issues more lately.

He made an extra note: *Ginger? Tea? Candy?
Will it help? Ask Dr. Fridley.*

The Becca Bible, as he privately called it, let him
keep track of how things were going and let him
be as supportive as possible during the experience.
He couldn't carry the baby for her, but he could do
everything possible to lighten the load.

"Hey! What are you doing?" His dad was at his
shoulder, frowning down.

"Oh. Hey." Jackson clicked out of the pregnancy
website, but that just revealed the daily surf cam
video that was up in the other tab. *Shit.* He closed
that too and pointed at the spreadsheet. "I'm just

trying to make sense of some accounting. I can't get a few columns to match up."

He'd never been bad at math, but the idea of managing all these spreadsheets, from scheduling to invoices to stock takes, felt as much fun as getting papercuts to the eyeballs. He understood how a guy like his dad, who enjoyed dotting every *i* and crossing every *t,* would get a bang out of doing this.

"Look, son, billing is essential to get right, so you need to be focused. You can't be surfing the web, or mentally surfing out on Heart's Hope Bay when you're doing that level of detail work. You make a blunder, and it will cost profit. The longer we take to get billing out, the more easily a client can forget a task we did and want to dispute the bill. Steady cash flow is security. You need to take it seriously."

"I'm doing my best, Dad." The trouble was, he wasn't really. But he wasn't lying either. This was the best he could do in this role he didn't want. Every day he woke up feeling the weight of dread slowly building. He missed being around the crew. He missed even more working outside. And most of all, he missed the sense that he was in control of his life. Now it felt as if he was stuck in some sort of box of expectation, and he couldn't shake the thought that this was his dad's life. Not his.

He loved his father. And respected him. But that didn't mean he wanted to *be* him.

"Maybe this isn't for me."

Alan leaned against the metal bookcase across from him. "And where does that leave Becca? Sofia? The baby? You want to have fun? Get a hobby. But life is hard work, and nothing comes for free. I did my best to see that my family got to be happy. It's your turn now. You're the provider. So do it. Provide. And if it's not here, you know what? I can live with that. I'd be disappointed, but who cares? I can sell the business. But I don't want you kicking yourself if you let this pass you by and then have nothing else going on."

"I hear you, Dad. I want that too."

"Then get it done." His dad left the back office, slamming the door so hard the windows rattled.

Jackson did his best to focus for the rest of the afternoon, even as his eyes dried and his back began to ache. At five on the dot, he was out of the door and walking fast to his truck. His phone rang as he was opening his door.

"Hey, Aaron,"

"What's up, man?" his brother asked.

"Was going to go check the waves," Jackson answered.

"Already ahead of you. It's messy. Nothing worth coming out for. Wanna grab a beer?"

"Last Chance?" Jackson could use a pitcher and some banter.

"You know it. Heading there now?"

"Yep. See you with bells on."

The bar was busy for a Tuesday night, so Jackson

and Aaron took a table away from the bar, leaving Ben and his staff to field the summer rush.

"What's got you looking like you drank cat piss?" Aaron asked.

"You ever wonder if Dad likes you? I mean, I know he loves us all and whatever. But if he truly likes you as a person."

Aaron frowned. "I guess so. I mean, what's not to like?"

Jackson burst out laughing and raised his glass. "Cheers to that."

"Work getting you down again?" Aaron topped him up.

"You wanna take it on?" Jackson heaved back in his chair.

"That would be a no thanks. But I'm surprised you aren't feeling it. You worked for the old man for years. I figured that was your plan."

"Not at all. I can't say I had a plan even. I just worked to live, not lived to work. Today the old man backed off a little. He said he'd be open to selling the business. He just wants me to make a plan."

"You're over thirty now. Surely you have some things you wanna do. Right? What about the surf lessons? Those were popular, and you just stopped them cold turkey."

"I mean, yeah. We used to talk about doing that all the time when we were younger, remember? I'd do lessons. You'd handle the shop. What was the name we'd picked out again?"

"Bros." Aaron snickered. "Cool name."

"We are the coolest." Jackson could be as fluent as his brother when it came to sarcasm.

"What are you into?" Ben slid into the empty seat. "I told my crew I was taking five. Wanted to say hey to you fine gentlemanly specimens."

"Just Aaron here, reminding me how we used to talk about a surf shop. Do surf lessons. Rent and sell boards. That sort of thing."

"I remember that. It's a killer idea. Heart's Hope Bay doesn't need another home goods shop or ice cream parlor. But it does need a surf shop, and has ever since Go Ride a Wave closed. Whoever gets in first is going to do great."

"That's exactly what I've been thinking about lately," Jackson said animatedly, as he turned to Aaron. "I just don't know if I could do it alone. But maybe if it was…Two Bros Surf Shop. What do you think, bro?"

Aaron leaned in. "For real?" He looked at Jackson contemplatively. "What are you thinking?"

For the next hour, they talked through logistics. Ben brought over pens and paper and Aaron charted out a SWOT analysis and a loose budget.

"Look, at first glance, the math here makes sense," Aaron asked slowly. "I think we need to crunch more numbers and go talk to the bank, but this idea has real potential."

"Well…" Ben mulled it over. "I'd say that the timing is auspicious. Earlier I had Yousif in here, and his real estate biz is on fire. He mentioned that the old fisherman's cottage near Main Beach is coming on the market. It can be housing, but it's also zoned commercial. It's a killer location, right where all the action is in town."

"That place has been empty since we were kids," Jackson said.

"Right. It was left to a bunch of grown-up kids when the owner died. They all live out of state, and no one wanted to live in it or fix it up. But I guess they all also didn't want to let another sibling get more than their fair share."

"They sound like real nice people." Jackson shook his head.

"Right?" Ben snorted, pushing back the chair. "Hey, I gotta get back to it. But according to Yousif, it's a dump, but not a dump-dump."

"What's that supposed to mean?" Jackson asked.

"It needs a lot of work, but it's not a teardown. I guess the bones are good."

"Those older houses were built differently," Aaron said thoughtfully. "Hey, J, you wanna take a look? Just for shits and giggles."

"Yeah, I'm down." Jackson kept his voice cool. He didn't want to get overly excited at the dream Aaron had so casually spoken into possibility. If he outright said he was interested, maybe he'd jinx it.

The sun was dropping as they parked in front of the old cottage. The yard had been overgrown since Jackson was a boy. The roof was missing a few cedar shingles but didn't have a sag. The framed-in porch had intact windows, just peeling paint.

"The driveway could be expanded," Aaron pointed out. "This is a double lot, so we could make customer parking, no problem."

Jackson turned and looked out. Across the road, the ocean beckoned. Imagine working day in and day out with that view? Even better, having a job where he could be out there most of the time.

They wandered around the property, looking in the windows.

"If we took out those two small bedrooms and combined them with the living room, that could be the retail space. We could do the boards over here in the backyard, build a shed. Have outdoor showers for customers to rinse off after." Jackson couldn't pretend to play it cool anymore. He was certifiably buzzing. He could see it. While the place looked like a time capsule from 1960, there was a classic beach shack vibe to the place. He could do construction and get the landscaping whipped into shape. "What do you think?" he asked Aaron.

"I think I like it." He flashed Jackson a broad smile. "We'd need to get a loan. I have a lot of savings that I could live on too." His brother had always been a saver; Jackson guessed it was paying off in spades.

"That's right." Jackson reflected on his situation too. "Here's the deal, though. I don't have a lot of savings. And I have the baby coming. But I could see if I could get back on the crew, at least part-time, to keep some income flowing while we get this set up."

"I like what I'm hearing." Aaron held up a hand. Jackson clasped it, and they chest bumped.

"And if I'm doing it with you, Dad probably won't freak as much. He likes you better. Say it was your idea." Jackson grinned.

"Likes me better? Hardly. But he does like when family comes together. While he might not love it, he's going to support us. And at the end of the day, you are a grown-ass man who can make his own choices. He'll have to respect that."

They turned around, hands on their hips and looked out at the view again. Jackson didn't have to close his eyes to see the future. Even though they had a lot of logistical work ahead of them to pull this off, his gut sense knew this was a great plan— a surf school and shop he ran with the brother he was closest to. A parking lot full of tourists eager for a chance to try a new adventure. Making people happy for a living. And best of all, getting a chance to share what he loved, the thing that drove him forward, with the people he loved best. Becca could learn to surf. Sofia would get in on the action. And imagine the baby? In a few years they could be out there too.

A whole family affair that felt healthy and authentic. Win and win.

Maybe dreams really could come true.

Chapter Twenty-Five

Becca stepped back, squinting at the four different color swatches that she had pinned to the spare room wall. There was Beach Breeze...a softer shade of baby blue. Then came Greige Glam, a soothing but sort of boring gray and beige mix. She loved Watermelon Summer, which was a vivid coral, but it didn't really fit with the minimalist vibe of the rest of her home. Finally, there was Mint Julep, a barely there green that felt like a kiss of summer.

Why was it hard to make a decision? Since she'd crossed into the third trimester, her brain had become more and more scattered. She didn't want to create a space in the house that was overtly committed to a gender, but she couldn't help but think of the envelope she'd put in her bedside table—

the note from Dr. Fridley that revealed the baby's biological sex.

If she peeked, maybe then she'd be able to decide what paint to purchase. It wasn't like she had to tell anyone.

She took a step toward the door and then froze.

"What am I doing?" she said to the empty space. Maybe she should eat another pickle. The cravings had been kicking in too. This time it was pickles and bean burritos.

Better to eat her feelings than peek. It meant a lot to Jackson to have this news be a surprise. If she found out, that felt like a violation, even though she knew that he'd understand in a heartbeat.

No. She'd wait. And in the meantime? She walked over and took down the mint and the blue. It was going to be a toss-up between the bold watermelon and the quiet greige.

But she'd wait another day to make the decision.

She walked over to her walk-in closet and peered inside with a grimace. This was the spot in the house where she'd kept all the things that didn't have a proper place anywhere else. Should she do a garage sale? The very idea made her want to take a nap. It felt like such a petty thing to be annoyed at herself for, having one closet in her house that was out of control. But it also felt like a stupid metaphor for herself—put together and managed and yet with secret pockets of mess.

"Mama!"

Becca yelped as Sofia's voice startled her. "Why

did you scream?" Her daughter cocked her head, looking past her as if there were hidden monsters.

"Sorry, baby. I was thinking about something and didn't hear you come in. When you said my name, it made me jump."

"I wanted to tell you that Jackson is here." She shifted her weight back and forth. "And I have to pee, so bye."

As her daughter ran to the bathroom, Becca went to the living room. Jackson was walking up her front walkway. He looked different somehow, like a kid on Christmas morning.

She opened the door. "Hey! What's up?"

"Hello, beautiful." Jackson grabbed her by the waist and lifted her off the ground, planting a kiss on her forehead and then raining pecks down her temple and along her cheekbone to her mouth.

"You seem happy." She grinned, relieved. Lately he'd been duller after work. Not drained, but not energized. Maybe he had finally turned a corner and figured out a way to connect to the business.

"I'm always happy to see my girls," he said, putting her down and then picking up Sofia, who had joined Becca at the door, holding her over the top of his head and tickling her tummy until she burst into a deep barrel laugh.

"Stop, I'm going to pee again."

"All right, all right." He lowered her down quickly. "It's all fun and games until someone pees on you."

"Come build Legos with me," Sofia commanded.

"Honey, hang on a second. Jackson just got here. Let's check and see what he wants to do, okay?" Becca loved how comfortable Sofia was with Jackson, but manners were manners.

"That's all right. I do need to talk to you. But first, Princess Sofia is commanding me to build her another castle, right?" He gave Sofia a mock bow.

"Right!" Sofia grabbed his hand. "Let's go."

"As you wish," Jackson said, glancing over his shoulder to Becca with a soft wink.

Sofia kept Jackson busy all the way through dinner and talked him into not one, not two, but four bedtime stories.

Once Becca made it clear it was absolutely lights-out, Jackson sat beside her on the couch.

"What's going on?" she asked. "I can read you like a book, and you're full of news."

"You'll never guess what happened today." He turned to her and took both of her hands. "Aaron and I went and looked at that old cottage across the street from Main Beach—you know, the one that has been empty forever."

"The haunted-looking place?" Becca frowned. Where was he going with all of this?

"We are going to buy it! I mean, of course, we need to talk to the bank, and write up a business plan, but I really think it's going to work out."

She stopped breathing.

"We want to turn it into a surf shop and school. Sell and rent boards and wet suits and do lessons. Isn't that amazing? I had thought of the idea a few times, but it seemed out of reach. But if Aaron does it with me, we can support each other and make it happen. I'm a better surfer, and I like dealing with customers. But he's got the legal know-how to pull off the business side."

"You are going to quit your job?" Questions reeled through her head. She was having a baby in less than three months, and he was going to walk away from a stable job and become a small business owner.

"I was thinking I'd tell my dad I can't take over the business, but I'd do the crew part-time so I could keep some income coming in while we get set up. Be able to help you out."

"Help me out with a part-time job?" She hadn't felt nauseous since the start of the second trimester, but right now she might lose her lunch. Was this real life? What was he talking about? "What about insurance?"

"What about it?" Jackson looked puzzled.

"Uh... you need health insurance. If you work part-time, how would you get it?"

He shrugged. "Don't know. I'll figure it out. I'm pretty healthy."

"But what if something happens?" Becca's voice went up an octave. "And then you'll have a pile of bills. And there's the baby."

"Whoa, whoa, whoa. Becca! Nothing has happened to me. And I told you, we have lots of planning to do before it's a done deal."

"What about registering the business. Insurance?

A website? Billing? Marketing? It's not just being in the water, Jackson."

"Hey, hey now." His smile faded. "I know there is a lot to work out. I don't have all the answers yet, but Aaron and I will figure this out."

"You can't just trust things will simply magically work out," she snapped. "Bad things can happen if you don't have a plan."

"I know. Becca, I know all of this. Don't you trust that I'll figure it out? I'm not going to just run off and be an idiot."

"I just can't handle the idea of you being this irresponsible." She shook herself free from his touch and crossed the room. "Look, if you can't step up and take responsibility, just say so."

"So, what you're saying is that you don't trust me? That you do think I'm an idiot?" Now he looked more angry than surprised. "I am doing this for us. So I can be a provider."

"No." She turned away. "No. No. No. You aren't doing it for us. You have a good job right now. But you want to blow it up because it isn't fun. And now you want to start a job that feels fun. I work at the bank. Guess how many small businesses fail? Spoiler: a lot."

"But there is no one else in town doing this. It's a great opportunity."

"It's a risk. And one you're willing to take right now?" She rolled her head back. "I . . . I don't know, Jackson. I guess I shouldn't be surprised. This was always going to be the outcome, wasn't it?"

"I can't believe you're talking to me like this."

She couldn't either. She wasn't even sure if she meant these terrible words. It's just that she was so tired. She'd carried the load for her dad after their mom died. Then Graham got her pregnant, and she was a single mom and didn't complain. Now it was happening to her again with Jackson and...she was just at capacity.

If he broke his leg or got hit in the head with a surfboard...medical bills would add up quickly, and he wouldn't be there to help. He might want to. He might intend to. But the road to hell was paved with good intentions.

"Maybe it would be better if you left," she said wearily.

"Don't you do this." He approached her warily, like she was an animal who would lash out or run away any moment. "Don't push me away."

"I'm not pushing anyone," she snapped. "You're the one who is looking for the escape hatch."

"I think you're worried that I'm not going to go the distance. But Becca...I am here. I—damn it, I'm in love with you. I've loved you since I've known what love is. I didn't even have a word for it with you because it felt so natural, it's like breathing."

The words pierced her defenses, but she wouldn't flinch. Not right now. Maybe not ever. She had to make herself stone and ice, a fortress to protect her little family.

When she didn't respond, he spoke up, his voice ragged. "Does that mean nothing to you? What I just said?" Jackson was a foot away. "I've never told a woman I love her in my life. Just you. Because you're it for me. No matter what. This..." He gestured at the space between them. "This means everything to me. And I'm not looking to set up this business because I want to run away from responsibility. I want to do what fits me, what will make me the best version of myself. I want to bring that version home to you, and Sofia, and this baby. I know there is a little uncertainty. There is a little risk. But guess what? That's life."

"I'm sorry," she whispered. "I just... I need time to think over what you are saying." Everything felt like it was going too fast and yet also stuck in quicksand.

"Fine. I'm going to go. Being here is just making it worse."

She closed her eyes. And when she opened them again... she was alone.

Chapter Twenty-Six

And then, wait…You just left?" Aaron asked, his brows up by his hairline. "After you said you loved her."

Jackson stopped pacing and looked at Spencer, Aaron, and Noah. He'd put out a bat call for his boys when he got home, and they'd come fast. "If I'd stayed there, it could have gotten worse. What if she said more stuff she didn't mean? She'd feel horrible later," he mumbled.

"I hope she feels horrible now." Spencer folded his arms. "No offense. I like Becca. But she just did you dirty."

"Hell yeah." Aaron nodded.

"Look." Noah held up his hands. "I'm going to

play devil's advocate for a second. I'm still Team Jackson, but hear me out."

"First, there are no teams." Jackson shook his head, jaw tight, his back molars grinding over each other. "I'll hear you out, but let's make sure that's crystal clear. I'm Team Becca. Always."

"Fair enough. I respect that." Noah dipped his head, conceding. "Here's the deal. Becca is pregnant. And like third trimester pregnant. She is in the shit with it all. I'm sure she's not sleeping. Eating probably sucks, as her stomach is running outta room. The baby is using her spinal cord as a kick bar. And she's probably feeling vulnerable and wants safety. Humans are animals, we have base level instincts. What if she's not trying to bust your balls? It's just she's hardwired to want a protector who is going to create a safe space for her. She wants security. Look at the way her dad was, and how she had to shoulder everything alone as a single mom. Now here along comes another baby and more life changes. She wants to feel stable and safe with you to see a future. If not, she's going to put up defenses."

Spencer and Aaron stared, their mouths hanging open.

"Jesus, dude," Spencer said at last. "I hear people call Hilde the baby whisperer. Well…you're the frigging woman whisperer."

"You talk like this with Savannah?" Aaron cocked his head, before waving him off. "Actually, never mind. I try to forget that you and Savannah aren't just platonic roommates like Bert and Ernie."

Jackson perched on the edge of the couch. "I hear you, man." And he did. Noah made sense. And helped Jackson to make sense out of the situation. "What are my options? To just...stick around with Dad and take over the landscaping business?"

"I'm not sure it would come to that," Noah said slowly. "But I guess you should think about what you are willing to do to make a future with Rebecca Hayes."

"Anything." Jackson didn't have to think. "Whatever it takes."

* * *

"She never stops crying." Abby sat on a yoga ball in a pair of Mighty Ducks pajama pants, bouncing up and down while Ava howled. "I feel like people must think I'm pinching her all the time. Why doesn't she stop?"

"Colic takes time, honey." Today Hilde was wearing mauve linen pants and a white silk shirt. She looked as if she was a museum patron or an elegant art therapist. Despite the baby crying and the panic that seemed to be oozing out of Abby, the baby whisperer of Heart's Hope Bay looked serene. "Ava is still just getting adjusted to the world. All she ever knew was being safe and protected inside your body. She was never cold. Or hungry. Or tired. And now she has to experience sensations. But this too will pass."

Carter came into the room holding a tray with three mugs of tea.

"Want me to take our little rager out for a walk? She falls asleep in the carrier."

"Okay, that would be great. Then I can at least hear your sister talking to me." Abby handed over Ava, who arched her back and waved her tiny fists in fury.

"Hi there, good girl," Carter murmured dotingly, kissing the ginger fuzz on the top of her head.

After he left, Abby buried her face in her hands. "I don't know what I did to deserve that man. He's honestly a saint. I'm just hopeless."

"You? Abby? Hopeless?" Becca sat straighter, back stiffened with irritation. "You need to cut yourself a little slack. You are exactly the mama that Ava Olivia needs. You just need to keep the faith. And it's okay to rely on other people. My brother is a rock. All he wants to do is to be there for you. And look, you have Hilde. Your grandma is the famous baby whisperer of Heart's Hope Bay, for Pete's sake. You aren't in this alone. You have a village. You just need to take a deep breath and reach out and trust that we have your back, and that all good things are coming your way."

Abby began to cry; big silent tears streaked her cheeks. "You're right. How are you so smart?"

"I'm not." Becca looked down. "Because I can tell you all those things, and they are true by the way, and yet I have a hard time believing them myself. Why is that? Why can't we ask for help as women and trust we are going to get it?"

Jackson's stricken face appeared in her mind. *Don't you trust me?*

And she hadn't.

Maybe it wasn't just women who needed that trust. Maybe it was a two-way street.

Abby cried harder, and when Hilde moved closer, Abby fell to her knees, putting her face in her grandmother's lap. As Hilde stroked Abby's hair, she glanced at Becca and mouthed a silent *thank-you.*

But Becca couldn't feel any pride in the words she spoke. She might believe them, but that made it even worse. Yesterday, when she felt the fear of uncertainty, what did she do? Lean in for support from Jackson? No. She pushed him away with both hands. And what had he done? Had he raged? No. He had let her do it, and then honored her need for space.

She needed to see him.

Quickly excusing herself, she drove to the landscaping company. But no one was there except for the administrative assistant. She went to Jackson's desk to leave him a note, to ask him to call her. Next to his keyboard was a notebook. She opened it to scrawl out the message and froze, seeing her name written on the top line.

"What is this?" She picked it up, flipping through the pages. Jackson had been making observations on her pregnancy, recording the growth of Bolt, taking notes on books he'd been reading, and writing down tips from the birthing class.

If she ever needed proof that Jackson took his responsibilities seriously, here it was, in black and white. He'd done it quietly, and daily, from the looks of it, and she hadn't had an idea. Worse, she hadn't allowed herself to trust that he'd come through when it counted.

The reality of the situation struck with the force of the Pacific Ocean just a few blocks away. She didn't need Jackson to provide for her. She had a stable job that made her happy. She had created a stable life, unlike the life she'd had after her mom died. But what good was all that stability if she didn't have someone to share it with, especially someone who made her laugh and reminded her that life didn't have to be oh so serious? She knew her concerns had been valid. She needed to know he had her back. That he had Sofia's back. That he had Bolt's back. If he wanted to be in a family with her, they all had to do their part. But he was ready. She just needed to give him the chance to live out the promise that he'd written down.

And she hadn't. Instead, she'd thrown up defenses, and messed up.

The question was, would he ever forgive her?

Chapter Twenty-Seven

Jackson climbed out of his truck and stood in front of the empty cottage. He'd come to say goodbye. While the idea of opening up a surf shop with his brother aligned with his passions, he didn't have that privilege right now. What he needed to do more than anything was ensure that Becca felt like he was all in, with her, her life, and their baby.

He sighed.

He'd been too eager, excitement getting the best of him. He knew how Becca operated. He'd needed to go in with a PowerPoint presentation, not just a good feeling. He had shared everything because it felt good to him, and he neglected to communicate to her in the way she needed to truly be given a chance to get on board.

He'd blown it. And it was too bad. He could see how this could all come together. The idea of creating something himself felt invigorating. And doing it with his brother was even better. His dad would be disappointed, of course, but ultimately, Jackson knew he could earn the old man's respect. His dad had built the landscaping business from the ground up, so how could he deny his children the same opportunity?

Soon someone else would get the same idea. And there would be a surf shop in Heart's Hope Bay again. It was just a matter of time.

But he'd have to content himself with chasing another dream, one that he'd barely hoped to have since a teenager, one that came with dark hair, big eyes, and a smile that seemed to hold all that was good in the world.

"It's okay," he whispered to himself. "This is enough now."

As he turned to walk back to the truck, he saw the face he'd been thinking about.

Becca was standing a few feet away, her hair a little wild and her eyes wide. She was breathing hard, as if she'd been running, and one hand braced the side of her baby bump.

"What's wrong?" He crossed the space between them in less than a second. "Something happened. What? How can I help?"

She held up a finger, drawing in another gulp of air. "I parked over at the beach. I thought you might be there. But then I saw you here and didn't want to miss you."

"Something is wrong." He reached out and smoothed back a windblown wave of her black hair.

"Yeah. Something is very wrong. I'm a giant idiot." Holding her arms out, she gingerly dropped to one knee. "Jackson Marcus Lowe, will you forgive me for being such a jerk? And will you marry me?"

He hadn't run a step, and still the breath whooshed out of him. He sank down in front of her. "Did I just hear you right? Because it sounds like you just said—"

"Marry me. Please." Her lower lip trembled. "I realized that I don't need you to support me as some big provider. I can provide for myself. I always have. It's that I needed to be able to trust you'd be there, in good times or bad. When I'm up or down. What I haven't ever had is a man who will have my back, who won't let me fall, who will make me laugh, and lift me up, and, even more important, be the best dad ever. And there is only one person who can be that for me. And that's you. You're my person. You always have been, even when I haven't been able to see it. And once I realized how stupid I've been, I didn't want to wait one more second without telling you that I love you. To tell you that I only now realized I've always loved you. And if there is one thing I know, it's that I'm always going to love you."

His chest felt like it was cracking open, as if a bolt of lightning thundered down from the sky. His gaze traced over each of her features—eyes, lips, nose. He wanted—no, needed to memorize this one perfect moment.

"Aren't you going to say something?" She offered a hesitant smile. "Don't leave me hanging."

"Say it again. Tell me that you love me." His voice was husky. He might cry right here in the middle of this yard with friends and neighbors driving by. He didn't care. He didn't care about anything but this woman here in front of him offering the most precious gift in the world, her heart.

"I love you," she whispered, reaching out to hold his face between her hands. "I love you. I love you. I love you."

"And marriage?" He grasped one of her wrists, her quick pulse thrumming against his fingertips.

"I want you to do whatever it is that your heart desires. And if it's starting this business...then go for it. I know you'll do an amazing job. I trust you. Yes, I was scared about the whole not having insurance situation, but you know what? Here, on this single thing, I can protect you. You might be bigger and stronger, but I bring to the table one hell of a benefits package."

"Wait." He ducked his chin. "Are you proposing to me to get me health care?"

"No, but it's a perk, right?"

"Okay, hold up. Then can you do it all again, but this time imitating a gecko with a British accent? Really sell me on this. What's the deductible? Can I keep my doctor?"

She squeezed her eyes shut and started giggling.

"I'm being ridiculous, aren't I? But for real, we can just go to the courthouse tomorrow and get this done."

"You? Ridiculous? Always. But I wouldn't have it any other way. You know, I'm happy to give you the peace of mind by staying at the landscaping business. Your happiness and well-being are worth everything to me."

"Then do this surf shop." She was firm. "Because while I was scared of the unknown, I need to be able to trust. After all, I'd never planned for you and me, and look how good this is."

"Are you sure?" Was it possible that he could get it all, everything he ever wanted? Was he that lucky?

"Cross my heart."

"Okay, except I'm not marrying you. Not like this. And it's not because I don't love you, it's because I do . . . so, so much. But I don't have to lose insurance. I can still get it working part-time for my dad, and then I can figure out how to offer it to everyone here at this business. And if it works out that I end up on yours, great, but it's not going to be the driving reason. Nor do I want to haul you to the courthouse tomorrow. We're only doing this once, you and me, and I wanna do it right, and I wanna do it when our child can be there along with Sofia."

Her kiss was soft. "What did I do to deserve you?"

"I've been wondering this exact same thing." He kissed her back, harder, with more urgency before pulling back. "Let's spend the rest of our lives figuring it out."

Epilogue

I have the pumpkin pie," Savannah announced as she breezed into the hospital room, Noah and Rosie in her wake. The engagement ring on her left hand winked in the fluorescent light.

"And I have the turkey and mashed potatoes." Abby followed behind with Carter, who had baby Ava strapped to his chest. The baby was cooing to herself, the colic long since gone, and both mother and daughter looked more rested and happy.

"Hilde, you did it again," Becca said as the baby whisperer brought up the rear with a bottle of sparkling apple juice. Just as predicted, Becca went into labor the day before Thanksgiving, pushing out their little bundle of gratitude a few minutes after midnight. Everyone waited until the next day to give the new family time to get adjusted, but then the race was on to meet Maverick Kai Lowe. Their beautiful baby boy had black hair like his mama and wide blue eyes like his father.

"I didn't do anything," Hilde protested. "You did all the hard work."

"She was amazing." Jackson had been repeating that mantra to anyone who would listen. It was cute, but also the nurses were starting to go "Yeah, we get it, so is every woman in here."

"And I'm so glad you're going to have so much time together," Savannah said. "Dad told me that you're going to take advantage of the winter slow-down to focus on setting up the shop and being a house dad."

"That's the plan," Jackson said. "And if the last few months are any indication, we'll be booked out with lessons on a solid basis." He'd been busier than he'd ever been, but he told anyone who would listen that he was happier than he'd ever been, and as he had moved in, Becca knew there was no lie to his words. He went to bed smiling and woke up whistling.

"I'm so excited for you and Aaron." Savannah held up a hand. "Oh! That reminds me. Dad also told Aaron ~~during~~ lunch today that he would sign up for lessons. You somehow got him on board."

"I think he finally understood how much I was struggling and realized that he and I were on different sides of the same coin. It's cool. We're cool."

"Well, it's still a lovely surprise," Savannah said.

"As for another lovely surprise." Hilde gave her a slow once-over. "Fourth of July. You're going to have your very own firecracker."

Noah went the same color of Becca's hospital sheets. "Are you saying—"

"The baby whisperer never lies," Becca sang out.

Savannah pressed a hand to her forehead as she wagged a finger at Hilde. "You're bad." But her voice was tender, as if this was news she'd been hoping for.

"Well, Maverick, it won't be long before you make a new friend," Jackson said, leaning over to stare down at his tiny son.

"I'm his friend too, right, Mama?" Sofia was snuggled in at the foot of the bed, where she'd been keeping careful watch since the morning.

"You're even better," Carter said. "You're his sister. And let me tell you something, as a brother, it's the best feeling in the world to have a sister."

The gang stayed for a few more minutes, snapping pictures, offering to babysit, and cooing over the new baby. Hilde ensured that Becca ate a little bit of Thanksgiving dinner, encouraging her to get her strength back post-labor. Sofia left with Noah and her aunt to have a sleepover with Rosie.

When they left, the room was quiet until Maverick gave a small squeak. His eyes opened and he went cross-eyed before he yawned and went back to sleep.

"I couldn't be happier than I am right now," Becca whispered, breathing in the addictive newborn smell from the top of his head. Her body might be sore, but it was a *good* sore that spoke of transformation and a job well done.

"Oh, that's too bad." Jackson sat next to her on the bed, and held out a small velvet box. "Because I wanted to give you this."

A pulse of heat flowed through her. "Are you serious?"

"Of course I am." He didn't take his gaze off her face, a soft lock of hair falling across his forehead. "I would have married you this summer, but not for health insurance. But because we are going to make an awesome life together. Let's do it. Let's go all in. The big dress. The party. The bells and whistles. And then the life together. What do you say?"

He opened the box and inside was a small, perfect pearl ring.

"I say of course I'll marry you," Becca said, getting choked up. "Look how cute our baby is. We can make a whole surf team."

"You serious?" Jackson's whole face lit up.

"Whoa there, tiger!" Becca burst out laughing. "One thing at a time, deal? I need some semblance of order here."

"Deal." He leaned in, blue eyes bright. "Let's seal it with a kiss, shall we, Fun Size?"

And that's just what they did.

Read from the beginning of the series!

About the Author

Phoebe Mills lives near the Great Lakes and loves her family, coffee, and binge-watching, in that order. During the day she wrangles kids, and by night she dreams up strong women, dreamy men, and ways to wreak havoc on their lives—before making sure everyone lives happily ever after, of course! It's a tough job, but there's nothing else she'd rather do.

You can learn more at:
    AuthorPhoebeMills.com
    Twitter @Phoebe_writes
    Facebook.com/AuthorPhoebeMills
    Instagram.com/AuthorPhoebeMills/

Looking for more second chances and small towns? Check out Forever's heartwarming contemporary romances!

THE TRUE LOVE BOOKSHOP
by Annie Rains

For Tess Lane, owning Lakeside Books is a dream come true, but it's the weekly book club she hosts for the women in town that Tess enjoys the most. The gatherings have been her lifeline over the past three years, since she became a widow. But when secrets surrounding her husband's death are revealed, can Tess find it in her heart to forgive the mistakes of the past...and maybe even open herself up to love again?

THE MAGNOLIA SISTERS
by Alys Murray

Harper Anderson has one priority: caring for her family's farm. So when an arrogant tech mogul insists the farm host his sister's wedding, she turns him *and* his money down flat—an event like that would wreck their crops! But then Luke makes an offer she can't refuse: He'll work *for free* if Harper just considers his deal. Neither is prepared for chemistry to bloom between them as they labor side by side...but can Harper trust this city boy to put down country roots?

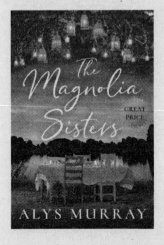

HER AMISH PATCHWORK FAMILY
by Winnie Griggs

Martha Eicher, formerly a school-teacher in Hope's Haven, has always put her family first. But now everyone's happily married, and Martha isn't sure where she fits in...until she hears that Asher Lantz needs a nanny. As a single father to his niece and nephews, Asher struggles to be enough for his new family. Although a misunderstanding ended their childhood friendship, he's grateful for Martha's help. Slowly both begin to realize Martha is exactly what his family needs. Could together be where they belong?

FALLING IN LOVE ON SWEETWATER LANE
by Belle Calhoune

Nick Keegan knows all about unexpected, life-altering detours. He lost his wife in the blink of an eye, and he's spent the years since being the best single dad he can be. He's also learned to not take anything for granted, so when sparks start to fly with Harlow, the new veterinarian, Nick is all in. He senses Harlow feels it too, but she insists romance isn't on her agenda. He'll have to pull out all the stops to show her that love is worth changing the best-laid plans.

RETURN TO HUMMINGBIRD WAY
by Reese Ryan

Ambitious real estate agent Sinclair Buchanan is thrilled her childhood best friend is marrying her first love. But the former beauty queen and party planner extraordinaire hadn't anticipated being asked to work with her high-school hate crush, Garrett Davenport, to plan the wedding. Five years ago, they spent one *incredible* night together—a mistake she won't make again. But when her plans for partnership in her firm require her to work with Rett to renovate his grandmother's seaside cottage, it becomes much harder to ignore their complicated history.

THE HOUSE ON MULBERRY STREET
by Jeannie Chin

Between helping at her family's inn and teaching painting, Elizabeth Wu has put her dream of being an artist on the back burner. But her plan to launch an arts festival will boost the local Blue Cedar Falls arts scene and give her a showcase for her own work. If only she can get the town council on board. At least she can rely on her dependable best friend, Graham, to support her. Except lately, he hasn't been acting like his old self, and she has no idea why…

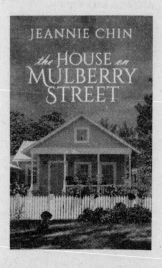

Discover bonus content and more on
read-forever.com

STARTING OVER ON SUNSHINE CORNER
by Phoebe Mills

Single mom Rebecca Hayes isn't getting her hopes up after she has one unforgettable night with Jackson, a very close—and very attractive—friend. She knows Jackson's unattached bachelor lifestyle too well. But in his heart, Jackson Lowe longs to build a family with Rebecca—his secret crush and the real reason he never settled down. So when Rebecca discovers she's pregnant with his baby, he knows he's got a lot of work to do before he can prove he's ready to be the man she needs.

A TABLE FOR TWO
(MM reissue) by Sheryl Lister

Serenity Wheeler's Supper Club is all about great friends, incredible food, and a whole lot of dishing—not hooking up. So when Serenity invites her friend's brother to one of her dinners, it's just good manners. But the ultra-fine, hazel-eyed Gabriel Cunningham has a gift for saying all the wrong things, causing heated exchanges and even hotter chemistry between them. But Serenity can't let herself fall for Gabriel. Cooking with love is one thing, but trusting it is quite another...